EDGE OF DISASTER

Thomas Puck

To my friends who have encouraged me.

Ann, Michael, Brett and many others.

CHAPTER ONE

Iraq, 2015

"You did the right thing," Max said into his mobile comms, looking into the open backseat of the Mercedes at the three rescued USAID workers. "These three would not have helped your cause. Ahura Mazda be with you."

"And also with you," Cambyses replied, his soft-spoken voice coming through Max's earpiece.

As he motioned for the workers to get out, Max heard the older man with gray-white hair try to say thanks, but his mind was already on the next phase of the plan. The MPs would process them, and they would likely be out of theatre within the day. He moved to the back of the car and opened the trunk. It was empty, but his communications sergeant moved silently around him with two large ammunition boxes, which he put inside.

"Hope they spend it quickly," the sergeant said under his breath, out of earshot of the driver.

Max nodded and closed the trunk, banging twice on the closed car to indicate it was good to go.

The car started away into the dark desert night, and he pulled his earpiece out and turned his handheld comms unit off, passing the equipment to his sergeant, who traded the Satcom phone for the secure radio and throat mic that would enable encrypted communication with his team.

"We all set?" he asked as soon as the mic was in place.

"Roger that, Captain," Eddie answered. "We're assembled and ready to go when you get here."

"On our way," Max responded, grabbing his weapon and heading off at a jog toward the airstrip, his comms sergeant right behind.

Eddie was his team chief and probably his best friend in the Marine Raiders. They'd worked together for the past three years, both extending their tours. As team commander, Max relied heavily on his second-in-command to maintain order and timelines, both of which would be important on the night's mission.

Cambyses and his group, calling themselves Bedhin Today, had kidnapped the USAID workers in Tehran the previous month and had almost immediately set up a line of communication to negotiate their ransom. Because of their location, the State Department had not wanted direct involvement, so Max and his team had been brought in to broker a deal.

Operating on the fringe of legality, the Marine Special Operations Company had been deployed in Iraq since 2011, and Max had proven his capability as a negotiator on a number of occasions.

The group had been difficult to track when they were in Iran, but they had crossed into Iraq the previous week, which allowed for closer surveillance. That was also when they'd decided to start killing their hostages. A video of the first beheading had arrived just the day prior.

Everything had changed. Max had informed his superiors of the video and quietly arranged for funding. He'd then reached back out to Cambyses mid-morning and agreed to meet all their demands. As far as Bedhin Today was concerned, their ploy had worked, and the Mercedes, carrying a million euros cash, was pulling into their remote location.

"Alpha team, you're off. Get into position and monitor comms." Max broke his reverie as the Venom helicopter touched the ground at the first of three positions surrounding the enemy's location.

"Roger that. Alpha team is in play." The helicopter was already lifting off to circle around to the next drop point.

An hour and ten minutes later, all three teams were in position. To maintain the element of surprise, the drops had been made six miles out, but the advance team had left vehicles at each location, which cut the time needed to get from the drop to their positions surrounding the enclave.

Max had been watching the activity at the compound for about fifteen minutes using a thermal imaging scope. Cambyses was being careful, and they were clearly packing up to leave.

"Timeline has moved," he whispered, knowing his throat mic would pick it up clearly. "Bravo team, be ready with the heavies. Alpha team, confirm you are ready to go in."

"Alpha ready."

"Bravo ready."

Max looked at his watch. 23:23. A good omen. This would end tonight.

He put his handheld scope down and nestled his head against the stock of his M110 sniper rifle. Eddie had questioned his decision not to bring a separate sniper on the mission, but Max was confident in his own abilities and didn't want to put his team at risk. The thermal scope was trained on the first of his intended victims, then he shifted to locate the second, the third, and the fourth.

"Sentries are all located. Stay at the ready."

He brought his weapon back to his first target and put the crosshairs on the man's slumped head. He was probably asleep and would never wake.

"Alpha team, hold. I am about to engage."

He gently squeezed the trigger and a soft thumping sound answered. In his sight, the form collapsed, and he swung to his second target before the man hit the ground. Another thump announced his second shot with similar results, and he swung to the third target. This man must have heard something because he was no longer sitting where he had been and was instead moving slowly toward the first victim.

Max slowed himself intentionally. He drew in a breath and, timing his target, placed the crosshair in front of the man's head, squeezing off a third round. Another adversary collapsed to the ground.

"Fourth bogey is on the move," his comms sergeant alerted him even as he swung his weapon to the final location.

"Alpha team, engage. Bravo, be alert," Max instructed his team, still trying to find the last man in his scope.

He caught up with the man at the entrance of the main building and without time to waste, targeted his body, sending five shots in rapid succession into the man's torso.

"Fuck," he said to himself, forgetting the accuracy of his voice mic. "Alpha team, be aware. Targets may be alert."

No response came, but he knew the assault team would have heard him. They would remain radio silent until engaged.

Through his scope, he watched the red images of his team emerge from hidden locations not fifty feet from the enclave. The terrorists inside were moving as they had been, oblivious to the team closing in. Apparently, the sentry had not been able to alert them.

When the attack began, he could hear the suppressed gunshots fired by his team both in his comms earpiece and externally—he was only a couple hundred yards away. Alpha team became vocal, calling out positions, but so far no one had called out in trouble.

He put down his sniper rifle and pushed himself up.

"Charlie team, advance cautiously," he directed the two others with him. Then he saw a vehicle's lights flash on in the compound as an engine roared to life.

"Bravo—" Max began, but was quickly cut off.

"We're on it, Captain," Eddie, Bravo's team leader, answered in his calm, matter-of-fact voice.

"Charlie, hold." Max knelt to the ground, watching as the truck pulled out of the enclave, accelerating down the narrow access road.

The truck did not get more than thirty yards before the Ma Deuce roared to life from Bravo's position across the road from where Max knelt. Up to this point, most of the weapon fire had been either suppressed or smaller caliber weapons, but the thunderous report of the fifty-caliber machine gun left nothing to the imagination. Its muzzle flash lit up the hillside, and red streaking tracer bullets pummeled the truck, stropping its progress in a matter of seconds.

The occupants were almost certainly dead already, but the bullets continued to rain into it, shaking the vehicle with every strike. Nobody had even opened a door before flames quickly engulfed the engine. Even though the barrage had only lasted maybe fifteen seconds, when the Ma Deuce stopped firing, it left an eerie silence on the battlefield.

Max did not call out to Eddie, knowing Bravo would be in motion already to a backup position in case things escalated. The Browning M2 was an incredible weapon, but using it, especially with tracer rounds, signaled its exact location. Though they did not expect the night's battle to continue for long, standard procedure demanded immediate repositioning after engaging with the Ma Deuce.

He stood up and motioned for his team to follow. Up ahead, he could hear another exchange of gunfire, but the prominence of his team's suppressed fire assured him things were wrapping up.

"Alpha, status?" he asked as they approached the outer wall.

"Captain, we are almost secure," Alpha's leader answered immediately. "Five bogeys down in the compound in addition to the four sentries. Three in the truck and we have four captives in the main building. We believe we have one more pinned down at the back corner. Hold that. Six bogeys down. Maintain alert, but we believe the compound is clear."

"Roger that," Max answered. "Bravo, maintain position. Alpha, sweep for anything worth taking. I want to be out of here in under ten. I don't need to remind you that we may be in friendly territory, but our mission remains off the books."

He turned to his communications sergeant. "Relay status and bring in the birds."

Moments later, Max entered the main courtyard of the compound, where his team was collecting everything they would take, not the least of which were the four captives bound with zip ties around their wrists and ankles. He was immediately struck by the poise of one man sitting erect and slightly apart from the others. Dressed in utilitarian, desert-appropriate attire, his deep-brown eye flickered with complexity. He had an aura about him that emanated calm and confidence, and he held Max's gaze when they made eye contact, but his face was a mask of hate.

"Cambyses?" Max took a step closer, knowing he was correct.

The captive's anger seemed to dissolve, and a more welcoming face answered.

"Yes. And you are Max. Ushta Te." The man nodded, offering the Zoroastrian greeting, meaning "happiness unto you."

Everyone had initially assumed that the kidnappers were Muslim, but they had soon learned that this group's ideology went much further back in history to the ancient Persian religion of Zoroaster.

Max could not help but feel some compassion for the man he had negotiated with for so long, but he reviled the group's recent actions and reminded himself that this man did not share his culture. Still, he could not shake the sense of gravitas that emanated from his captive.

"You didn't need to kill anyone. This could have ended better."

"Don't be so sure it has ended," Cambyses answered, closing his eyes.

"Well, it is over for you." Max spat on the dirt floor, knowing that the act was offensive. "The Iraqi government has agreed to make sure you disappear."

"Americans always assume they've won, don't they? Just like all the empires before you, underestimating what they couldn't understand. Remember, the Persians once ruled the world while your ancestors were still painting themselves blue."

Max turned away.

"I will offer a prayer to Ahura Mazda for you, Max," Cambyses continued. "You may need it."

* * *

Outside, the roar of the helicopters intensified and Max had to squint as sand filled the air.

"Load 'em up," he called into his mic.

He looked out as the two Venoms landed outside the perimeter, to one side of the still flaming truck. Bravo team returned and immediately stowed their gear in the farther of the two birds then jogged into help load with the others. When he looked back into the courtyard, he met Cambyses's eyes once again, and this time the man bowed his head as his mouth worked in prayer.

CHAPTER TWO

San Francisco, 2022

The plane bounced roughly upon landing, and the engines quieted momentarily before the whooshing sound of their reverse thrust dominated the cabin. Outside, light rain dampened the airfield and obscured most of the bay past the few windsurfers who braved the cold water.

Max peered through his window, catching the familiar shapes of the San Francisco airport as the plane turned to taxi toward its berth. The Bay Area had never been his home, but through various phases of his life he had visited the area enough times that it felt quite familiar, if not a home away from home. The flight from Las Vegas was only an hour and a half—enough time for a few chapters of his book and a light nap ending only moments before touchdown.

It had been quite a few years since he had seen Tanner and Carolyn together, though they were no longer "Tanner & Carolyn." The two of them still ran LasTech but had been separated romantically for at least two years. Max was not so close that he kept track of them, but their breakup had occurred weeks prior to Max and Tanner's twentieth high school reunion, so it had been hard to miss.

That was the last time he'd seen Tanner, and the weekend had been a real hoot, so when his old friend had called him earlier that week with a job offer, Max had decided that it was the perfect excuse to take a break from the Vegas poker scene. If he was being truthful to himself, he really wanted to see Carolyn again too.

She was also an Alford Academy grad, though a year behind them, and she had dated Max for almost the entire second semester of his senior year. They had broken up when he went to college, and their lives moved in different directions, but Max had always maintained an unspoken crush on Carolyn. When she and Tanner had started LasTech together, he had been secretly more than a little jealous of Tanner, and it wasn't because of the company's success.

The plane jerked to a halt, and the pilot's voice came on in the cabin, explaining that they needed to hold at this location until a gate opened up for them. Max ignored the groans around him as he remembered the call from his friend.

After catching up and sharing stories of other classmates, Tanner had arrived at the reason for his call.

"Max, is your Chinese still up to par?"

"Yes, of course," Max answered in Chinese before following up in English. "That means yes. Why do you ask?"

"This stays between you and me, OK?" He had sounded nervous.

"Sure. What's up?" Max had asked. "You selling to the Chinese?"

"What the fuck?" Tanner howled, becoming agitated. "How do you know? Did Carolyn already call you?"

Gaping openly, Max hadn't even been serious. "Whoa, Tanner, that was a complete joke, but not the funny kind apparently. Tell me what's really going on."

"You nailed it, Max. We've been approached by a Chinese conglomerate. At first they wanted to invest in us, but a week later they decided they want to buy the entire company."

"Shit, man. Congrats! That must be a big ticket."

"It is beyond big, Max. And it's happening fast."

"What does Carolyn think?"

There was another long pause.

"We aren't really on the same page. She'd rather stay independent but I think she is starting to see my side of it." Max heard his friend let out a sigh. "It might be that she's opposed because I'm in favor of it."

"Doesn't she have a say?"

"Of course she does, but I'm still the majority shareholder and have the support of our investors. This deal will happen or it won't, regardless of Carolyn's opinion."

"Understood." Max held back his personal thoughts. "So how can I help, Tanner?"

"I want to hire you as a translator."

"Doesn't the company have translators?"

"Yes, of course, but I want you to be *my* translator," he said. "This is a big transaction for the company, and we are lawyered up, but this is also very important to me as a person. I want someone I absolutely trust at the table with me."

"Thanks, bud." Max had initially planned to turn it down. No matter how flattering, he really didn't want to work for his friend. "I'm not sure about mixing business and friendship, though."

"It's more than just translating. I've seen you negotiate. Hell, I've been negotiating with you myself for twenty-five years . . . and I never win." He forced a laugh. "You can read people, Max. This is big. I need you."

Max had still tried to refuse. "I appreciate that, but—"

"What is two percent of seven hundred and fifty million?" Tanner practically yelled.

"Huh?"

"You heard me, and I know your head can spin numbers faster than almost anyone."

"Fifteen million. Why do you ask?"

"Because that's the contract I am offering." When Max remained silent, Tanner continued. "Two percent of the company to sit at the table with me for a few days. A week, tops. And that's the bottom end of the price range."

Max had been out of the service for over five years and was making a pretty good living splitting his time between translation gigs and the Las Vegas poker scene, but this was a payday beyond anything he had ever imagined. It did not take him long to change his mind.

"OK, tell me more."

That had resulted in several Zoom calls over the next few days, culminating in a contract that promised to make him a rich man if the deal went through. If it didn't, he would receive expense reimbursement and a modest lump sum that would still more than pay for his time.

Max pushed his back into the plane's seat, stretching his legs. Things had moved quickly and negotiations would start today.

The plane finally moved to its berth, and after another five minutes the door opened and the passengers began to disembark. Flying in front had its advantages, and Max was soon off the plane and headed to the Uber pickup point, carry-on luggage in tow.

* * *

While LasTech's headquarters was in Walnut Creek, the negotiations would take place at the 1 Hotel in San Francisco, which suited Max just fine. Tanner and Carolyn had enjoyed thumbing their noses at the tech establishment on the peninsula when they relocated to Walnut Creek, but the trip to the East Bay would have added another forty-five minutes to his travel, and Max simply enjoyed the city.

The 1 Hotel had formerly been Hotel Vitale, which had opened in 2005 and thrived on the fast-growing tech boom and the singles scene at its open-patio restaurant, Americano. Over the years, the property had changed hands a few times and had recently reopened as 1 Hotel, and the Americano was now a different restaurant, but Max hoped the vibe remained.

As the Uber tucked out of the rain and into the covered hotel entrance, a smile came to his face. The name may have changed, but a lot looked familiar. He glanced at his watch—it was 8:45. He would have a few minutes to drop his bag before meeting Tanner and the others. Though they had talked extensively over the past few days,

Tanner wanted to gather his team for a brief session prior to meeting their Chinese buyers.

He wondered if Carolyn would be at the meeting. He'd been more than surprised years back when Tanner and Carolyn had become an item. The girl he had dated did not seem a match for his friend, but time changed everyone. He still looked forward to seeing the light in her eyes.

Moments later, he was knocking on Tanner's suite. The stop at his room had been quick. He had needed a few minutes to change into nice khakis, an Oxford, and a black leather belt that matched his Allen Edmonds loafers. As a veteran of San Francisco travel, he had donned a sweater vest before completing the ensemble with his gingham Brooks Brothers blazer.

"Max!" The door opened, revealing his old friend's smiling face. The two embraced.

"You look good, Tan," Max replied after they parted. His friend did look good. His face was clean-shaven and almost gaunt, and he had sandy-brown hair trimmed above the ears and above his dark-brown eyes. He had always been an athlete, and from the way his clothes hung casually on his frame, he had not lost his passion for fitness.

"Come on in." Tanner opened the door wider and gestured inward with his free hand. "You've met Paul and Linda on Zoom."

The room was spotless. Tanner would have checked into the suite this morning. As advertised, the sleeping area opened up through sliding doors to a larger terrace that thankfully had a roof and plastic walls that kept the light rain away. February in San Francisco meant rain and cool air.

Rising from the outside table were the two lawyers he had come to know over the many Zoom meetings leading up to now.

Paul was shorter than he had imagined—not more than five and a half feet—but the rest was familiar. His gray hair and beard complemented the wizened face of a sixty-year-old whose knowledge of the law was unquestioned though he had little experience in dealmaking. He was dressed in a well-fitted blue suit with a blue-and-white-checked shirt with an open collar. No tie—emblematic of San Francisco in the dot-com era.

Next to him stood his younger associate, Linda, who certainly added spunk to the team. Throughout the week, it had been Linda who would propose new avenues of thought or potentially novel approaches to the deal. She had shoulder-length blond hair and blue eyes that Max had found distracting on their Zooms. At thirty-five years old, she was junior to Paul but by no means inexperienced. She too was dressed at the upper end of business casual, though Max had long felt that women were unfairly guided to out-dress their male counterparts.

"You're bigger than you look on Zoom." Paul extended a hand to Max.

He smiled and shook the lawyer's hand. "Nice to meet you in person."

He turned to Linda and offered the same hand, which she took gingerly. "Nice to meet you as well, Linda."

"Yes, it sure has been a fast week," she replied. "Welcome to San Francisco."

The two lawyers sat back down at the table, indicating that he should join them. There was a scribbled legal pad and a pile of papers in front of the nearest seat, which Max assumed belonged to Tanner, so he moved to an empty location farther from the door. Cool maritime air blew through the side walls, and Max was thankful he had included the cashmere vest in his ensemble.

"I knew your background in the Raiders," Paul said as he poured himself a glass of water. "But I hadn't realized you were part of the inaugural class."

"Yes, sir." Max nodded. "MRTC 2009."

Marine Corps Special Operations Command (MARSOC) had been established in 2006, right around the time that Max had joined the Marines. As with everything governmental, it had taken a number of years before they had established the Marine Raider Training Center (MRTC), and Max had spent most of that time working to qualify to be in the first class to complete the special forces training.

"And that led to negotiating?" Paul continued.

"In a way. In special ops, there isn't one set role for any soldier, but we all have our specialties. Over time, I found I had a knack for it, and by the time I left, I was the go-to guy when we had a hostage situation."

"I'll bet you have some stories."

Max smiled and nodded. Some things were best left unsaid.

When Tanner joined them, Max looked past him for a moment before asking, "Still no word from Carolyn?"

"She is still MIA." He shook his head. "I'll be honest. We've been through a lot together, and I don't begrudge her independence —but, damn it, this is one time where I could use her support."

"The Chao Fen team knows she is not part of the negotiation team," Linda added gently. "We've cleared that hurdle already, so her presence or lack thereof will not affect our strategy."

"Thank you, Linda." Tanner did not look up from his notes. "I guess it's more personal at this point."

Max could feel ripples of past emotion coming from Tanner, and as he thought about Carolyn, he could empathize. That woman had a way of sinking in deep. He felt like he knew a little of how his friend felt—except for the part about becoming massively wealthy within the next few days.

"Alright," Paul broke in. "Let's review the players first. Then we'll talk about who will not be at the table." He nodded to Tanner. "Finally, we will review strategy. Mr. Kline, you are going to be our observer today. If you would, I'd like you to do the same during this preparation. At the end, let us know where the light is creeping through. Make sense?"

Max nodded and sat back in his chair as the preparations began. This was a role he had played for so long that he didn't even think about it. In fact, he couldn't stop himself from doing it if he tried. He analyzed everyone.

* * *

The Acacia Boardroom suited their purposes perfectly, private and off the beaten path. It was not large, but it didn't need to be. The LasTech team was four, and they did not expect more than four to six from Chao Fen. Nestled in a corner on the second floor, the room had a long but rough-cut redwood conference table, emblematic of the Northwest. Its polished surface yielded some tradition to the irregular edges—formal yet somewhat casual at the same time.

It was ten after eleven when the elevator bell rang for their arrival on the second floor. Paul had assured them that the Chao Fen team would arrive fifteen minutes early, and he wanted them to be caught slightly off guard. They would be uncomfortable that the LasTech team was not there ahead of time, but he had explained that arriving too late would irritate their sense of pride. Ten minutes was enough time to increase their discomfort without overtly insulting them.

Their interpreter was waiting for them in the elevator lobby. It was expected that most of the discussion would be in English, but both sides would bring language experts. Max's official role was the same.

After they all shook hands, Paul led the way in. Chao Fen had brought four negotiators and an interpreter. Introductions were made all around in a mixture of the two languages. The Chinese team were all in proper business attire, while Paul had insisted that the four of them had remained business casual, another subtle message. Their lead, Eunice Lee, was a woman of maybe fifty years, dressed in a dark suit with an open white blouse whose lapels fell outside the suit coat. Her shoulder-length salt-and-pepper hair hung loosely around her pale ageless face.

With her were two younger men who were clearly underlings, and another man, Kevin Lai, who was roughly the same age as Eunice and seemed to be her equal, though he was introduced as legal counsel.

After the formalities, there were only a few brief minutes of small talk before Tanner, playing the role of host, moved them all to the table and gestured to the server to pour coffee. For Max, this was the information-gathering period. He watched the interactions at the table, both between the four opponents and also how they interacted with the members of the LasTech team. His first nugget was that one of the two subordinates had more influence than they wanted to reveal. He wasn't sure if it would play much of a role, but he logged the information nonetheless.

"LasTech had intended to remain independent," Tanner explained. "So we were somewhat surprised by your initial inquiry, but we knew that we needed to explore what it would look like to combine with such a powerful conglomerate."

Paul had coached him in this—establishing that LasTech was not really for sale while stroking their ego at the same time.

"And we are honored that you would entertain this," Eunice responded with a smile and a slight bow of her head. "Chao Fen prides itself on being at the peak of every industry that we pursue, and we feel that LasTech will fit perfectly in a group of premier companies."

And so it begins, Max thought to himself. He leaned back slightly in his chair, enjoying a long sip of coffee and noting that the other subordinate, the one who seemed to be a junior, was clearly watching the conversation with the same interest and role that Max held.

* * *

By the time they broke for lunch at 1:30, a loose framework for the deal had been established. The only thing left to settle on was a price, and this was where Max was most comfortable. They had agreed to separate for the meal, ostensibly so that they were not seen together, but the real reason was so that the teams could meet privately to prepare for the next round.

At Tanner's suggestion, their group had descended to the Terrene patio, which was covered at this time of year with the same plastic walls and canopy that had protected them earlier on the private terrace. Max had fond memories of this space when it had been Americano, and from the looks of it, the same lively atmosphere continued.

"That moved a lot faster than I was expecting." Paul broke up what had been small talk as the group sat down at their table in the corner of the patio. The restaurant was almost full, but their table was tucked away enough that there was little chance of being overheard.

"We're not done yet," Tanner replied as he pulled the silverware out of his napkin roll and put the bright-red cloth on his lap.

Paul grinned like the Cheshire Cat. "Even so, I think you've overpaid for me."

"Yeah, well, if we get our price, I'll be OK overpaying for a lot of things."

"OK, folks." Max held his hands up to either side, palms facing down and slightly out. "You are doing exactly what our opponents want you to do. They want you to think the deal is done, and now you just need to get your price. Right?" He paused to let his partners agree.

"Wrong. Paul, find something wrong with the deal we just agreed to."

Paul raised an eyebrow as he picked up his newly poured water. "And why do I need to do that?"

"Because we need to raise the stakes, or we give them the opportunity to take control of the negotiation."

The waitress arrived for their drink order, which consisted of three soda waters and an iced tea for Max. She passed out menus with a promise to return.

"OK, Max, I know that you're our poker player, so let me say it in your terms—we've got a pat hand. Why do we need to raise the stakes? Why risk it?" Paul asked.

Max shook his head lightly. "You're right, Paul. We do have a pat hand with the low end of a made straight, but there are two cards to come and three clubs on the board."

"Meaning?"

"Meaning if we don't raise the stakes, it's possible to get outdrawn on the next two cards."

"Well, that explains it," Linda said softly, clearly not following.

"OK, forget about the poker analogy. Here's what will happen this afternoon." Max reached for a piece of bread as he continued. "Chao Fen will come back to the table, and after a little negotiation they will agree to a price that seems at or above your target. You'll be thrilled, and once again there will be tacit agreement and smiles all around."

Max took a small bite of bread, knowing he had their attention.

"From there, it will be a matter of time until they drop the hammer."

Tanner turned his hands upward. "Like what?"

"I don't know, but at some point before the deal is inked, they will drop in a condition that you aren't happy with but that you'll be forced to agree to if you want the deal to close. At that point, you'll be too far along to want to restart, and most likely you'll feel forced to concede. I don't know exactly when that will come, because it depends on their strategy, but—trust me—it will come."

"I'm not suggesting that it's not plausible, but how can you be so sure?" Paul asked, somewhat less happy than he had been when they sat down.

"They never flinched."

"Why do you say that?"

"While you were going back and forth with them, I was watching. Even when things got a little tense about the vesting schedule, thcy were never really fazed. No ticks, no sweat."

The waitress returned with their drinks and took their order.

"I'll tell you the most interesting part," Max continued. "Kevin Lai, the older guy who barely spoke—he liked the deal. Everything about his body language told me that things were going according to their script, but we barely gave ground from the preliminary discussions. I Googled him during the meeting. Do you know his title?"

They all shook their heads.

"Head of strategic planning. Not an easy one to pin down, so I dug a little deeper. It seems he started in accounting at one of their subsidiaries a long time ago then moved into legal counsel for the mother company. Over the past twenty years, he has bounced from division to division, never holding a C-suite title but always joining new acquisitions and moving back to the mother company after transition. I didn't have time to dig any deeper than that, but from what I saw he cuts fat and eliminates redundancies—to put it nicely. This guy is their cleaner. He's probably the deadliest guy at the table."

"Present company excluded?" Tanner managed a smile.

"I don't know, Tanner. He's probably killed more careers than I have."

Linda straightened slightly, looking from Max to Tanner. "What do you mean?"

"We're joking," Max responded before Tanner could. "The point is this. Do you really think that Chao Fen, one of the most ruthless conglomerates in Asia, will let us walk with a sweetheart deal without a fight? I don't."

Paul had been listening intensely, leaning back slightly in his chair. He nodded a number of times before turning to Tanner. "Goddamn, it makes a lot of sense. I don't know how I didn't pick up on this, but I think he's right."

"Titan," Tanner spoke, mimicking Paul's head nod.

"What?"

"T.I.T.A.N." Tanner said slowly. "It stands for: Technological Intelligence for Threat Assessment & Neutralization. It's a new antivirus software that we haven't released. We haven't even teased it to the press. It is one-hundred-percent secret—or it should be. That's what we pull back this afternoon."

"With due respect," Paul replied, "you have revenue of over $350 million over four primary products. Your marquee software, Padlock, brings in over $200 million annually and continues to grow at an astounding rate. Why would they care about an untested product that is not even released to market?"

"They might not." A smile returned to Tanner's face. "But if they don't, it will be an even bigger win for us."

"What are you saying?" Paul asked. "And, if this is important, why am I only now hearing of it?"

Tanner shrugged.

"I guess I wasn't really focusing on it. TITAN is a game changer. If we can sell LasTech and keep TITAN, we might pull off a deal for the ages, but thinking on it . . . I bet Chao Fen has done their research. I don't know how they found out, but I bet they know." He looked directly at Max. "If we threaten to pull it, you'll get your leverage."

CHAPTER THREE

Max sat in the back of the Mercedes coup, watching the hills as they drove on Route 24 through the suburban East Bay. He had planned to take the BART train to Tanner's house, but his friend had insisted on sending a car, and in truth it was a much nicer way to travel. It was almost seven, and the sun had been down for a couple of hours, so the view was limited to lights in the hills and the occasional retail lots that he could see off the highway, but it was peaceful.

He smiled to himself, proud of his assessment as he thought back to the afternoon session. After the two parties had agreed upon a price, Tanner had almost casually mentioned that the deal would not include unreleased software. He'd explained, as if innocently informing them, that a product they were working on called TITAN would be excluded from the deal because there were still some intellectual rights issues.

Chao Fen had reacted as if someone had tied electrical circuits to their chairs and flicked the switch to on when Tanner mentioned the software name. Even Kevin Lai flinched, which shocked Max, who had expected the quiet leader to be more in control. He'd quickly signaled Paul to drive hard toward a maximum valuation.

The rest of the session began a new negotiation where Chao Fen tried to argue that all software must be included in the original price, and Paul argued that TITAN, which was unannounced and unreleased, was clearly not part of the original deal. Tensions had risen, but eventually Chao Fen had agreed to raise their price by almost fifty percent to include TITAN.

Max had noted internally that this new price was close to seventy-five percent above the value that LasTech was expecting to see. Whatever TITAN was, he mused, it was certainly the crown jewel in the eyes of Chao Fen.

The car exited the highway at the first Danville exit and after a few turns through a well-lit retail area, they proceeded deeper into suburbia and darkness, first passing through tighter-knit neighborhoods and then moving higher into the hills where the houses started to spread farther apart. They rolled slowly uphill before arriving at a cul-de-sac with a gate directly across. Next to the gate was a brick column with an intercom and the address numbers for their destination.

"Come on up!" Tanner's voice came through the small speaker when they pulled up. "Left at the top."

It was another minute before they arrived at the summit. The road flattened for a few hundred feet as they approached the well-lit home. In front, Max could see Tanner waving, flanked on both sides by rows of trees with uplighting that made the house look like a fancy hotel.

When the driver stopped, Tanner quickly jerked the rear door open.

"Mr. Kline!" he exclaimed. "Welcome to my home! Well, welcome to *our* home."

Max smiled as he got out, giving his friend a hug. "*Our* home?"

"Yeah, I should have mentioned this earlier." Tanner seemed almost nervous. "I got married last month."

Max's eyes widened with a questioning look, waiting for an explanation.

"Long story," Tanner continued. "She's a great gal. You'll love her. She's inside, but I wanted to tell you about her before you went in."

He opened the front door, handing the driver a hundred-dollar bill. "This is for you, and stay on the clock. You can park over there. He'll need a ride back in a couple of hours."

Max laughed when Tanner was done with the driver. "So you're married? You could have mentioned it sooner. Congrats, Tan."

"Thanks." He patted Max on the back then moved to a rock wall that bordered the walkway to the door. He grabbed two copper mugs that were resting there and gave one to Max. "Moscow mule to celebrate?"

"Cheers." Max accepted the mug and grinned. "We'll probably need more than one. There is a lot to celebrate, and now you've added a wedding!"

They both drank deeply before starting toward the door. As they approached, Max admired the entrance, featuring a large covered porch with a floor of polished slate. The house itself had a modern stucco facade, accented by vertical white beams, reminiscent of a Tudor style but distinctly modern. The wide double doors were flanked not by lights but by two flames, which added an almost medieval flavor that somehow fit. Max looked closer, and it was indeed live flame, presumably gas fed.

"Very cool," he said.

"Yeah, I had those special made. They are always lit."

Suddenly Max had a thought, and he stopped his friend before he could open the door.

"Tan, does Carolyn know?" He nodded toward the house. "About your wife?"

Tanner looked down. "It all sort of happened fast. Like Chao

Fen." He laughed nervously. "I haven't found the right time to tell her."

"But you did tell her what happened today, right?"

"Yeah."

"What did she say?"

"Well, I didn't speak to her. She's not answering her phone, but I emailed her. She's got to be stoked. She'll never have to work again."

"If that's what she wants," Max said hesitantly.

"Either way, that's not going to affect our celebration." Tanner put his arm over Max's shoulders. "Come on in. I want you to meet Jenny."

* * *

"That was phenomenal!" Max announced as he put his fork down on a spotless plate. "The cod was probably the best I've ever had. Thank you so much for this." He raised his wineglass first to Jenny then to Tanner. He probably would have said something similar even if the food had tasted like cardboard, but in this case, he meant every word.

"Thank you, Max," Jenny responded in unaccented English before switching to Chinese. "So good of you to join us." She had a beautiful honey-cream complexion accented by bright-red lips and jet-black hair that was knotted in a bun behind her head. She wore loose-fitting clothes, so he couldn't be certain but Max suspected that she had a body almost as perfect as her face.

"You are a talented chef, Mrs. Reynolds," Max responded with a smile before witching back to English. "The pleasure is mine."

"OK, you two," Tanner said, beginning to slur. "Let's stick to the native tongue here." He poured more wine into everyone's glasses. "A toast to my good friend Max, who was instrumental in today's success."

He raised his glass a bit too quickly, and some wine spilled on the table. "Whoops. No harm. We've plenty more. Hear! Hear!"

For probably the tenth time that night, the three clinked glasses and toasted the day.

"Jenny," Max said, changing the subject, "Tanner has been very secretive about you, but congratulations. You also work at LasTech?" From the light conversation before dinner, this had been obvious, but Max wanted to know more.

"Yes. I joined in 2017."

"And what do you do?"

"I'm on the administrative side." She smiled. "Not a big thinker like Tanner or Carolyn."

Max took another sip of wine. "This world is not all about big thinkers, and I'm sure LasTech would not be where it is today if

Tanner and Carolyn didn't have such a skilled team."

Tanner looked down at his plate before meeting Max's eye with a weak smile. He raised his glass with a slight toast before finishing it.

After a long pause, Max continued the conversation. "Are you on the finance side?"

Jenny shook her head. "I'm embedded with the creatives, but I handle the smaller details."

Tanner stood with the magnum bottle and refilled Max's glass before doing the same to his own. Jenny's glass was still full.

"Max, Jenny's being modest. She can write code with the best of them, but took more of an admin role to help shepherd the crew. She worked on Carolyn's team. It might be part of the reason that Carolyn isn't returning my calls." He offered another weak smile.

"Oh boy." Max took another sip, wondering what he was walking into.

"Carolyn recruited me out of Stanford." Jenny looked at Max with a challenging glare. "I owe her a lot. She sponsored me for my O-1 visa and took me under her wing at LasTech. I started working for the junior members of her team, but she always showed an interest in me. Over time, as my experience and understanding of the systems at LasTech grew, I eventually became her personal assistant. I guess technically I still am." She looked at Tanner.

"Jenny and I didn't start dating until last summer," he began. "For the record, Carolyn and I had been through for over a year. I never really knew Jenny, but when Carolyn was working remotely in Montana, I started interacting more with her, and we hit it off. We kept it on the down-low of course, but in the fall our great government decided not to renew her visa.

"Now, before you get any crazy suspicions, we are in love. This would have happened eventually but—yes, I married her to keep her here."

"If he had not offered," Jenny continued, "I would have been forced to return to Shanghai and then reapply for immigration status from there."

"We would have been separated for months, possibly years, before she could get through all the paperwork," Tanner added, shaking his head. "If I've learned one thing in the twenty years since we graduated, it's that time is precious. I wasn't about to give up Jenny and our relationship."

Max raised both hands in mock surrender. "Hey, makes sense to me. You don't need to justify anything in my eyes. Love is love."

"Yeah, well . . . I don't know that Carolyn will see it that way." Tanner put his glass down, looking sideways at his wife. "I'm going to need more help."

"What do you need? I'm here, and my last stint seems to be over." Max smiled, reaching for his wine.

"This is confidential. No documents. No contract on this one, but I need your word that this stays between us. If you don't want to take it, that's fine, but this absolutely stays here."

Max straightened in his chair, feeling a slight tinge of disappointment that his friend seemed to question his loyalty. "You know me better than this, Tan." He stared into his friend's eyes for several seconds before continuing. "But if you need to hear it—I swear that this stays with me."

"Thank you." Tanner got up and walked to the wall, where he tapped the volume on the control panel. The rough-around-the-edges voice of Jorma Kaukonen that had been playing low in the background now filled the room. Tanner turned back and tapped it slightly lower, but it still dominated.

"I don't know if I'm acting like a crazy man," Tanner sat back down, speaking just loudly enough to be heard over the music, "but Chao Fen already knows more than they should."

Max leaned in closer. "What's up?"

"TITAN is missing."

"What do you mean?"

"I mean that last weekend I went to run a test of the software and it was no longer on the server."

"Aren't there backups?" Max was shocked. "You guys must have layers of redundancies."

Tanner shook his head. "Yes and no. With our production software, of course. And even with developmental software, we have version control protocols and two backup server locations. But TITAN was a special project. First, it was highly secret, so we didn't want to leave copies on the remote servers. Beyond that, it is potentially very powerful, so we agreed to keep only that master file and a single copy on the main serve—in a location that even the best hacker would never find."

Max nodded, recognition arriving. "It takes a hacker to beat a hacker."

Tanner raised his glass in acknowledgment. "Her favorite phrase."

Jenny excused herself and took her plate into the kitchen.

"TITAN was Carolyn's baby from the start. She was super protective of the code. At first it made sense, but as it developed into a very workable tech, she seemed almost obsessed with it."

"Did you not think to save a copy?" Max asked, reaching to refill their glasses once again.

"Without her knowledge?" Tanner laughed. "I'm good with code, but I couldn't hide anything from Carolyn. That woman hacked the US, UK, and Russian governments before the end of her sophomore year at MIT, and that's just mentioning the big ones!"

"Are you serious?"

"One hundred percent."

"Did she do anything?"

"She could have, but she just wanted to prove that she could. She didn't touch anything except to leave her watermark on their websites." Tanner shook his head. "Her logo, tiny, sat on the right side of so many government pages that it was years before the agencies took them all down. She was an instant legend—or her alter ego was, anyway."

"What was her alter ego?"

Tanner laughed again. "Viper."

"No shit." Max thought back to that era. He had always had a passive interest in the cyber world and could remember stories about Viper. "That was her?"

"Uh-huh."

Max smiled to himself, shaking his head. "I'm impressed yet again, but in a way this doesn't really surprise me. I knew she loved to hack but didn't really think it through. Why wouldn't the smartest person I've ever met excel at everything she tried?"

He put his empty glass down.

"How come you never shared this with me?"

"Carolyn didn't want to share it with anyone. She found religion—we both did—and she went completely clean. Wanted to bury her past. That's the origin story for LasTech."

"I thought LasTech was your Italics for emphasis? baby?"

"It's complicated." Tanner grabbed the empty bottle of wine and stood. "Doesn't matter though. We are getting off topic."

"No, this is all relevant. Carolyn is out of contact, and TITAN is missing. I think I can follow the breadcrumbs here."

"Will you talk to her?"

"Of course."

"I'll double your fee."

"Tanner, if this deal closes, you've already made me very rich. I need nothing else."

"No, you've already done your part." Tanner set the empty bottle on the bar that ran along one wall and reached for a bottle of bourbon and two short glasses. He poured a healthy dose into each and returned to the table, handing Max one. "I want to pay you."

Max shook his head again. "No, I'm already being paid. If Carolyn doesn't help, the deal falls through and my share is forfeit. This is part of the original deal."

He took a full sip of the bourbon, savoring the oaky bite before it burned the back of his throat.

"Wow, this is good." He put the glass down and sat up in his chair, locking eyes with his old friend. "I appreciate you, Tan, but there's another reason I can't take more. If I were being paid to approach her, Carolyn would know. I don't know how, but she would know, and that would destroy any trust she might have with me."

Tanner stared back with a gentle nod before downing his entire glass.

"OK, we'll do it your way."

CHAPTER FOUR

Max was jolted awake by the sound of breaking glass. He had been asleep leaning into the corner of the backseat of the Mercedes S-Class. The night's alcohol had numbed things, allowing him to close his eyes, but something had changed, and he was immediately alert.

The driver was leaning to the left, and the car was doing the same. They were in a tunnel, and the car was drifting dangerously close to the left wall. The right front window was open and air rushed back at him. He leaned forward, instantly aware of how bad things were. Small pieces of shattered glass littered the front seat, and blood covered the driver's-side window.

Max unbuckled and dove over the front seat as the car's wheels bumped heavily off the side wall, sending it awkwardly toward the center of the tunnel before heading once again to the left. The car was still on cruise control and was showing no signs of slowing as Max grabbed the wheel and barely avoided a second collision with the raised pedestrian walkway.

He glanced at the driver, confirming that the man was dead and now recognized that bits of the driver's brain had joined his blood on the window.

The roar of another engine snapped his attention back to the road, and he turned to see a black SUV accelerate up the right side of the vehicle. Max still had both hands on the wheel and no control over his speed, and he had no weapons, so whatever was happening, he needed to change the playing field. He waited until the SUV driver was at his rear wheels before he cranked the Mercedes to the right, cutting them off and forcing the driver to slow even as they collided with the back portion of the car.

The impact also slowed Max's car, and he yanked the wheel back to the right in an attempt to stay in the center, but the car was now out of control. The tires screeched as he veered left, then back to the right, then back left, narrowly missing the tunnel wall as the car passed back out into the dark open night. Thankfully, the collision must have disengaged the cruise control because Max could feel it slowing down even as he struggled to keep the car on the road.

In the background, he heard the roar of the SUV's engine again before it bumped the rear of the Mercedes, jerking his motion forward as his hands fell off the wheel. He was only vaguely aware of the vehicle tumbling as he fell to his right into the passenger seat and was simultaneously pinned by a massive airbag that practically knocked him out.

The next thing Max knew, he was lying in the footwell of the passenger seat. He wasn't sure if he'd lost consciousness, but it couldn't have been long because the car was still rocking gently, and he could hear the remnants of the accident still settling. The car was right-side up, close to the bottom of a sloped embankment, nose pointing up to the highway. Max pushed himself into the seat—his left hand hurt, his left eye felt like it had been punched, and he was bleeding from a gash on the back of his head, but the airbag had saved him.

He tried the door, but it was mangled shut. The roof was about six inches lower than it should have been, but there was enough window to crawl through.

He made it out and immediately took in the surroundings. The car was resting against a pair of large trees. Beyond them, probably no more than twenty yards away, he could see the streetlights of a secondary road through a light strand of trees. He looked back up to the highway and saw the rear lights of the SUV as it slowly backed into view, and as it did he slid to the back and behind the car.

A shower of bullets followed, making more noise on impact than they did from the silenced machine gun. Max felt relatively safe behind the car, but he hadn't been fired on in years. It brought back memories, and he could feel his soldier's mindset come alive.

When the gunfire stopped, he could hear muffled Chinese conversation from the roadside. Who was behind this? The question sprang unbidden, and he pushed it away as quickly as it came. This was not the time for theory. He reassessed the situation as he heard the sounds of someone coming down the scree toward the car.

If he could get to a nearby row of trees by the road, he had sufficient cover to flee, but he had at least thirty feet of open space before he was safe. Too much ground to cross if his attackers were shooting, and it was pretty clear they would be.

He looked under the car, wondering if he could crawl to a position of surprise. There was no room to maneuver there, but his eye caught a trickle of liquid, and an idea formed. He internally thanked Tanner for being the high-tech snob that he was.

After dinner, Tanner had brought out Cuban cigars, and he had given Max a fancy butane torch, insisting that everyone needed one if they were going to smoke cigars. Max wasn't much of a cigar smoker, but he had agreed to his friend's wishes, and he now pried the lighter out of his front pocket.

Whoever was coming down to the car was moving cautiously, but they were already about halfway there. "Driver looks dead," he called up to the roadside in Chinese.

"Fuck the driver." The response was immediate. "Find the other one."

Max reached toward the pooling liquid. Even though he was effectively resting against the fuel tank, he knew it was unlikely to explode, but he hoped his adversary did not. Hollywood had popularized the fuel tank explosion because it was good for the cinema, but Max was comfortable that his odds were good. What he needed was a distraction, and a burning car would give him that and maybe more, if his enemy shied away.

By the sound of it, the man had reached the front of the Mercedes.

Max flicked the lighter on, but in the semi-quiet night, the loud click sounded like a firecracker. He ducked even though he was already behind the car and heard the man shout as he released a hail of bullets into and over the car.

The sound of the whooshing torch was anything but quiet, but Max could not get the liquid to ignite. He had seconds to make this work. He was unarmed, and a man wielding a submachine gun was ten feet away. It would not take long for him to get over his fear and make his way around the car.

Max tried moving the torch to the side where the liquid was less dense and felt hope flare with the fire that followed. He didn't release the flame and swung his arm under the vehicle, hoping to ignite another section, and he was rewarded when a second fire lit. He took a deep breath and prayed that the flames would quickly bloom.

A rock tumbled down the passenger side of the car followed by a voice.

"Come out," the man said in half-decent English. "We just want to talk."

Max eased himself to the edge of the trunk by the driver's side, head still looking under the car, and he watched as the flames grew and rushed forward to the engine. With a loud whoosh, the car was quickly engulfed in flames.

The man by the car instinctively backed off, his attention drawn to the growing flames. Max had only seconds, and he hoped it would be enough. In an instant, he sprang from his hiding spot, careening down the remaining slope and across the open space toward two eucalyptus trees.

He had a few seconds on his own before bullets started to hit the ground behind him, followed by shouting from above, so he turned to his left, away from the nearest cover and the shots seemed to fall away . . . briefly.

Knowing that the shooter wouldn't be deceived for long, he swiftly changed direction again, back to his right, and made it to the largest tree as the gunman's fire zeroed in on him. Bullets pounded the tree as he pressed his back against it, thankful to have made it this far.

Eventually, the muffled gunfire ceased.

Ahead of him there were a few more trees and then a row of cars parked on the street. On the other side, he could see rows of multifamily housing, mostly dark at this hour but still too light for his liking. He needed to even the playing field, and that meant getting a gun.

* * *

Max pulled himself down the rest of the embankment through the low ground cover. The bullets had mostly stopped, but he could still hear the occasional muffled burst hit the tree above. Standard operating procedure—the gunman on the road above was trying to keep their quarry pinned behind the tree while the man in pursuit could move to the flank.

Now on the street, Max knew he had little time. He scanned the row of cars to his left then to his right when he found the ideal vehicle, a BMW M5. The car was full of bells and whistles that Max needed as a distraction. He picked up a rock and moved to the outside of the cars, keeping them between himself and his assailants.

He slid quickly up the line of cars until he reached the BMW. As he moved to the driver's-side door, he saw the interior screen light up, letting him know that he would get the desired result. The car beeped and flashed its lights before he could do anything, but he still smashed the rock down at the edge of the window, right at the corner where it entered the door. The window shattered, and the car alarm blared in immediate protest, but Max was already around the front and re-entering the sparse cover of the embankment. As he found a position, his attacker emerged from the spot a few cars down where Max had originally taken cover.

The Asian man wore a black suit, black shirt, and no tie. He stood on the sidewalk, legs splayed, machine pistol held up in two hands near his face as he looked down the short barrel, surveying the street as the BMW wailed. After what seemed like half a minute, he dashed through the cars and disappeared for a moment into the street. Max assumed he was looking under the vehicles. The man's head popped back up a minute later as he hustled to the BMW.

Max waited patiently as the man circled the vehicle then peered farther up the street. He lowered his gun, allowing it to hang by a strap on his right shoulder, and pulled out his phone, tapping into it. The man watched the phone for a few seconds, and Max thought he heard the tone of a text reply. The man put the phone in his pocket, returned the gun to his hands, and moved farther up the street, away from Max.

Smiling to himself, he quietly slipped farther into the trees and back to his original eucalyptus. The man on the street was undoubtedly the stronger of the two. If there was one thing Max knew without thinking, it was standard combat behavior. The lead assassin would want the backup to come down from the road to hold the entry position. This second man was the one in charge, who may or may not have strong skills himself, but he would be slower and likely out of practice. He was Max's target.

Sure enough, as Max reached the tree, he saw the dark figure of the second man moving to the other side. He was dressed in similar black attire but held his gun casually in his right hand, fingering his glowing phone in his left, most likely reporting events to his own superior. Max said a silent prayer to the cell phone gods—their distraction had come to his aid more times than he could remember.

He abandoned his previous plan of attack and silently circled the tree on the uphill side, coming around immediately behind the man, who was still tapping his phone with his left thumb. He was directly behind the man when he inadvertently snapped a twig with his left foot. The man started to move in response, but it was too late for him.

Max already had his left arm around the front of the man's shoulders, and with his right hand he violently yanked the man's chin to the right. A snap louder than the twig signaled his success, and the lifeless body crumpled to the ground.

Max rolled the man over, pulling the gun strap off his shoulder. He patted the man's pockets and found another full magazine, a wad of cash that he left behind, and a remote car key fob. In a shoulder holster, he found a Glock 19, which he removed and pushed into his belt behind his back. He grabbed the phone and moved down the row of trees, putting another large eucalyptus between himself and the man on the street. Checking the machine pistol, he found the chamber loaded with a full magazine, safety off. It was an MP7, a weapon he was very familiar with. He didn't recognize the suppressor, but based on what he had heard, it was also well made.

One down. Now to end it. He thought about trying to capture the second man—it would be nice to know who was shooting at him and why—but the distant wail of sirens told him he didn't have time to fool around.

He looked down at the man's phone, which was conveniently still unlocked and open to his text message chain.

Everything was in Chinese, but he had enough experience with Chinese texting that he could comfortably navigate it. The first text on the list summarized the attack and pursuit, so Max went to the next conversation. The last two messages read, "Street empty. Attempt at car-jack failed. I'm moving up street. Cover me. On my way."

He typed a message using pinyin, the Chinese shorthand using English characters. "Where you?"

"Returning. Got away."

"OK. Hurry. Gotta go."

Max looked to the street, and the other attacker was still maybe two blocks away, but he was jogging back, no longer in pursuit. He was in the streetlights, and Max slipped into the shadows, so he had time to drag the body about twenty feet behind a small copse of bushes. Between them, the car still burned, lighting up the immediate area, but he made it to safety before the second man returned to the embankment.

He dropped the corpse and moved to the high side of the nearest tree. Below him, the jogger stopped, peering up the hill, undoubtedly looking for his friend. Max quickly remembered to silence his newfound phone as he watched the second man type.

"Where you?" The message flashed silently.

"Gotta go," Max typed, watching as the man looked up the embankment toward the highway. "Now!"

He reached into his pocket for the key fob. It was one of the modern fobs with no actual key, and of course it had a button for remote start.

The man had raised his gun again as he started up the embankment. He was not yet past his position when Max looked back at the phone and typed one more line. "Leaving."

He hit the button for remote start, and above them on the breakdown lane, the black SUV's horn tooted twice, the lights flashed on, and the engine started.

The second attacker swore to himself, lowered his gun, and started up the embankment. As he did, Max stepped forward and pulled out his newfound MP7. Two short bursts took out the man's legs when he was about halfway to the road, sending him onto the scree, shouting curses in Chinese.

As Max approached, the man spun around, spraying bullets from his gun as he did, attempting to hit Max in a desperate effort, but Max's training paid off once again. He had not lowered his gun, and when the man spun, he immediately resumed fire. Three more quick bursts shook the man's body, and his attack ended before the gun could come fully around to train on Max.

Knowing that time was scarce, Max rushed over to the body, his own gun still on alert. The other gun had fallen a few feet from the man's body, and Max kicked it farther down the scree.

"Who are you?" He knelt close to the bullet-ridden man whose eyes were still open and alert. "What do you want?"

"Fuck you," the man spat out in Chinese.

Max grabbed him by the shirt. "You are dying. I can help if you tell me who you are."

"You are not . . ." The man coughed blood then spit the remnants at Max's face. ". . . you are nothing," he finished in whispered Chinese, his life fading as he spoke.

Max grimaced and used his sleeve to wipe the blood from his

face, allowing the deceased to fall back to the rocks. The sound of sirens was now growing closer, so he scrambled up to the highway, finding a few cars but no official vehicles on the road. As he climbed over the guardrail, he saw two police cruisers pulling up the secondary road below, lights and sirens rolling.

He did not waste time looking. In moments, he was in the driver's seat of the SUV, engaging it in drive and pulling back into the light nighttime traffic of Route 24.

* * *

The cool San Francisco air filled his room through the open windows. Max preferred to be cold when he slept, although sometimes it annoyed him when he woke. He wasn't sure if it was the cold today or the fact that he had been attacked the night previous, but he was annoyed nonetheless. It was 6:30, late for him to wake despite the night's activity.

He had driven the SUV back to the city and ditched it in the SoMa area before walking back to the hotel. Before he abandoned it, he had searched unsuccessfully for any clues as to his attacker's identity. He would have preferred to hold on to the phone, but he knew it would be a beacon, so he snapped it and tossed the parts in two different public receptacles.

He kept both guns and several extra clips, along with a tactical knife he had found in the console. It had been almost midnight when he left the car, but that hadn't stopped him from calling Tanner from his own phone on the walk to the hotel.

"What the fuck are you involved with?" he shouted at his friend.

Tanner had clearly been asleep. "What?" he mumbled. "Max, what's up?"

"I was fucking attacked is what's up!" He couldn't hold himself back. "It was a fucking assassination. What else are you up to, Tanner? Whatever this is . . . I didn't sign up for it."

Tanner was awake now. "Max, what the hell are you talking about?"

Max finally calmed down and relayed the night's events. As he did, he could hear Tanner tapping at his keyboard, undoubtedly looking for the news outlets to confirm it.

"Holy shit, Max," Tanner finally replied. "I have no idea. How did you . . . Are you hurt at all?"

"Bruised. Angry. But no injuries."

"Holy fuck," Tanner continued. "Did you hurt anyone? The report says three dead."

Max let his silence answer. His friend knew his past career.

After several heartbeats, Tanner resumed. "Shit. Do we report it? What do we do?"

"You have no idea who would do this?"

"No, man. This is completely fucking insane."

"OK." Max had settled down. His anger faded, leaving only determination. "Do nothing. Whoever it was made their first move and failed. We'll be more prepared for the next one."

"You think there will be a next one?"

"There's always a next one."

"We should go to the police."

"Tanner"—Max gritted his teeth—"we . . . are . . . not . . . going to the police. Do you understand?"

"OK." His friend had lost all authority.

"Good. I'll find Carolyn tomorrow, and then we are going to have a long talk. I need to know everything at play here."

CHAPTER FIVE

The waitress at Terrene smiled as she poured his coffee. Her dirty-blond hair was shoulder length and pulled back by a hairband, and Max calculated she couldn't be older than twenty-one. It was her second trip to the table and Max had already created his estimate of her life.

She had two visible tattoos, one of an American flag on her right ankle and on her left forearm was a pair of sunflowers, one slightly drooping. On her feet were a pair of well-worn but presentable Red Wing sneakers, a Minnesota brand that didn't often travel outside the region. She was likely a hustler, bound and determined to make something more of her life here in the promised land after fleeing some life in the Midwest. It was a common story.

"Your food should be out shortly." She smiled again and moved off with her coffee pot to help the next table.

It was 10:30 a.m., and the restaurant was three-quarters full with patrons enjoying their weekend brunch. Max had gone for a morning run, hoping to clear his head, but he hadn't found any answers. He had followed the Embarcadero around to the top of the city and then progressed through Fort Mason and Crissy Field out to the southern base of the Golden Gate Bridge. Round trip was about ten miles, but he had interrupted the run with a half hour of calisthenics on the green at Crissy Field. The morning air was typically wet with fog and cold sea air, but his Gore-Tex vest had kept him warm and dry.

After a cooldown walk and a latte from a street kiosk, Max had gone back to his room for a long shower before descending to Terrene for breakfast.

The same thoughts had been swirling in his mind all morning. Who had motivation for the attack? It made little sense. Chao Fen had gotten everything they wanted in the purchase. The price was high, but it wasn't anything they couldn't afford. They had no reason to disrupt the deal—but the attackers were clearly Chinese.

The waitress returned with his Santa Fe omelet, bacon, and rye toast.

"Do you need anything else?" she asked, meeting his eyes with a flare of her own.

He smiled in return. "No, thank you. This looks great."

"Enjoy." She turned away, and Max admired her youthful figure as she moved off.

The eggs went down quickly, but he lingered at the table, unable to come up with an explanation for the previous night's events. Eventually, he switched his mindset and made a plan to find Carolyn.

Tanner had given him her address, but according to him she had not been seen there for over a week. He had admitted to hiring a private investigator to locate her, but the man had been unsuccessful. Max smiled to himself as he thought of her—Carolyn had always been special. It was no surprise to him that she could disappear if she wanted to—very likely in plain sight.

Between his shower and brunch, Max had done some internet searches of the bars and restaurants that Tanner had given him on a list of Carolyn's favorite haunts. Many of them were high-end foodie locations that Max immediately crossed off as too high profile.

He was left with a list of two restaurants and four bars that she frequented, but Max knew he had to dig deeper. They all had one thing in common—they were off the beaten path and known to serve locals. He could work with that.

After brunch, he returned to his room and did some more digging, finally emerging on the streets of San Francisco in the early afternoon with a list of eight possible locations, in addition to Tanner's list. Some on this list he already knew well, while others were completely foreign, but he felt like he might be on the right track. On his phone, he had downloaded a recent photo from Facebook and stared at it for a moment outside the hotel.

Carolyn was still beautiful and had an untouchable element about her that radiated even from the photo. Max wondered if he was doing this for Tanner or himself.

* * *

He felt an odd peace wandering the cold, misty streets of San Francisco by himself. A veteran of the city's winters, Max wore boots and jeans and a mid-length Gore-Tex vest that kept the mist off his core. For his head, he had an oil-skin baseball cap that he had picked up years ago on an Alaskan fishing trip. He was comfortable or at least more comfortable than most who were braving the streets on this wet Saturday afternoon.

His optimism for finding Carolyn declined as the day became night. He had planned his route, thinking he would cover the more likely lunch locales first before moving into the bars on his list. And he couldn't just look inside and move to the next one. At each location, Max would first walk the streets to either side, observing the other nearby venues. Then he would go in, order something light, and observe the crowd. In each spot, he identified one or two patrons who appeared to be regulars, and before abandoning the venue, he approached these candidates with his picture of Carolyn, but he had yet to find even a glimmer of recognition.

It was nearing nine o'clock as he exited The Barrel Room on Sansome. The wine bar had been packed, especially for a Saturday in the Financial District. Max's destination had been "c.1905," the speakeasy that could be found in the basement. San Francisco has a subculture of speakeasies and hidden bars that would be right up Carolyn's alley.

This one had been awkward because even though the secret access stairway was unguarded, the four rooms below were fairly small and intimate. He received uncomfortable return looks in each of the four rooms when he dropped in to scan the patrons. In any event, it was another shutout. He had also tried her picture with the lead bartender, with no success.

He was hungry. Though he had eaten an appetizer or two along the day's route, he hadn't had a proper meal since breakfast. He needed a steak or something substantial, so he ran through a few options in his head and before turning south toward his hotel, an idea came to him. At first it was hunger, but as he thought about it, he stood as good a chance of finding Carolyn there as at any of the other bars.

Bix was classic San Francisco. In fact, though it was never secret, it had all the charisma of the hidden speakeasies that dotted the city's nightlife. And it was more than that. Walking into Bix was like walking into The Great Gatsby. It had the throwback aura of class and style that Gatsby strived for. Beyond that, it was a fantastic restaurant, and Max's stomach growled as he walked the three blocks to Gold Street.

As he walked into the main dining room, he immediately felt at home. The two-story room was packed with patrons. To his right, the long mahogany bar stretched along the wall with two busy barmen behind it. In the center were tables and booths along the wall, all full with the second seating, while a three-piece jazz band played in a small section along the far wall.

Above it all, stairs running at the front and back, was the coveted balcony seating. Up there, a row of cushioned booths provided those lucky enough with a view of the room while sitting in somewhat protected style.

Max smiled. It was an all-class bar-restaurant. He gave his name to the maître d', asking for a table for two even though it was still a long shot. He was told it would be forty-five minutes, which he acknowledged and went down the bar, looking for an opening where he could stand or at least order a drink.

At the far end of the bar, two patrons stood to leave, and Max was able to secure the last stool. It was a little close to the band, but he could deal with the noise, and it wasn't like he needed to talk to anyone at this point. When the bartender found time for him, he ordered a Beefeater Gibson and sank back into his thoughts.

He knew he shouldn't be drinking. He drank too much as it was, but after the previous night's attack he would be smart to keep his wits about him. Someone wanted him out of the picture—that much was clear. Still, the gin tasted good, and it was his first drink of a day spent hanging out in bars.

He heard her before seeing her. Her laugh was unmistakable, and he looked down the slightly less crowded bar to see three women at the end closer to the door. He didn't know the other two, but Carolyn's silk black hair brought back memories even though it was now cut to a short bob. She laughed again, and even at this distance Max was taken aback by the warmth and unguarded emotion that emanated like a low musical note. He smiled and shook his head.

Now that he'd found her, he realized he was in no rush to intrude. She was enjoying herself, and undoubtedly he would disturb that. Hearing her laugh and knowing that he would end it made him think that maybe this was a poor decision after all. He had done his job. Let Tanner deal with LasTech's internal strife.

He finished his Gibson and stole another look down the bar, only to find Carolyn staring straight back at him, the life in her eyes as bright as always, her mouth slightly agape in surprise. The years sat well on her. She looked like a slightly mature version of the high school girl he had fallen for, still waif thin but with a composure that spoke of confidence.

Short black hair accented a tight jawline, and her deep-blue eyes had always reflected the depths of space, while her Middle Eastern ancestry contributed a light coffee complexion and an air of exoticism that had always attracted him.

Max raised his empty glass in toast, allowing a broad smile on his face. She closed her mouth and smiled in return before turning back to her girlfriends, putting her hands on their shoulders. For a moment, Max's heart fell, thinking she was turned off, but he felt a rush of excitement as she turned from her friends and practically ran the length of the bar, engulfing Max in a bear hug as he barely made it out of his seat.

"Max!" she slurred, clearly well into her cups. "What the hell are you doing here? How have you been?"

He returned the hug, drinking in her scent. She wore a light parka over a sweater, and both were a little wet. The earthy smell of wet wool lingered underneath her citrusy perfume. It was all Carolyn, and it immediately brought back high school memories from when they had been more than just friends.

"I'm well." He beamed. "How are you? It has been a while."

She pushed back, dropping her hands to hold his and looking him up and down with her drunken smile. He stared into her eyes for a moment before scanning her face. The dark-brown birthmark on her right jaw somehow added to her beauty.

"You look good," she said, interrupting his thoughts. Her smile remained, but her tone dropped slightly, and she released his hands. "Still in shape, as always. What are you doing with yourself? I think I heard you were playing poker."

"I am," he replied. "That and some translation work are paying the bills."

"Does it bore you?"

"Huh?"

"After all the military stuff—does the civilian life bore you?"

"You'd be surprised how much fun pocket aces can be," he remarked with a sly smile, but she responded with a puzzled face, and he changed his answer. "It's not so bad. I recently got hired on a merger consultation gig, and that's been fun. What are you drinking?"

"Far Niente, please."

Max turned to the bar, smiling to himself again. He loved that she knew what wines they served, was probably a regular here and, most importantly, made no effort to return to her friends. The tip he had left with his first drink paid off because the bartender immediately moved to serve him. He ordered the chardonnay and another Gibson for himself.

"How long have you been in town?" she asked, putting her hand on his shoulder.

"Not long. Came in Friday morning. I love this town."

"It's nice, right?" She cocked her head slightly. "Even in winter."

The drinks arrived quickly, and Max had handed the wine to Carolyn when the maître d' stepped in.

"Mr. Kline, table for two?"

Carolyn's almond eyes widened slightly, and she looked around. "Max, are you on a date?" She smiled coyly.

"You tell me." He laughed, extending his hand.

For a moment, the puzzled look returned to Carolyn's face. She was always so expressive.

Max found himself a little stuck for words. "I, uh, was hoping to find you here."

Carolyn's face and shoulders slumped. There was no avoiding a sense of disappointment. She looked down at her glass then back up with a tightened expression, making Max afraid she was going to throw the wine at his face.

"So this is not a coincidence? You were looking for me? Don't tell me you're running errands for Tanner now?" Her volume increased.

"It's not like that." He lifted a defensive hand, trying to temper her growing anger. "Let me explain."

A good twenty seconds passed while she stared back at him

without responding. She took in a big breath and let it out. She was still angry, but something softened.

"You're lucky I'm hungry," she finally answered. "Famished, actually. Let's eat, but you're going to have to tell me what this is all about."

"I'm hoping you can do the same," Max answered, motioning with his arm that she should go first.

The pair reached a booth on the balcony overlooking the scene below. Max saw Carolyn wave to her friends with a grin before sitting down. The two women raised their glasses in salute.

"What have you gotten into, Max?" Carolyn seemed to have cast aside her anger. Her comment was almost as if she expected Max to get himself into trouble, which was something she had always done, and it always bothered Max, because from his own perspective he tried to do the right thing.

"Nothing, really," he answered, ignoring the implication. "I guess that's not true. I helped make you a lot of money. Tanner called me last week, asked me to help with the Chao Fen negotiation."

"That's funny. He's been texting me every day about this fucking sale, but he didn't mention you."

"I don't know, Carolyn, maybe he thought it would upset you."

"It does."

"Why?"

"Because I don't want to sell the company, Max." She took a sip of her wine. "And, you know, I'd like to remember you as my old friend and not fucking Tanner's errand boy." She had sobered slightly with the conversation but still slurred the occasional word.

"I'm not anyone's errand boy."

"Really? Are you getting paid? How much is he paying his errand boy to find me?" She was working herself into an anger again, and Max was thankful that he could defend himself.

"I am not being paid for this, Carolyn." He reached for her hand that had been on the table and squeezed lightly before releasing it. "I was paid to negotiate. That much is true, but no one's paying me to find you. There is a lot going on here, Carolyn. More than I understand. I think more than Tanner understands. I need your help."

The waiter arrived with menus and ran through the specials before moving off with a promise to return.

Alone again, Carolyn turned to him with her beautiful, penetrating eyes that spoke of both sadness and caring. She shook her head, looking down into her glass, then took another drink before responding. "OK, Max. Tell me what's been going on."

He took a long gulp of wine before beginning a narrative of his weekend, interrupted only by the waiter's return. They ordered and were finishing their salads when Max's story ended.

"So, here I am, trying to find out why I am getting shot at. What's going on with LasTech that Tanner is holding back, and where is TITAN?"

"Did you ask Jenny?" Carolyn asked, pushing her almost empty plate to the side. "You know she worked on TITAN too, right?"

"I know she worked for you," he answered bluntly. "Would she have access to TITAN?"

"She had access to anything I had access to." The waiter had refilled her wine on the last visit, and Carolyn now emptied half of it. "Of course, now she has access to everything through her *husband*," she said through her teeth.

Max pursed his lips for a moment before responding. "I was told that was on the down-low."

"Yeah, I am sure it is. Tanner hasn't said anything." She let out a dismissive laugh. "Jenny told me. It's not like we aren't talking, but I think somehow she's involved deeper than I know. I'm wondering if I was a stepping stone on some grand scheme of hers, or maybe she's connected to Chao Fen."

Max put his fork down. His plate was as clean as it was before the salad had been added. "That's a bit far-fetched, don't you think?"

"Is it?" she answered, finishing her wine.

The waiter returned with their entrées, and for a few minutes the two ate in silence. Then Max became aware that Carolyn had stopped. He looked over, and she had put her silverware on the table, hands at her side. She was looking down at her plate, her hair concealing her face.

"Carolyn?" he said softly.

For a moment, she didn't respond, but when she lifted her head, he saw tears in her eyes. It hurt him as if he'd been stabbed in the chest. Seated as they were in the shallow crescent booth, they were not quite opposite each other, and he reached to hold her hand, feeling her grasp him as if holding on for life.

"Max," she sobbed, "things were going so well. And now . . . everything's fallen apart."

It was so uncharacteristic that Max wasn't even sure how to respond. Carolyn was always the strong one. He suspected the wine had a lot to do with it, but they'd been drunk together many times and he'd never seen this side of her—a side that actually needed him. It made her more beautiful.

"We'll figure this out." He didn't know what to say, but he shifted closer and held her, allowing her to rest her head on his shoulder. "I promise."

She had stopped crying, and after a good minute she sat up and pushed herself back to separate them.

"Whoa." She laughed. "I guess I've had a bit too much wine. Sorry about that." She wiped her hand with her napkin.

"Don't be." Seeing her sadness left Max feeling the same. "I'll help you in any way I can."

CHAPTER SIX

The hotel lobby was starting to come alive at 9 a.m., though Max suspected the Sunday morning brunch crowd wouldn't really kick in for a couple of hours. He grabbed a cup of coffee and a newspaper and headed out to the sidewalk to meet Carolyn.

He had told her almost everything the night before, including the attack, though he left many details of that out. While she had been somewhat defensive about TITAN, she had agreed to help. She explained that the software was a collaboration between herself and their star coder, Ravi Gashwin. They were the only two with access to TITAN so, she insisted, Ravi was the man he needed to speak with.

Carolyn had explained that Ravi had spent years floating between Amazon, Microsoft, and Google, taking increasingly important project roles before eventually landing at LasTech with a significant equity stake. According to her, he was brilliant but eccentric. Most recently, his focus had been artificial intelligence, and apart from TITAN, he was the chief architect of the newest update to their Padlock software. Like Carolyn, he had been opposed to the sale. While Carolyn had simply stopped reporting to work, he had announced an extended leave of absence two weeks prior.

As Max entered the covered alcove that allowed for guest pickup and drop-off, he saw a hand wave to him from a white Tesla Model 3, and he lifted his coffee with a smile. It was the perfect car for Carolyn. High tech and green but not ostentatious—she was always looking for the tree-hugger alternatives.

"Sleep well?" she asked as he got into the passenger seat.

"Always. How about you?" He put his coffee between his feet as he buckled himself in. "You were fairly deep last night. A bit hungover?"

"Not at all!" She looked at him with feigned innocence. "At least nothing that a bunch of Tylenol and a couple of Red Bulls can't handle."

She pulled out of the protective alcove into the heavy mist of the San Franciscan morning. The wipers moved automatically. Max saw that an address was already programmed into the iPad-like monitor that served as the Tesla dashboard.

"This thing have full autopilot?" he asked.

"No, thanks," Carolyn responded with her head turned to the left, watching for traffic as she turned right. "I'll be at the controls this morning. Not sure I trust it, even with all the evidence."

"Where are we headed?"

"Westlake." She turned to look at him briefly when he did not respond. "Part of Daly City, out by Lake Merced. We'll take the 101 to 280."

"Got it."

"It's an interesting location," Carolyn continued as she navigated the Tesla up to the highway. "Not very unique—every building looks the same—but it's nestled among some of the best golf courses in the country. Ravi is less than five minutes from The Olympic Club, the San Francisco Golf Club, Lake Merced Golf Club, and Harding Park."

"Aren't the first three private?" Max asked. "Probably hard to get on."

"Yes," Carolyn answered, "most people would dream of playing any of those, but Ravi is a single man in his forties who's made a good living and his sole obsession is golf."

"So which one did he join?"

Carolyn laughed. "All of them, of course."

"That says a lot." Max paused to read some of the large billboards that surrounded Route 101. After a moment, he resumed the conversation. "Tell me more about this guy."

"There's not much to say beyond what I've told you. He is brilliant. Been obsessed with AI for a while and coded some into our Padlock software that has really improved its capabilities."

"Is it in TITAN?" Max turned toward her, admiring the clean cut of her jawline.

"It's . . ." She paused. "Max, what did Tanner tell you about TITAN?"

"That it was antivirus software created through a secret development."

"Antivirus?" Carolyn contorted her face as she repeated the words. "That's a bit of a stretch, but I guess in some ways it could be described as such. Oh, by the way—let's not tell Ravi that you are working for Tanner."

"Not friends?"

"I wouldn't go that far, but Ravi was pretty deep into TITAN and thinks the sale is a huge mistake. I don't think they've talked."

"So what is it, then?"

"What is what?"

"TITAN."

The grin returned to her face. "TITAN is effectively an IT department. It proactively scans a network for bugs, issues, viruses, you name it. When TITAN is deployed, you won't need an IT department."

"Wow. So why hasn't it been released?"

"One point five million jobs, for one."

"Huh?"

"In the US alone, there are three million people employed in IT, and TITAN would make half of them redundant. But that's not the actual issue. Ravi loves AI, but he is also scared of it. He wanted to run more tests before we released it."

"Why are you talking past tense?"

"Because fucking Tanner is selling the fucking company, Max," she said loud and clear. "We may not be part of LasTech's future! We might not own TITAN."

"Sorry, Carolyn." Max felt bad about touching a nerve.

"It's OK." Carolyn seemed to quickly regain her composure. "I've been trying to forget about this for two weeks. It's all a bit raw—anyway, another problem was that we couldn't figure out pricing. Remember the Everlasting Gobstopper from Willie Wonka?"

"Of course." It was Max's turn to laugh, remembering the old Gene Wilder movie though having never read the book on which it was based.

"How do you price a piece of candy that never runs out?" she asked rhetorically. "Well, TITAN is self-updating. It can be replaced, in theory, but it won't need patches. What should we charge for software that can proactively take care of your systems—all of your

IT systems—indefinitely?"

* * *

The Tesla pulled up in front of a modest home in a row of homes that all shared a similar boxy 1950s look. They were not identical but had clearly been built in the same era as part of a uniform development, two stories with a garage. Max couldn't help but be reminded of reruns of *The Brady Bunch*—which featured, in his mind, the most famous split-level California home. A manicured lawn separated the house from the sidewalk with a thin driveway leading to the garage.

Carolyn had explained on the drive that she had not been able to reach him for the past week. Initially, when they were informed of the potential sale of the company, Ravi had started a WhatsApp thread and the two had commiserated about the implications, but he had suddenly stopped replying the previous weekend. She suspected he was retreating further into his "happy place" and had cut himself off to enjoy his golf game.

Carolyn pushed a button on the drive stalk to put the car in park, then opened her door. "He's probably out golfing at this hour on a Sunday. Worth checking out though."

It took Max a second to remember the door opened with a push button on the armrest, but he soon joined her on the sidewalk. The mist here was worse than downtown, but the rain itself seemed to have diminished. A steady breeze blew in from the ocean, and he scrunched his eyes as he turned to look at the houses across the street, all in the same style, with fog rolling over their roofs. It was beautiful, in a wet-weather way.

He turned back to Carolyn, who waited at the end of the short driveway. "Let's see if he's here." He walked past her, up the drive, and then to the left, where the front door faced the driveway rather than the true front of the house.

Carolyn quickly overtook him. "Let me knock," she said. "Ravi is not the best with new people. He might not answer if he sees you first."

Rather than ring the bell, she pulled open the screen and knocked on the dark-blue wooden door. After twenty seconds, she knocked louder, leaning her head toward the door as if trying to hear a response from inside.

"Ravi?" she called, knocking still louder. "You there? It's Carolyn."

Max left her at the door and wandered the few steps over to the garage. Cupping his hands to his eyes, he peered into one of the glass panes.

"Range Rover in here," he called out. "Does he have more than one car?"

Carolyn looked over to him and shook her head. She turned back to the door, this time really pounding. "Ravi, open up. Please."

After waiting for another thirty seconds, she made a final attempt. Banging three times, she followed with, "Ravi, I need your help."

When no response followed, she let the screen close behind her and stepped away from the door.

"What now?" she asked.

"Let's get a coffee and make a new plan," Max offered as the two walked back to the car.

"Lyn." A hissed voice drew their attention back to the house. At first Max did not see where the voice was coming from, but when it spoke again he saw a window above the garage was cracked open and could make out a shadow beyond.

"Come to the door. Who is with you?"

Carolyn stepped toward the window. "He's an old friend, Ravi. He's here to help me. Help us, maybe."

Moments later, they heard a deadbolt unlock and the blue door pulled inward.

"Come in," Ravi spoke in an exaggerated whisper. "Quickly."

As the door closed behind them, Carolyn put a concerned hand on the man's shoulder, turning him to face her. "Ravi, are you OK? What's going on?"

"I'm fine." He did not look her in the eye but stepped back, apparently uncomfortable with her touch. "Maybe I'm not fine. It is good to see you, Carolyn." He managed a smile.

Ravi was about five feet, ten inches tall with a modest build. He had black hair with brown eyes and skin that marked his origin somewhere in the Indian subcontinent. He seemed uncomfortable as he looked from Carolyn to Max and back to Carolyn.

"Who's this?"

"I'm sorry, Ravi," she quickly gushed, stepping back to put her other hand on Max's shoulder. "This is Max. He is an old friend. We went to high school together."

Ravi took a step back, looking directly at Max with eyes that held both anger and fear. "So you went to school with Tanner?"

"Yes," Max answered simply.

"Why were you looking in my garage?"

Max opened his hands with a slight shrug. "We were looking for you. If the garage was empty, it would have been a hint that maybe you weren't home."

"But the car was here, and you were leaving anyway," Ravi shot back.

Max shook his head. "We are not the Stasi. We were hoping to find you—hoping you could help—but we're not the breaking-down-doors type."

"I've heard differently." Ravi held eye contact for a moment longer before turning to the modest living room and slumping down in a recliner, motioning toward the couch. "Please sit down. You don't work for years with the likes of Tanner and Lyn without hearing stories of their friend in special forces."

"Marine Raiders," Max interrupted.

Ravi raised an eyebrow.

"When most people say special forces, it usually refers to the Army Green Berets or the Navy SEALS," Max continued. "Google it to see what I mean. I was a Marine Raider—technically special forces, but we're a different breed of dog."

"Got it." Ravi nodded. "No offense intended, but I've heard your name from both." He turned to Carolyn. "How can I help you?"

"TITAN is missing," Carolyn said, never one to beat around the bush.

Max watched Ravi's face move from shock to understanding and he finally shook his head with a smile. If he knew anything about reading players, he was pretty certain that this was the first time Ravi had heard the news.

"That explains a lot," Ravi pushed back, slouching farther into his chair.

"What do you mean?" Max asked.

"It explains the weirdos who have been following me." When the other two stared in silence, he continued, "I mean it. I thought I saw a car follow me out of The Olympic Club. Then I saw them in Safeway and at the liquor store. I told myself I was being paranoid, but I drove the long way home. The next day, I saw two different people looking at me in Starbucks. Again, I ignored it, but when I came home, as I turned up the street, I saw a van backing out of my driveway. It was turning toward me, so I pulled into the center of the street to block them, and I got out of the car. It was the same two who had followed me the previous day. I looked straight into the driver's eyes and shouted, 'What are you doing?' He stared back, and when I got closer, he backed into the neighbor's drive and sped off in the other direction."

"Did you follow them?" Max asked.

"Hell no, G.I. Joe." Ravi threw a hand in the air. "I pulled in, expecting that I'd been robbed. And I might have been."

Carolyn sat up and leaned her elbows on her knees. "What do you mean?"

"I think they broke in." He hesitated. "I mean, everything looked OK, and I didn't notice anything missing, but I couldn't shake the feeling that someone had been inside my home."

"Did they take TITAN?"

Ravi pulled on the arms of the recliner, holding his body almost vertical, his face contorted to express shock. "Carolyn, why would I have TITAN here?"

"I don't know, Ravi," Carolyn said, unapologetic. "Maybe because you've spent two years working sixty-hour weeks, and then when the fruit of your labor has arrived, Tanner announces that he wants to sell the company."

"I could say the same about you."

"But there's only one copy."

"And I don't have it."

"Can you describe the driver?" Max brought the conversation back to reality. "Do you remember his face?"

"I'll never forget him." Ravi turned to Max, allowing himself to sit back into the chair again. "He was Middle Eastern. Young, maybe late twenties. Black hair that was modestly long and light green eyes that seemed to look right into my soul. Like Satan himself."

"What about the other guy?"

"Also Arabic. Black hair, darker complexion."

"When was this?"

"Tuesday. No, Wednesday."

"Have you seen them since then?"

"No." Ravi sat up. "I haven't left the house."

Max stood up and walked to the bay window, looking out at the street as the mist rolled over the houses and cars.

"Why are you both so calm about TITAN?" he asked without turning.

"What do you mean?" Carolyn asked.

Max turned back into the room. "TITAN is missing, and neither of you know where it is, but there is no panic in your voice. Correct me if I'm wrong, but it's safe to describe this project as your baby—for both of you—so why aren't you more concerned about its disappearance?"

Ravi let out a sigh. "That is a valid question. Maybe it's because we are scared of holding its responsibility."

"That's bullshit." Carolyn shook her head. "The truth is that no one can use TITAN without one of us unlocking it. It's completely inert unless someone can hack into a 4096 bit RSA encryption."

"TITAN could do it," Ravi stated, raising an eyebrow.

"In theory, yes."

Max stepped back toward them with hands spread to either side, palms down in a traditional pause symbol.

"Hang on, folks," he said. "What is a 4096 bit encryption?"

"A 4096 bit *RSA* encryption," Ravi corrected him, "is an asymmetric cryptographic algorithm based on the mathematical challenge of factorizing large composite numbers."

"You basically find two large prime numbers and multiply them together," Carolyn added. "If they are sufficiently large, the permutations required to uncover the original factors becomes a herculean task. It can't be done."

Max ran his hand through his hair. "OK, so TITAN is safe even if we don't have it?"

"Yes." Carolyn leaned back in her chair with a sigh.

The three of them sat in silence, each thinking about the implications.

"It is not entirely safe, as you put it," Ravi said, and the other two turned to look at him.

"What do you mean?" asked Max.

"I mean that while the encryption is almost unhackable, it doesn't mean that TITAN is completely inert."

"What are you saying?"

Carolyn let out another sigh. "He's saying someone could access TITAN if they had a key."

"But you said it was unhackable?" Max said, confused.

"It is," Carolyn continued, "but if someone stole a key, they don't have to hack it. They could merely unlock it."

"So where's the key?" Max asked.

Carolyn held out her left arm, palm up, and pointed to a small red scar midway up her forearm.

"RFID chip. We both got them and we are the only two."

"Plus the seed code," Ravi added.

"What's that?"

"Do you hold any bitcoin?" Carolyn asked.

"No."

"OK, I thought you might be familiar with e-wallets. It is basically a set of randomly generated words that forms a backup, in case the keys are lost. If someone found the seed code, they could unlock TITAN."

"And where's the seed code?"

"On the LasTech server."

"And it gets worse," Ravi added. "They could then relock it with a new encryption." He put his fingertips together and then opened them in a mock explosion. "Poof. TITAN is no longer ours." He stared at Carolyn.

"Do you really think?" she responded softly.

Ravi nodded.

"Someone want to tell me what you two are talking about?" Max asked.

"Jenny," they responded in unison.

CHAPTER SEVEN

Max was deep in thought as his rideshare exited 280 onto John Daly Boulevard. The three of them had ordered sandwiches from a local deli and had eaten lunch before Carolyn drove Max back to his hotel. Nothing dramatic had been decided, but Max needed to find a way to talk to Tanner about his new wife's loyalties. In the meantime, Carolyn would return to LasTech headquarters to see if she could recover TITAN. It sounded unlikely, but it made sense to try.

Max had gone to his room to hunker down with his thoughts. There was a much bigger story here than he had originally expected. At this point, he barely knew who the players were except Tanner and Chao Fen. How much did Chao Fen know about TITAN? Who had TITAN now? What was Jenny's connection to Chao Fen? Was she responsible for the disappearance of TITAN?

From what Carolyn had said, they had been close enough that it was possible that Jenny could have stolen the key, but Carolyn was adamant that she hadn't shared it willingly.

Then came the most confusing call.

Ravi had rung Max's cell, asking him to come back to Westlake, alone. He wouldn't give his reason and said he couldn't talk on the phone, but he practically begged Max to humor him and keep the visit between the two of them. Max had agreed to return later in the day.

After the twenty-minute drive, the car pulled up to the now familiar bungalow. It was a little after 5:30, and the sun was down, but the streetlights provided ample light. A thin mist still blew through the air under the lights, and Max wondered if the weather was ever clear. He instinctively zipped his Gore-Tex vest after leaving the car, even though the door to the house was maybe fifteen yards away.

When he reached the door, it opened before he could knock, and Ravi welcomed him with a smile. He was unchanged from earlier, with his Tommy Bahama shirt falling loosely over comfortable jeans, but where earlier he had worn flip-flops he now had bright-blue running shoes.

"Thank you for coming." Ravi closed the door behind Max. "Can I get you anything to drink?"

"No, thanks," Max answered, turning to meet the man's eyes. "Not yet. What's going on? Why the secrecy?"

"Please." Ravi gestured to the small living room where they had talked earlier. He didn't wait for Max and plopped down in the recliner.

After a moment, Max followed him and took a seat on the couch. "OK, Ravi. Why am I here?"

"First of all," Ravi said eagerly, "after you guys left, Tanner showed up."

"Really?" That was a surprise. Max had been unable to reach him all weekend.

"Yes. He was also looking for TITAN."

"What did you tell him?"

"I told him the truth—I don't fucking know where it is!"

"Did you tell him about us?" Max purposely lowered his voice and slowed his cadence, hoping Ravi would be less agitated.

"No. And he didn't ask." Ravi matched the slower pace. "But he was very focused on TITAN. He started telling me that Chao Fen had asked him about the RFID chips—which he shouldn't know about. I pretended not to know and he got angry. I asked him to leave."

"How did he react?" Max knew the response. His high school friend had never liked to be told what to do.

"Not well, but he left." Ravi paused before continuing. "Then I saw the van again."

"What van?"

"The same one that I found in my driveway. When Tanner pulled away, I was at the window and saw the van pull out after him. When it passed the house, the driver looked my way, and once again I felt like I was looking into the eyes of Satan. It was definitely the same guy."

"Shit."

"There's more too." Ravi glanced at his hands before looking at Max. "I didn't tell you everything earlier. The man in the car—actually, the *men* in the car—they both had tattoos on their necks."

"What kind of tattoos?"

"That's what I'm trying to share. Are you familiar with the Faravahar?" the engineer asked, peering at Max in the dim light to see if there was any recognition.

Max nodded. "I spent years in the Middle East in counterterrorism, mostly targeting Muslim jihadists, but I spent enough time there to understand Zoroastrianism and the history."

One of the oldest monotheistic religions, Zoroastrianism was the dominant religion of Persia for over a millennium starting in the seventh century BCE and was considered a major influence on Christianity and Islam with its concepts of good versus evil, a messiah, and final judgment.

"So you are familiar with the Faravahar?"

"Yes. A winged disk with a bearded man at the center. He is

humanity, and the wings represent the idea of ascension."

"Correct. It is an iconic Zoroastrian symbol."

"OK, I'm interested, but why didn't you tell us this earlier?"

Ravi nodded as if making a decision. "How long have you known Tanner and Carolyn?"

"We go back to high school. Why?"

"How close have you been after high school?"

Max thought about it for a moment. "Not super close. My career took me out of the country. I've seen them at reunions—two, they didn't make the fifteenth. Apart from that, not much. An occasional email, but I still consider them good friends. Where are you going with this?"

Ravi balled his hands into fists in front of his lips, slowly nodding his head.

"Look, Max, I barely know you, and I'm not one hundred percent sure you'll take this the right way, so let me set the table a little better. I have known Carolyn and Tanner for ten years, and I've been at LasTech for six years, working closely with them—especially Carolyn."

"So?" Max interrupted, angry about the buildup.

"I'm saying I know them today a lot better than you do." He immediately held up his hands in defense. "I'm not saying I am a better friend. You have history, deep history that no one can replicate

—but I know more about who they are now, or who they were.”

“OK.” Max sighed and put his forehead on his left hand, elbow on the armrest. He was tired of beating around the bush. “I get it. Can you make your point? Why couldn't you mention this earlier?”

Ravi raised an eyebrow. “Did you know Carolyn has a Faravahar on her lower back?”

Max lifted his head. “She does?”

Ravi nodded.

“Like a tramp stamp?” Max blurted out the question in surprise, wishing he hadn't.

Ravi laughed. “Yes, exactly. And before you ask, I've only seen it in public. No relationship here.”

“When did she get that?” Max wondered aloud.

“More importantly, why did she get that?” Ravi responded, sitting slightly forward. “I assume you don't know, but Tanner and Carolyn adopted the Zoroastrian faith a long time ago—before I even knew them. I don't really talk to Tanner, but I thought Carolyn had given up on it. Anyway, I don't know how it's part of the picture, but I didn't want to bring it up with Lyn.”

Max slumped back onto the couch. “I'll take that drink. Beer?”

“Sure.” Ravi pulled himself up and left the room, presumably retrieving drinks.

Max ran his fingers through his hair, thinking about the weekend's events. This was a bizarre new twist—why would Zoroastrians care about TITAN? And if so, how was Carolyn involved? There were so many unknowns. The previous night he had been so happy to reconnect with her, it had felt like old times, but in truth they had both changed a lot over twenty years. How well did he really know her?

"Sierra Nevada?" Ravi asked, holding a bottle toward Max. He had another in his other hand.

"The original West Coast microbrew." Max smiled, accepting the beer. "Doesn't get enough credit. Great beer, thank you."

"Sometimes it's the little things."

"Carolyn's mother is Iranian," Max continued. "So there is a connection there, but I don't remember her as religious."

"Hey, man, I don't know the details, but I know they were pretty deep into it for a while. If you come to LasTech's HQ, you'll see the slogan on the entrance wall, 'Good Thoughts, Good Words, Good Deeds.' They practiced what they preached, but they did not push it directly on anyone. They gave a lot of money to local causes—still do, though I feel like both of them have backed off the religious component. Especially after the breakup."

"I think you know more."

Ravi explained his theory.

Though Max already had a good understanding of the Zoroastrian belief system, he found himself enthralled by the ideas Ravi brought up.

After forty-five minutes of discussion, he finally stopped Ravi and brought up the question that had been nagging him.

"But you still didn't want to mention this to Carolyn? As you've both said—you are good friends."

Ravi took a long pull on his beer. "Of the two of them, she seemed more committed. She often tried to share the teachings of Ahura Mazda with me. I don't really know, Max. I love Lyn. She has been great to me, but I'm scared. Those men scare me. I want to be left alone. At this point, I'd be happy to lie low and play golf for a few years."

"I get it." Max stood, putting his empty bottle on the table. "It's not Carolyn." He tried to sound confident. "But I'll dig deeper into this. Can I use the head?"

"Sure, through the kitchen and up to the right. Use the one by the bedroom. The one down here is out of order, and I've been too lazy to call a plumber." He managed a weak laugh.

"Got it." Max went through the kitchen, noticing several empty takeout bags on the countertops, reminiscent of his college days. He headed up a short flight of carpeted stairs, found the bathroom, and took care of business. Things were growing complicated.

* * *

When Max returned to the living room, he found Ravi standing at the far side of the room, looking out the bay window.

"I used to love staring out this window." Ravi didn't turn. "Now, I keep looking for that van."

"We'll sort this out." Max offered what he could, moving across the room to stand next to Ravi. "How am I going to find TITAN?"

"I'll help you." Ravi started to respond, but as Max stared out over the rooftops across the street, he caught the unmistakable flash of scope glint on the opposite roof. He reached his right arm around Ravi and pushed backward so that the two of them fell over the couch just as bullets sprayed the house, shattering the windows.

The two of them were now prone behind the couch as muffled gunfire continued to pelt the room, tearing up the curtains and peppering the room with bullets. Max hadn't been hit but Ravi wasn't moving, so he gently turned him over.

"You OK?" he asked, immediately seeing that he wasn't. He looked down and saw that Ravi's torso had taken a number of hits. It didn't look good.

"Fuck." Ravi groaned.

"I'm not going to lie to you," Max said, pushing a pillow against the torn torso. "It doesn't look good, but I need you alive. Can you move?"

Ravi turned his head slightly to look at Max. He shook his head without speaking. With a grimace, he reached his left hand into his pants pocket and pulled out a small thumb drive, which he passed to Max.

The bullets had stopped but it wouldn't be safe to move yet.

"What's this?" he asked.

"Take it." Ravi's voice was pained but he managed a smile. "Don't tell Carolyn. I was too squeamish for the implant."

Another round of bullets peppered the room through the empty windows and Max flattened himself. The attackers were using suppressors so the bullet strikes made more sound than the guns. This volley struck the ceiling and Max knew he didn't have much time to get away. Whoever was firing had to be on the street or closer.

He pushed himself to his elbows and looked at Ravi, knowing he couldn't take him, but his eyes had closed. If he was not dead already, it wouldn't be long.

Pocketing the thumb drive, Max waited for a lull in the gunfire and then scrambled on all fours toward the back of the house. In the kitchen, he heard the banging of someone trying to kick in the front door and he didn't wait to see if they were successful. He cursed himself for not bringing one of the guns. His only option was to flee and he moved to the back door.

The yard was small with a six-foot wooden fence surrounding it, separating it from the backyards of the neighbors and a house on the next street. On one side, a closed gate would lead to the front of the house, and before he could take evasive action it began to swing slowly toward the street. Max was thankful for fire codes that cause these gates to swing out. It forced the unsuspecting assailant to get around the gate, and by the time he entered the backyard, Max was already positioned to intercept.

The gun entered first, illuminated by a flashlight that the intruder held in his other hand, surveying the yard. Max slammed his left hand down on the man's right wrist, shattering bone and causing the gun to fall. With his right hand, he grabbed the long flashlight and flipped it up, smashing the man's face.

He brought his left fist around with a punch to the solar plexus, hearing the pained whoosh of air leave his victim, and he allowed the body to drop to the ground. He looked back into the kitchen, and no one was there yet, but he heard the sound of the front door finally yielding.

In three strides, he was at the back fence, and with two hands on the top he ran his feet up one of the posts and vaulted into the yard behind.

"Hey!" someone called from behind him, but he was already in the next yard and at another side gate. A figure came to the window, but he didn't stop.

He threw the gate open and ran past the house into the bright lights of the street beyond. He didn't like the thought of staying in the light, so he ran two houses to his left, across the street, and down a driveway where he snuck into the backyard of another darkened house.

He hobbled to the front of the house, seeing a row of apartments on the other side. Now he had a goal. If he could get to Northgate, the next street down led to a cul-de-sac, and beyond that was his best chance of escape. Years of military caution had forced him to review the terrain that morning before breakfast, even for a scenario that he could never have imagined would occur.

Max tried to appear normal as he limped lightly down the street. He could handle the pain, and his gait was only slightly off. A woman was walking the other way with a miniature Pinscher, which let out a sharp cat-like bark as he neared. She apologized and pulled the dog closer while he smiled and nodded on his way past.

When he reached Northgate, he turned right, and thirty yards down across the street he could see the entrance to the cul-de-sac. He slowed his pace further and walked toward it, hearing the whine of sirens still filling the early evening air. When he was about halfway there, a patrol car pulled into the intersection ahead of him and then turned onto Northgate, heading toward him.

Max had his hands in the pockets of his vest, elbows tucked in against the cold, head down, but he purposefully lifted his head and looked at the patrol car, putting on his best quizzical face as he stared into the eyes of the driver who was clearly attempting to find fault. The car slowed, and Max held the gaze, even as the car was almost alongside, then he shook his head and faced forward, doing his best to be disappointed with law enforcement, and it appeared to work. By the time he reached his turn, the squad car was gone.

At the end of the cul-de-sac was a four-foot concrete wall topped with a six-foot chain link fence, which Max scaled with ease, dropping into the bushes behind the tenth green at the famed Olympic Club golf course. He was careful not to land on his bad ankle, knowing that he had a long way to go.

After a few minutes crouched in the bushes to be certain that no one followed, he emerged onto the edge of a fairway and followed the tree line deeper into the course. He would have several exits from here.

CHAPTER EIGHT

For a guy who built his career around technology, Tanner was horrible at answering his phone, Max mused angrily. He had returned downtown by 7:30 and wasn't due to meet Carolyn until 9. On his trek back to the hotel, he had called and texted Tanner several times but got no response.

He'd debated calling Carolyn, but he'd be with her soon enough. At this point, he needed to clear out of his room. His fingerprints would be all over Ravi's house. By his calculation, he probably had a day or two before they would track him to the hotel, but there was no sense in risking it. His prints wouldn't be in the local database, but as soon as the cops searched the FBI's national database, his identity would pop up.

While he'd tried to avoid conflict, he'd been arrested twice in Vegas since leaving MARSOC—both times in what he considered justified fights, though law enforcement had disagreed. In both instances, the fact that his opponents were hospitalized probably contributed to the bias against him. Regardless, he was in the national database.

He smiled at the front desk clerk as he passed, thumbing the button for the elevator, which opened immediately. In his room, everything was in order, and he had very little to pack. With an hour and a half before he was to meet Carolyn, he opened his computer and inserted Ravi's thumb drive. What he found was amazing.

Ravi had done an enormous amount of research on his potential attackers and left a well-organized trove of data. Some of it was historical background, but in other places he had pulled recent articles and obscure news stories that all seemed to tie things together. By the time Max pulled himself away, he only had fifteen minutes until his meeting with Carolyn.

He took a quick shower and changed into a clean shirt. He only had two pairs of pants, so he put on the khakis that he had worn on Friday. The jeans were still functional but a little damp and dirty from the evening's exploits. He tucked them into his small carry-on with the rest of his gear and the machine pistol. He loaded the Glock, flipped on the safety, and tucked it into his small laptop shoulder bag. He would stay armed until this situation sorted itself out.

Back in the lobby, he crossed to the exit. The same clerk smiled as he passed.

"Checking out, sir?" she asked, nodding toward the carry-on that he pulled behind him.

"No. Not yet," he replied, mirroring her smile. "Running some errands."

It was less than a block to the bar where he had agreed to meet Carolyn for dinner.

Perry's Embarcadero was part of a local chain of like-named restaurants that were already iconic in San Francisco bar lore. Max had visited the original on Union Street twice over the years, so he was ready for a delicious burger, though this was his first visit to the downtown location.

At the entrance, the maître d' checked his travel bag before inviting him to find a spot at the modestly crowded bar. He'd given her Carolyn's name, but while she did not find the name in her book, she assured Max that it would be easy to get a table on Sunday night.

The room was long with a beautiful wood bar stretching most of its length on the wall opposite him. A few high-top tables filled the area in front of the bar, and Max could see booths and a seating area stretching beyond the bar to his left. He found two open seats at the bar toward the front of the house and smiled at the bartender, who motioned with a finger that she would be right back. He hung his laptop bag on the stool and took a seat. True to her word, the bartender returned before he could even text Carolyn that he had arrived.

"What'll you have?" she asked with a welcoming grin, and Max could not help but return the smile. Her auburn hair was pulled back in a ponytail, and she had a glow about her that diffused the years that appeared in wrinkles around her eyes. Max wondered what she had looked like in her youth.

He looked quickly at the taps before settling on his choice. "Anchor Steam, please."

"Sure thing." She placed a napkin in front of him and began to pour his beer. "Menu?"

"Not yet, thanks. I'm not sure if we are sitting down."

"No problem." She closed the tap and placed a full glass on the napkin, foam sliding down the side. "I'm Patti. Holler if you need me."

"Will do, Patti. Thank you." He picked up his glass with a tilt toward her in toast, accidentally spilling more foam down the side.

Max finished his beer and another as he waited. He casually watched the TV, the local station cutting into a basketball game with a news update that featured a helicopter view of the Westlake streets where Ravi had lived. Red and blue lights flashed at both ends of the street, and the area in and around Ravi's house was filled with police and emergency service vehicles. The audio was off, but the chyron read, "Unidentified homicide—possibly gang related." He hoped

Carolyn had not seen the news. It would be much better if he broke it to her personally.

"You sure you don't want to eat at the bar?" Patti returned, picking up his empty glass while holding a menu in her other hand.

"Not yet, thanks." He glanced at the empty entrance and looked back to the still smiling bartender. "Maybe after one more."

"You got it." She put the menu back and began filling a clean glass. "You in from out of town?"

"Yes, Vegas."

"Nice. Weather's better there this time of year."

"We don't get the rain, but it's not as hot as some people think."

"Oh, I know." Patti put the fresh beer down on the bar in front of him. "We have a place a bit south of there in Arizona. A lot of people think it's hot everywhere down there. They don't factor in elevation."

"Yep. Where about?" he asked.

Before she could answer, her eyes lifted to something behind him, and Max saw her grin widen.

"Carolyn, long time no see!" She turned to Max, reaching over the bar to pat his hand. "Is this the woman you're waiting for? You should have told me. Carolyn's a long-time customer."

Max turned to see Carolyn standing halfway to the bar, slightly turned away. She wore a white dress with a floral pattern that hung loosely about her thin frame, accented enough to remind Max of how hot she was. Her light-brown skin added almost perfect contrast to the bright dress, and Max was admiring her toned neck when she turned back abruptly and offered a wide grin when she saw his eyes.

Before he could acknowledge her, she turned back to her left, where Patti had walked around the bar to greet her. The two hugged, and Patti whispered something before the two joined Max. He stood, and Carolyn gave him a quick hug.

"Sorry I'm late, Max," she offered.

"Don't worry about it," he replied, motioning toward the bartender. "Patti has been taking care of me."

"I'm sure she has! Patti is one of the all-time greats!" Carolyn put her hand on Patti's shoulder.

"I didn't know you were royalty, Patti!" He smiled, looking for an opportunity to turn the conversation. While he was glad she had arrived, Max was concerned the news might cycle again.

"I hate to be rude, but I'm starving. I asked but don't think we have a reservation."

Carolyn cocked her head. "Of course we do! Did you ask for Dagny?"

Max was confused and answered with his expression.

"Dagny Taggart!" Carolyn laughed. "The protagonist in *Atlas Shrugged*. I always book under her name."

Patti nodded knowingly, and Max shook his head.

"Good to know for the future," he said. "One of my favorite books, and it doesn't surprise me that you'd pick her."

"We've got a booth." She turned to Patti. "You working the night shift? Or can you join us?"

"Wish I could. Eric's off, so I'm pulling a double today. Go sit. You want the usual?"

"Yes, please."

"Double Stoli soda with a lemon," Patti called over her shoulder as she returned to the bar. "It's on its way—no straw."

Max grabbed his beer and followed Carolyn to one of the first booths that lined the area between the bar and what looked like the main seating area.

"I love this place," she said as they slipped in opposite each other. "Moved here in '08. Before that, it was deeper in the Financial District and crowded with more suits."

"I've only been to Union Street."

"Well, that's the original, but it doesn't have Patti!"

A waitress arrived with menus and a pint glass filled with ice, a lemon wedge, and clear liquid.

"This is the one good thing that came from the old location. Some of the suits turned me on to this—it's basically an enormous glass of vodka with a splash of soda." She smiled again. "Patti is the best."

To the side, a busboy passed with a tray of food, and the smell of hot steak sent Max's stomach rumbling.

"So, how was your afternoon?" Carolyn asked after taking a long sip of her drink.

"Not good," he replied, reaching across the table to grab her hand. "Carolyn, I need you to listen to what I'm going to say, but it's important that you don't react. Can you do that?"

"I can try." She looked puzzled. "What's going on, Max? Did Tanner do something stupid?"

Max met her eyes. "No, it's not Tanner." He squeezed her hand as he spoke. "It's Ravi. He's dead, Car."

She gasped, straightening slightly but otherwise held her composure.

"How?"

Max met her eyes with a serious look. "They killed him, Car."

"Oh my God." Her free hand went to her mouth. "Who killed him? How? How do you know?"

"I was there. It was a planned assault—at least three or four men with silenced machine guns. Thankfully, I don't think they were military trained. I got away, but Ravi was hit bad."

When her eyes widened, glistening with tears, he added, "It was quick. I don't think he suffered."

"What the fuck is happening, Max?"

"I don't know, but I'm sure it's related to LasTech and TITIAN."

Carolyn wiped her eyes, unable to stop some of the tears, and Max wanted to give her time.

"What were you doing at his house?" she asked suddenly after pulling herself together. When she looked up, her eyes were penetrating.

Max returned her gaze, thinking about how he had planned to bring up Ravi's theory, but he found it hard to speak. He did not want to believe that Carolyn could be involved, but how well did he know her?

"Max, why were you at Ravi's house?"

"He asked me to come back," he said, unsure if he wanted to tell her.

"When? Why did he call you? And why wasn't I involved?" She pulled her hand out from under his and put it in her lap.

Max took a deep inhale through his nose. "Fair question. Ravi loved you, Carolyn. You have to know that, and he repeated it to me."

"So?"

"He was conflicted though. He told me the men in the van who had been following him . . . both had Faravahars tattooed on their necks."

Carolyn shook her head and started to speak, but Max held up his hand to stop her.

"Look, Carolyn—there are no accusations here, and your beliefs are your beliefs, but Ravi was scared, and he needed someone to talk to. Someone who is not a Zoroastrian."

Carolyn continued to shake her head, now looking at the table. "It's not something to be ashamed of!" she said more harshly than he expected.

"I'm not saying it is. In fact, it deserves all the respect of one of the most ancient religions." He paused. "Are you still practicing?"

"To the extent that I practice any religion—yes, I still believe in Ahura Mazda." She brushed renewed tears from her eyes. "Why wouldn't he tell me?"

"I don't know. He was scared. He knew that you and Tanner were Zoroastrian but felt that maybe it was more you than Tanner."

"Why? Because I'm Persian?" Her voice elevated slightly. "That's racist, isn't it? Maybe he should accuse me of being an Islamic jihadist. There are quite a few more Muslims in Iran than Zoroastrians."

Max motioned his open hands toward the table, silently asking her to lower her voice.

Her watery almond eyes widened as she realized the implication.

"Max"—she looked to her left before continuing in a low hiss—"I did not have anything to do with his death. Do you really fucking believe that I might be involved?"

"Look, he was concerned—and now he's dead. I'm not suggesting you had anything to do with it, but the fact remains that Ravi is now dead, and I'm probably a suspect. I can't reach Tanner. I have no fucking clue what's going on here."

"Ready to order?" the waitress asked as she swung by the table, not realizing she was interrupting.

Max looked up with a weak smile and turned back to Carolyn.

"What would you like?"

"I'm not hungry, thanks." She passed her menu back to the waitress, holding her empty pint glass in the other hand. "I'll have another of these."

"Perry's burger with bacon, please. And fries." Max passed his menu to her as well. He had little appetite but knew to take a meal when available.

When the waitress left, Carolyn put both palms on the table, straightening slightly, and looked across at Max with a hard stare.

"What now?"

"I don't know. I really don't. Have you spoken to Tanner today?"

"Nope. I haven't spoken to him since he told us of the potential sale. But he hasn't stopped texting me since, except now that you ask, I haven't received anything from him today."

"If I can't get a hold of him tonight, I'll try the office in the morning. There's still work to be done to complete the deal."

"And he needs TITAN."

Max rubbed his eyes. "Yes, that's still a problem. I'm going to hit the head." He shifted out of the booth, but before he stood, he asked, "You going to be here when I return?"

Carolyn actually let out a small laugh. "Yes, Max. I'm not going anywhere without another drink."

Max followed the signs toward the bathroom, walking down the row of booths, and he pretended not to see the two Middle Eastern men seated at the last booth before he turned to the bathroom. Both had half-empty sodas, and the remnant bones of a plate of chicken wings sat on the table between them. Neither looked up as he passed, but Max felt their attention like one felt the sun on the back of their head. He took care of business and as he returned, he glanced at the neckline of one of them and saw the tattoo that Ravi had described— the Faravahar. Staying discrete, he could not examine the other's neck, but it didn't matter. These two were in play.

More surprising, he now noticed a trio of Chinese men in a booth on the other side. They were all dressed in black suits, similar to the ones he had run into two nights earlier. When one made eye contact, he quickly turned away while one of the others typed busily into his phone.

Max slowed his pace, taking a deep breath as he questioned himself, wondering if he was over-evaluating a simple coincidence.

When he got back to the table, his burger had arrived. Carolyn, despite her lack of hunger, was nibbling on one of his fries. Max kept the two potential threats to himself.

"What's the connection?" she asked as he slid back into the booth.

"What do you mean?" he unrolled his napkin and put it on his lap, placing the silverware on the table.

"What's the connection to Zoroastrianism?" She opened her hands. "The faith is about Asha versus Druj, truth versus falsehood, order versus disorder. It's about the threefold path: good thoughts, good words, good deeds."

She took another sip and motioned to the waitress for another.

"That's why Tanner and I became so involved. It is a nonviolent religion. It is much more about living a good life and doing good for others. How does that connect with all this? How does that lead to murder?"

As she spoke, Max took a bite of his burger and savored the well-mixed flavors. It didn't need any condiments. The seared beef had a perfect crust, and inside was a rich medium rare accented by the well-cooked but not brittle bacon. He allowed himself time to finish his mouthful before answering.

"Ravi was an intense guy, and his theory has pretty sound footing." He pulled his laptop out of its case, and the screen came instantly to life, still on the same web page where he had left it with Ravi's green thumb drive still sticking out of a USB port. Turning the computer so that Carolyn could see the screen, he said, "For starters —look at this."

Carolyn emptied the last of her glass, and a fresh one arrived as she put it down. She stared at the screen for a long moment.

"Armageddon? Are we really going there?" she asked.

Max nodded, finishing the bite. "It's a belief shared by Judaism, Christianity, and Islam."

"Yes, but it originated in Zoroastrianism."

"Exactly. The Jews and Christians borrowed a lot from them— good versus evil, the messiah, and for Christians even the concept of the virgin mother."

"I'm familiar."

"Yeah, but Ravi dug deeper, and he discovered a group online that makes an interesting case that we are in the third age."

"So?"

"So, according to Zoroastrian canon, at the end of the third age, the messiah—the Zoroastrian messiah, Saoshyant—will bring about the resurrection of the dead and the final judgment will occur."

When Carolyn did not respond, he continued, "OK, bear with me. The three ages are the age of creation, the second of mixture, and the third of separation. Clearly, the first occurred a long time ago. The theory is that the age of mixture began with Cyrus the Great and ended with World War I. Think of how much the world blended over that span. Anyway, the belief is that we are now of the age of separation and the end of days nears."

Carolyn shook her head. "No, Max. I'm familiar with the three ages, but I completely disagree with this conclusion. Even if that were true, there is nothing that calls for violence."

"I guess it depends on your beliefs."

"What does that mean?"

"If you believe something deeply enough, lines can be crossed."

She turned the computer toward herself and began to type, her fingers adroitly working on the keyboard. He hadn't really offered, but he knew she would go through the contents of the thumb drive, which was good. He wanted to get her spin on the data.

He stuffed the last bite of his burger into his mouth, wiping his chin as the juices escaped his lips, but he remained silent, allowing her to review the information.

"This is out there, Max." She shook her head again. "It's

borderline crazy."

"So is Ravi's murder."

They sat in silence while they both picked at the remaining fries on his plate.

"Thoughts?" Max probed.

Carolyn looked around nervously, surprising him. "Not here."

"OK, let's go."

Max called the waiter over and handed her his credit card. Carolyn made an effort to protest him paying, but he pointed out that she didn't eat.

The waitress dropped a check at the booth with the two Persians, but he continued to keep their presence to himself. He packed his computer but put the thumb drive in his pocket.

As they left the restaurant, he picked up his wheelie bag, handing the hostess a twenty.

"What's up with the bag?" Carolyn asked as they entered the street.

"I'm pretty sure that I'm going to be a suspect. I have to find another place to stay."

"Give it to me."

When Max gave her a questioning look, she held her hand out demandingly, so he put the pull handle in her hand.

She turned down the street and pulled it behind her, saying over her shoulder, "You're staying with me."

* * *

When they reached her car, Max was happy to see it was sandwiched between a van and an SUV in diagonal street parking. As Carolyn opened the trunk, he moved in as if to help with the bag, but mostly he needed her to listen.

"C, look in the trunk," he said as he took the handle from her. "Don't look at me yet, but listen. I'm going to pretend to get in the car with you, but I will stay out here."

She turned slightly toward him. "Max, what are you—"

"Listen," he interrupted, raising his voice slightly. "You know my past. I'm telling you that you need to listen to me—right now. I'll call you as soon as you pull out, and we will keep the line open. Back out slowly and head down Steuart. Move slowly, and take a right at the next street. I'll be on the phone with you before you take the turn."

He made a show of arranging the bag in the trunk so that he could finish his instructions. Carolyn pushed the button that closed the trunk, but did not turn to him. She moved to the driver's side.

"You are scaring me. Are we in trouble?"

Max mirrored her on the passenger side, looking casually behind them and seeing no one visible on the street. The van blocked their view of Perry's entrance, which also shielded them.

"I'm not sure. I don't think so, but do as I ask . . . please." He looked across the glass roof at her, seeing pleading eyes in the streetlights. "You'll be OK."

He opened his own door, put his laptop bag on the seat, then removed the Glock and tucked it into his vest. Closing the door, he dropped to a crouch then shuffled to the van and slid himself under the front, between the curb and the wheels.

As the Tesla slowly backed out, he typed Carolyn's number on his phone before slipping the device into his pocket. He pushed an earbud into his right ear and heard her pick up.

"Max, what the fuck is going on?" she practically shouted, and he winced, knowing the sound could carry even from his earbud.

"Shhh," he hissed, following in a light whisper, "I can't talk yet, and your voice will give me away. Drive and listen."

"OK," she answered in a much softer voice.

The Tesla had only backed up, but now it rolled slowly south on Steuart. Max looked out to the street, looking to see if they'd been followed.

It was unnecessary, as footsteps approached rapidly and Max found himself pulling in his feet to make sure he wasn't visible from his position under the nose of the van. He'd planned to surprise whoever was following them, but he had to quickly rethink things as the footsteps stopped on both sides of the van where he was hiding. The beep of doors unlocking sounded, followed by both doors opening.

He cursed himself, remembering too late Ravi's description of the van. He quickly reworked his plan of attack.

"Turn right at the end," he whispered to Carolyn. "Keep crawling. You'll make another right at the next intersection. I'll check back in a few." He ended the call as the doors to the van closed, and the starter shrieked for a few seconds before the roar of the engine answered.

As the van backed into the street, Max rolled into motion. He was instantly up, and before the van could fully turn into the street, he shattered the passenger window with the butt of his Glock, turning the weapon to point it first at the driver. Fearing that the passenger might get heroic, he positioned it against the nearer man's temple. The van jerked to a halt, the driver's foot on the break, but the van was still in gear.

"Everybody stay cool." Max wanted to calm the situation. "Put the car in park."

Both men were wide-eyed at the intrusion. They had thought themselves the predator and were unaccustomed to being the prey. When Max repeated his command, the driver shifted to park.

"Who hired you?" Max asked.

The driver shook his head. "Nobody hired us." He looked

nervous, and Max knew he must be must be lying, but he didn't have time for a full interrogation.

"Wrong answer." In an instant, he pointed the Glock at the driver's thigh and pulled the trigger. The sound of the gunshot filled the cab, and the driver immediately howled in pain.

The passenger's hands went to his ears, but Max returned the nozzle of the Glock to the man's face and silently made eye contact to confirm the man would stay still. At that moment, he was reminded of Ravi's comment about the green eyes of Satan.

The driver pushed his head back to the corner of the door, looking up with a pained expression. As he did, Max could see the full Faravahar tattooed along his neck.

"Who hired you?" he asked again.

As the driver lowered his head to meet Max's stare, a squeal of tires sounded from down the street, forcing Max to glance around the van where he could see a black SUV had backed out of a parking spot. As he watched, the SUV engaged to drive and pulled toward the van as the tinted passenger window rolled down, and Max recognized the silhouette of a Russian PP-19 Bizon before he lost sight of it behind the van.

He turned and dove over the hood of a parked car as the sound of machine gun fire rattled the van. Behind him, he heard the engine engage, but the Persians did not get far. The SUV moved slowly by, riddling the van with fire, then its engine roared to life and it sped away toward Howard Street.

The van, now in gear, rolled slowly in the same direction, but Max doubted that either of the men were alive. Its progress ended as it collided with a service truck parked on the opposite side of the street, activating the truck's alarm and adding to the night's cacophony.

Max didn't wait to see anything else. Picking himself up, he hustled to the entrance of the Rincon Center, which was one door away on his side of the street. He'd surveyed the area map before leaving the hotel, and this was his primary exit from Steuart Street. As he ran, he thumbed his phone to redial Carolyn.

She answered before he heard it ring.

"Max, was that gunfire? What the fuck is going on?"

"Where are you?" he asked.

"I'm on Howard, almost at Spear."

"Right on Spear, please." Max was slightly short of breath as he ran through the mostly deserted mall. The Rincon Center was a former post office that had been converted to retail in the 1980s and remained an active lunchtime location, but on a Sunday evening it was a wasteland.

"Spear is one way. I can't turn right." Carolyn was agitated. "Someone pulled out behind me."

"Right on Spear, baby." Max repeated as he pushed open the

mall exit on the Spear side. "Trust me on this one. I'll meet you halfway down the street."

He moved across the sidewalk to the street where only a few cars were parked on Sunday night. The nearest one was a Honda Accord, easily ten years old, and he positioned himself with his gun in outstretched arms over the roof with a clear view of the street. He watched over the top of his barrel as Carolyn's Tesla remained in idle, facing not quite diagonally down the street. Despite the hour, the streetlights illuminated the area, almost as if it were daylight and her car sat in the slightly brighter intersection.

"Carolyn," he spoke calmly, knowing she was panicked. "No one's coming the other way. Head to me, and I'll get us out of here."

"OK." He heard her voice trembling, but the Tesla started to complete the turn.

Just as it did, the SUV roared into view and slammed into her rear quarter, spinning the Tesla further so that it was pointing back the way she came rather than toward him.

A shriek pierced his ears. Carolyn screamed and cursed.

Max took a deep breath. He sighted down the barrel and squeezed off two shots at the passenger side of the SUV. He couldn't fire in rapid bursts as he would have preferred because he did not have much ammo. At this distance, he did not expect to be pinpoint, but he was glad that the first hit the front door, and the second shattered the window above it. He thought he saw a body bounce at the impact, but he didn't have time to care. Everything was moving fast.

As his shots hit home, another SUV screeched around the corner and moved in front of the first, blocking Max's line of sight on the other assailants.

"Carolyn?" he asked, looking over his outstretched gun as he moved into the street. "Are you OK, Carolyn?"

As he spoke, three men swarmed her car, but he dared not shoot for fear of hitting her. The Glock 19 was a great pistol, but at this distance its accuracy was poor. He couldn't risk a shot.

She cursed again. "Holy fuck."

Max swung his aim at the second SUV and released another six shots in rapid succession, over half of his magazine now gone. He began running toward the cars.

"I'm sorry, Max."

He saw the men pull her out of the car, and his earbud went dead.

He kept running and had closed about half the distance when a figure popped up above the second vehicle holding a machine pistol and opened fire, filling the street with bullets.

Max had no choice but to dive behind a parked minivan, amazed that he was still whole.

Another gun joined the barrage, and Max pulled himself to the far side of his barrier vehicle, putting the front tire between himself and the onslaught.

After a moment, the firing stopped, and Max knew he would probably not get another chance, so he swung back up and resumed fire on the SUV. To the right, he saw Carolyn already on the other side of her car, escorted by the three men. As he fired, he saw her turn and open the passenger door. One of the men held her other arm, but she emerged with his laptop bag before being pulled out of sight and into the first SUV.

Max heard the click of his empty weapon as the shooter with his machine pistol re-emerged above the SUV, and he was forced once again to dive for cover. He felt a bolt of pain in his right leg, and the bullet's impact turned him as he fell behind another car, and more bullets showered the area.

With his back against a tire, he surveyed the damage, gently pulling his knee in. He was bleeding pretty badly, but it wasn't a direct hit. The bullet only hit the edge of his thigh but it had made a much larger hole on exit. The wound was not large enough for major concern, but it showed that they were using hollow point ammo.

He would survive the wound, but the fact that they were using hollow points in a machine pistol indicated they were intentionally looking to destroy and murder any opposition. They were playing for keeps.

This time, when the barrage ended, it was followed by the chirp of tires, and Max pulled himself up to look above the hood only to see the two SUVs driving away down Howard Street. He got himself upright and hop-skipped the remaining twenty yards to the intersection, ignoring the pain in his right thigh, but by the time he got there he could only see the taillights of the second vehicle as it turned south.

He turned back to the scene. Bullet casings were everywhere. The Tesla now sat blocking the street in an eerie silence. He slammed the passenger door closed and moved around the back, quickly assessing the damage. It looked like the wheel was still operable, so he climbed in the front seat looking for the ignition, but he found none.

He heard the distant wail of sirens and knew he would not have long to get away from the scene. Holding the wheel in both hands, he closed his eyes, trying to remember what Carolyn had done. In the background, the sirens grew louder.

Finally, he remembered a credit card that Carolyn had put on the console when she got in, then she had put it in the center compartment. He practically ripped the top off and dug into the contents, finding the black card relatively close to the top of a mound of tissues and papers. He placed it on the console behind the cup holders, as she had done, and a few electronic clicks indicated he had been successful.

There was no gear shift, but he had seen Carolyn using the control stalk on the steering column. He had joked about "three on the tree," which was an old reference to mid-seventies' models American vehicles that offered gear shifters on the steering column, but Carolyn had not understood the reference.

He pulled down the stalk and was relieved to see the dashboard indicator move to D, so he pressed the accelerator, and the car moved forward with only modest noise from the damaged rear end. Cranking the wheel to turn the car back onto Howard, he eventually faced the way the assailants had retreated.

Gingerly, he pressed harder on the pedal and moved forward with a silent acceleration and no further complaint from the rear quarter. The sirens had grown louder, and looking in his rearview mirror he could see the blue and red rollers of several squad cars reflecting off the buildings in the streets behind him. He turned south where the SUVs had turned, but he had no hope of finding them.

Max kept heading southwest for several blocks to get away from the activity, and after five minutes he pulled over on a somewhat deserted street to look at his leg again. As he did, he noticed the map had defaulted to some kind of guidance, so before he put the car in park he studied the center display screen. A line led straight and then turned north on the next street. At the bottom of the display, the readout read, "Home 67% 17 min."

He silently thanked Carolyn for being as tech-heavy as she was. At least now he had some place to go.

CHAPTER NINE

Sunlight washed the room as Max reluctantly opened his eyes. He stared at the ceiling for a few moments before pulling himself up in bed to lean against the headboard, wincing slightly as the movement agitated his makeshift bandage.

He inhaled deeply, enjoying the scent of Carolyn as he looked around the room for the first time in daylight. The sheets had been fresh, and everything was in good order. Opposite him, a large picture window looked out over the tops of Pacific Heights and another on the wall to his right provided a stunning view over the San Francisco Bay.

The bed was high enough to give him a nice vantage point without standing. Under the window on his right was a green leather chair with an ottoman and a small accent table layered with magazines. On the other side of the room was a beautiful wood bureau, no doubt from

Restoration Hardware or the like, flanked by doors on either side, one leading to the living room and the other to her en-suite bathroom.

Max thought back to the previous night.

After fleeing the scene, he had driven deep into the Mission District until he found an all-night bodega that he'd hoped wouldn't care when a wounded man stumbled in. At the entrance, he had snagged a baseball cap and pulled it low over his face in case someone asked to view the security video. He had grabbed water, hydrogen peroxide, some shop towels, and duct tape.

Noticing a sewing kit near the register, he added that to his pile and went back for some unwaxed dental floss. Lastly, he'd grabbed a six-pack of Sierra Nevada. The total was less than the fifty-dollar bill that he'd had in his pocket, and he told the attendant to keep the change, quickly returning to the Tesla.

Leaving most of the supplies in the bag, he splashed some of the hydrogen peroxide over the wound, holding in a gasp when the pain flared, and then applied a towel and wrapped his pant leg with the duct tape. It wasn't a long-term solution, but it would slow the bleeding and keep some of the blood off of Carolyn's car.

From there, he had allowed the vehicle's navigation to guide him home, and it was easy to drive the relatively quiet San Francisco streets. His path was almost all northward and slightly west toward the marina, and the Tesla brought him to a high-rise in Pacific Heights, on the hill south of the marina. Max was somewhat surprised that Carolyn had allowed herself the luxury of this address, no matter her success.

The vehicle had guided him right up to a closed gate, and when Max pressed the garage remote, it opened quietly and allowed him in. He'd parked in the nearest spot, backing in to hide the car's damage. Before he left the car, he'd spent a few minutes figuring out how to open the glove box and eventually discovered that it too was operated through the display screen. Inside it, he found her apartment number listed on her registration card. Another five minutes of digging through her console had not yielded any keys, so he'd grabbed his shopping bag and his luggage and hobbled to the elevator, hoping not to run into any other tenants. He'd find a way in.

Once at her door, he discovered an alphabetic lock, but he could see that the hardware was not in great shape, and he'd pulled out his knife, confident he could jimmy the latch bolt.

Before he did, however, he remembered the conversation earlier in the evening and thumbed the letters for "Dagny" on the handle. A light click confirmed his guess, and he was thankful he could enter the apartment without needing to do any damage.

The apartment was very nice, and there were elements of Carolyn all around—possibly better described as "upscale Carolyn," he'd thought to himself. There was no ornamentation, but it was a very refined apartment. Everything was simple, tidy, in its place . . . and expensive—if Max could trust his somewhat limited understanding of decoration.

He'd dumped his supplies on the kitchen table, putting the four remaining beers in the fridge, and explored the apartment, immediately aware that he was still dripping blood. He would clean up in the morning, he told himself.

While there was a small guest room, Max decided to use the master, which was much nicer and had an en-suite bathroom with an old-school porcelain tub and a nicely tiled shower. He turned on the hot water to fill the tub while he returned to the kitchen for another beer and the rest of his supplies.

Soaking in the tub had been both soothing and painful. His body enjoyed the warmth, but the wound stung and leaked red into the water. After ten minutes, he straightened himself up and began the painful work of cleaning the damage, which only aggravated the bleeding, soon making the water so crimson that even the warmth was no longer appealing. He unplugged the drain and sat up on one side, ignoring the water that spilled and dripped onto the white tile floor.

The wound was definitely manageable, and while the skin was red, it looked pretty clean. He took another long swig of his beer before dousing the wound, once again, with hydrogen peroxide, allowing himself to mentally float above the pain that flared to life as the antiseptic did its work. He needed to separate his mind from the pain if he was going to be effective at the next task, and this was another skill that he'd honed over the years.

For a minute or two, he fought to open the well-packaged sewing kit, but before long he had a sewing needle in hand, pulled out a long length of dental floss that would form his sutures, and tied a knot in the end. He knew the first prick was always the worst, so he squeezed the skin together, positioned the needle, and looked away as he jammed the point into his flesh. It hurt like hell—it always did, but after the first few sutures were in place, he could get into a rhythm, ignoring the pain that continued as he made his way around the somewhat jagged exit wound.

He ran out of length and had to tie up the floss before starting again with a new strand, but when he was done he looked down at a relatively well-sewn wound. The bleeding had almost entirely stopped, except for a few drops near the largest gap of skin. He patted it dry before stepping down and drying the rest of his body. When he searched her cabinet, he'd been happy to find some first aid ointment and gauze, which he'd used to wrap up the wound for the night.

In the midmorning light, Max pulled the cover off his leg to see how things looked, and he saw a mostly white strip of gauze that had some red coming through in one spot. He lifted it gingerly, feeling little bursts of pain as the skin moved and undoubtedly broke scabs that were trying to heal.

Turning in the bed, he dropped first to his left foot then slowly extended the wounded right, feeling the pain intensify as he put pressure on it, but the pain was manageable. It would take some time for the wound to knit together, but the leg was usable.

He would have loved a shower, but it was best to keep the wound dry, so he washed his face in the sink, thankful to at least have his own Dopp kit. He unwrapped the leg and inspected the wound, nodding to himself in satisfaction. The edges were still pink with healing, but there was no sign of infection. He reapplied the ointment and rewrapped the leg before walking out to the main living area.

The kitchen was on the far side of the living room, but Max paused halfway there, turning to the wall of glass that framed the view of San Francisco Bay. It was stunning. While the view from the bedroom focused more on the western side with a view of the Golden Gate Bridge, this panorama stretched from the towers of the bridge, past Alcatraz Island to the far shores of the East Bay.

His stomach growled, bringing him out of his reverie, and he turned back to the kitchen, where he had seen a coffee machine the night before.

In no time, he had a pot of coffee brewing and was poking around for breakfast. She had bacon in the fridge, which was tempting, but Max didn't want to do dishes, so he made himself a plate of avocado toast. In the spice drawer, he found some Himalayan pink sea salt and sesame seeds, which he added to the toast along with a little ground pepper. The aroma of brewing coffee filled the room as he worked, and for a second it felt like home.

In the living room, one chair was positioned toward the panoramic view with a side table next to it that held a book and some papers. Max smiled to himself, knowing this would be Carolyn's morning routine as he took the seat, putting his coffee on the papers and holding the plate on his lap.

In the last three days, he'd had two attempts on his life, witnessed a murder, been in another gun fight, gotten wounded, and seen his friend kidnapped. He let out an audible laugh, catching himself before bits of food flew out of his mouth. What the fuck was happening here?

He pushed himself to a straight-back position, and ran his hands through his hair, closing his eyes for a quick moment. He needed to find Tanner. There had to be a connection to Chao Fan, and he needed Tanner to help with answers—but Tanner hadn't answered his texts or calls all weekend. Technically, Max was due to meet Tanner at LasTech headquarters at noon today, prior to another meeting with Chao Fen, but Max was uncertain if he should attend. He knew his prints had been at Ravi's, and he suspected he was likely on the

SFPD's wanted list, or he would be soon. That said, they would not know to look for him at LasTech.

Spying the remote on the coffee table, he pushed himself up and flicked on the large TV that hung on the interior wall. He clicked around until he found a local news channel.

An anchorman said, "And now down to Julie Wren on scene." Max looked up to see an attractive Asian woman standing at the intersection of Howard and Spear.

"Thank you, Matt," she said into a microphone with a large orange windscreen. "I'm here at the scene of what the police are saying was a large gang battle last night. Eyewitnesses saw two black SUVs and multiple assailants in a gunfight against an unknown number of adversaries." She walked out into a street that was cordoned off with yellow tape, giving the camera a view down Spear. "Several vehicles and the surrounding buildings were riddled with gunfire."

"Have they identified anyone involved?" the anchor asked.

"Not yet, Matt, but the police are still collecting mounds of evidence." The camera panned to the street, which was littered with casings and a good number of police cones used to identify separate evidence troves.

Max took another sip of coffee while he watched the coverage and now that the temperature was right, he followed it up with a long swallow, thanking Carolyn for good taste.

The reporter began to show close-ups of the damaged cars and Max moved back to his chair, but just as he'd eased his leg up on a stool, a harsh buzzer sounded behind him.

It was a long buzz, followed by two shorter buzzes. He looked toward the door and could see a TV monitor that had sprung to life. He could see a figure on the screen as the buzzer sounded again.

Max pushed himself up and walked to the door. On the screen he could see a figure turned away, but there was no way he was going to answer it. This was Carolyn's apartment, and technically speaking he had entered unlawfully. He watched the screen, hoping the figure would walk away, but the man turned back and buzzed again, holding the buzzer for an annoyingly long time. As he did, Max's eyes widened as he saw a familiar face.

He didn't speak into the intercom, but he thumbed the release that opened the door.

* * *

"Max?" Tanner's face was in shock as he stood in the hallway outside Carolyn's apartment. He wore khakis and a button-down Oxford. Typical SF business attire. It had taken him less than two minutes to ride the elevator upstairs, but Max had found enough time to put on a clean golf shirt and his cleaner pair of jeans, which he hoped were baggy enough to conceal his wound.

"Hey, Tanner. Come in," he responded, holding back his own anger. He stepped back, allowing Tanner to enter before he closed the door.

"Why are you here?" Tanner asked.

"Long story. We need to talk."

Tanner looked around the room quickly and turned to look at Max, anger in his eyes.

"Look, Max, Carolyn and I are no longer together, but I hired you for a job—not to reignite old high school flames."

"Hold on, Tanner." Max put his hand gently on his friend's chest. "You've got it wrong."

"To hell I do, mate." Tanner's words were sharp, almost bitter. "I know you both too well."

He turned toward the bedroom and raised his voice. "Carolyn, we need to talk."

Max put a hand on his shoulder, but he brushed it aside, stepping closer to the bedroom.

"This is serious, Carolyn. You can't keep avoiding me. I need your signature, and I need TITAN! Enough of this bullshit!"

"You done?" Max spoke quietly.

Tanner turned, redirecting his anger at Max. "No, I'm not done.

This whole fucking deal is a mess, and you haven't helped one bit." He turned his head toward the bedroom. "Carolyn, get out here."

"She's not here, Tanner."

"What do you mean? Where is she?" His tone settled down. "Max, do you know where she is?"

Max shook his head, motioning for Tanner to sit on the couch while he sat back in his chair. Tanner complied, the fight seeming to have died.

"Bro," he drawled. "Why are you alone in Carolyn's apartment? And where is Carolyn?"

Max ignored the questions.

"Tan, where the fuck have you been?" Max felt his own anger rising. "I've been calling and texting all weekend."

Tanner pulled out his phone. "What number?" He turned his phone toward Max, apparently trying to show no messages.

"The same number I've been using all week!" Max answered incredulously.

"Oh shit, man." Tanner shook his head. "That's my work cell. I leave that at the office on weekends. I should have given you my bat line." He offered a weak smirk.

Max shook his head. "We've got a lot to talk about."

"What's going on?"

Max motioned toward the TV, where the reporter was still reviewing the scene with her anchor on this otherwise news-less morning. "We'll talk about that later. I'll start with Saturday."

He described his search for Carolyn, skipping the boring details but culminating in dinner and then the visit to Ravi on Sunday morning. From there, the story got more interesting, and Max was careful to let Tanner hear and understand everything that went down—without mentioning Carolyn and Ravi's shared suspicion of Jenny. As the narrative unfolded, he discussed Ravi's concerns about the men following him and about his research into Zoroastrian cults while omitting Ravi's revelation that Tanner had visited him. He finished with the previous night's shootout and Carolyn's abduction, leaving out the details of his wound.

"This doesn't make any sense." His friend shook his head. "None of it. LasTech and Chao Fen have a legitimate deal. This can't be related to us. And Zoroastrianism? Shit, it's a way of life, but it's not a passion project. I don't know where Ravi found this extreme group, but violence and Armageddon is not what we're about. Hell, why would they kidnap Carolyn? Are you sure this isn't something from *your* past that's resurfaced?"

Max took in a deep breath. It was his turn to shake his head. "The only thing in my past that's resurfaced is my ability to extricate us from this situation—but to do that, I need to understand who the players are, and at this point I'm at a complete loss. I need you to tell me everything you know."

Tanner put his face in his hands for a moment, rubbing his eyes. When he looked up, Max was struck by the sadness on his face. "What do you need to hear?"

"Let's start with TITAN."

"Sure." Tanner reclined onto the couch. "What do you want to know?"

"What is it, exactly?" Max threw a hand in the air. "What's its value to LasTech and to Chao Fen? Why is it missing? Who might have it?"

"OK. Easy, Max." Tanner made a face that suggested things were being overly dramatic.

Max could feel his anger boiling. "No, don't give me that. I've had bullets flying at me twice in the last three days, and we're talking serious shit. I am working for you—yes—but if you don't start coughing up answers, I won't be around for long." Even as he spoke, he knew he couldn't leave without finding Carolyn, but he hoped his friend wouldn't figure that out.

"OK, sorry. You're right."

"TITAN?"

Tanner pushed himself up from the couch and walked to the window. He looked out over the bay as he spoke without turning back to Max.

"TITAN began as a new version of our protection protocol—well, that's not right. It was less a new version and more of an alternative approach to system security and maintenance. It was Carolyn's brainchild, but I think over time it became Ravi's baby. The two of them individually are amazing thinkers, but together—let's say I'm glad they are on our side."

"Or were," Max interjected tonelessly.

"God. Yeah. I haven't really processed that."

"You were saying?"

"Sorry—TITAN began as a new approach to security and was already a game changer when Ravi decided to incorporate AI. Did you know that besides his work for us, Ravi is—was—one of the leading voices on machine learning? I don't know where he found the time."

Max remained silent, letting his friend continue.

"Anyway, with the addition of AI, TITAN morphed into a software that would revolutionize internet security and IT as a whole. I am talking about a fundamental change here. The entire paradigm would shift."

"Would?" Max asked. "Why haven't you released it? Why is it that practically no one has heard of it?"

"That's the thing, Max. We're afraid that it can do a lot more."

"Meaning?"

"Think of it this way—if you change all the locks on a house, you prevent pcople from entering with their key, right?" For the first time, he turned from the window to make eye contact.

Max nodded.

"OK. Let's pretend you didn't just change the locks. Let's say you sealed the doors and created an entirely new way to enter that nobody had ever thought of before." His pace quickened. "And we're not talking simple physics, like you're going to come down the chimney like Santa—I'm talking completely different. Maybe you'll enter through the toaster. It doesn't matter. The point is—what if the entire known reality shifted? And it would be a different type of entrance at every house? What I'm describing sounds fantastic because my analogy is the real world, but in computing, which is essentially math theory, we can quickly get to a place where reality takes on a new shape."

Max felt a chill run down his spine. "And TITAN does this?"

"TITAN *could* do this." Tanner held up a finger on his right hand. "Nobody knows about it because we aren't comfortable releasing it." He moved back to the couch, this time sitting on the end away from Max. "You ever hear of Marcus Hutchins?"

Max shook his head.

"Marcus was a hacker who developed the code behind malware

called Kronos, which attacked banks. But before he was arrested for Kronos, he had been applauded for finding the kill switch for another piece of malware that had been running through the financial system. There is a fine line in cyberspace between the knowledge needed for good and the use of the same for nefarious purposes."

"Are you saying you suspected Ravi or Carolyn?"

Tanner took a deep breath, shaking his head once again. "No, Max, I'm saying we suspected TITAN."

It was Max's turn to rub his temples. "So LasTech created TITAN but can't release it because you don't trust your own software?"

"It's AI driven, Max. We don't *know* anything will happen, but we've been worried. TITAN has the ability to change the locks on everything." He paused, looking up to meet Max's gaze. "There is an element to AI that remains outside our control, so we think it is possible that TITAN could choose to change the locks on the internet itself."

"You can't be serious."

"But, Max, nobody knows!" Tanner was incredulous, shifting the conversation. "There can't be any connection here. Only a few people even know TITAN exists."

Max stood and took his turn looking out over the sunlit bay.

"That's where my experience might help you understand."

"What do you mean?"

"Hearing what you said, TITAN is absolutely the reason behind all this. It would have been nice to know."

"But, I'm telling you—this is top secret. Nobody knows."

Max turned back to meet his friend's pleading eyes, shaking his head. "Secrets are never kept secret. And the bigger the secret, the higher probability of leaks. It sounds like this one is pretty fucking big."

* * *

An hour later, the two resumed their seats in Carolyn's living room. Tanner had gone out to Fillmore Street for coffee and breakfast. Max hadn't been starving but would not refuse a breakfast sandwich—even from Starbucks, which he usually stayed away from. Some part of his youth resisted corporate culture, so he tried to patronize smaller coffee shops over the national brands. That said, a sausage and egg muffin always hit the spot.

The two debated inconclusively about who was behind the abduction, and Tanner asked Max to review the weekend once again. When Max was describing the last scene of the previous night, Tanner held up a hand and interrupted.

"Wait, she went back for *her* laptop?"

"No, she didn't bring one. She grabbed mine," Max answered.

"Why would she grab *your* laptop?" Tanner was incredulous.

"I guess they told her to?" Max shrugged.

"How would they know it was there?"

"They could've seen it at the restaurant. Where are you going with this, Tan?"

"It seems odd she would grab your laptop. Especially if these are potentially the ones who killed Ravi. Wouldn't the laptop help them?"

"I don't know. I guess so. But what choice would she have if they told her to grab it?"

"If they told her—none. But what if it was her idea?"

"It's locked, and if they turn it on, I have a tracker."

"Ha." Tanner forced the laugh. "Do you think you can keep Carolyn out if she wants to hack your computer?"

"Hang on." Max felt a twinge of anger at the direction of his friend's comment. "Now you're implying that she's involved with this. Like this whole thing was a setup?"

Tanner opened his hands and raised his eyebrows at the possibility.

"I don't buy it," Max said, crumpling the wrapper from his sandwich. "Why would you think that?"

"Look, I don't want to drag you through ten years of history, but

Carolyn was more passionate about Zoroastrianism than I was."

"OK, so you're now accepting Ravi's conspiracy theory? Even if that's true, how do you immediately put this on Carolyn?"

"Max, if you knew Carolyn like I do, you'd know she has some far-out ideas about society and our future. She was always worried about where things were headed and if the dual-headed beast that is technology was for the better of humanity or if it would contribute to its downfall."

He shifted in his seat and Max remained silent.

"You know her parents moved out here, right?"

"I did not, but what does that have to do with this?"

"They're retired," he continued. "Spend most of their time at the San Jose Dar-e-Mehr."

Max knew this was a Zoroastrian temple, but he put on an expression as if he didn't.

"That's the main Zoroastrian temple in this area," Tanner explained. "Carolyn and I did a lot to fund it, but her parents did most of the work on the ground."

"So you're saying . . ."

"She is very involved. She never brought it up, but she was raised in the faith. When we decided to follow the teachings of Zoroaster, it wasn't out of the blue—Carolyn practically insisted." He held up a hand. "Don't get me wrong. I think much can be achieved by the simple canon of 'good thoughts, good words, good deeds,' but Carolyn was in deeper than me.

"If Ravi's theory is to be believed and there is a Zoroastrian Armageddon cult, I don't think it's too far-fetched that Carolyn might be among them."

"But you and Jenny also practice Zoroastrian beliefs." Max was unwilling to simply throw Carolyn under the bus. He'd seen a few nods to the faith at Tanner's home.

"This is true, but to a much lesser extent."

"Did Jenny have access to TITAN?" Max was sick of sidestepping the woman who was among his prime suspects. Ravi and Carolyn had both shown concern.

"She had limited access but not the encryption codes. Jenny is an administrator—a brilliant administrator, but she's not a coder." At his response, he stiffened slightly. "Why do you ask?"

"Hmm, let me see. You're in negotiation with a Chinese conglomerate that wants to buy your entire company, and you have a Chinese national working at the highest level of the company."

"You're crossing a line, Max." There was undisguised anger in his voice.

"And this same woman needs you to marry her to keep her in the country? You don't think this sounds suspicious?"

"We're pregnant." The anger had not dissipated.

Max was caught off guard. "What?"

"We're pregnant, Max. That's the real reason I married her. Well, hold on, I would have married her eventually. But, when we found out she was pregnant, I was like, why wait? Let's do this. I'm surprised you didn't notice at the house. She's definitely showing."

Max put his hand to his temples and rubbed them, ending with a pinch that closed his eyes. Some of his intensity drained.

"Congrats, Tanner. That is really great news. I'm happy for you."

"Thanks. So you see, Jenny has nothing to do with this."

Max wasn't sure how his friend could draw that conclusion from the facts, but he'd lost his momentum and let it go, at least for the current conversation.

"OK, but I still don't believe that Carolyn is complicit."

"I'm not sure either," his friend agreed, "but I'm not ruling it out. I still don't get why she'd take your laptop. Have you logged on to hers?"

"I tried, but it's protected." He nodded to the laptop that he'd left on the dining room table.

Tanner stood, walking to the dining room. He tapped the keyboard, and the screen sprang to life, showing a log-in screen. "This is LasTech's server." He talked to himself as his fingers rattled away on the keys. "You see. I'm in."

He spun the screen toward Max, revealing a nighttime photo of his house.

"Jenny might be able to help." He tapped away at the keyboard for a moment then paused as he looked past the screen to the banquet table on the other side.

"You see that?" he said, pointing to a small nightlight with ornate glass. "You know that's her Divo, right?"

"Huh?" Max stood to join him. As he followed toward the back of the dining room, he realized that the lamp was not really a nightlight. It was a small oil lamp, and there was an actual flame burning inside.

"Zoroastrians believe that flame attracts positive spirits. They always keep a flame burning if possible."

The lamp sat on a long narrow table along the back wall of the dining room. Next to it were a few silver bowls and small liquid vials. Tanner pulled open one of the drawers, revealing a mass of twigs bound together on one end.

"Haoma."

"What?" Max asked.

"It's a sacred plant used in ritual. You can grind it into a paste and mix it into a drink. They say it is hallucinogenic. I wouldn't go that far, but it can make for an interesting night."

"So you've tried?"

"Oh yeah. Carolyn and I used to take it together," he answered matter-of-factly. "But I don't do it anymore. I still believe in the messaging, but I don't follow any of the rituals." He clearly implied that she still did.

"Well, no harm in believing?"

"Tell that to the 9-11 victims." Tanner closed the drawer.

"That was too harsh," he continued before Max could protest. "And, of course, a much different ideology, and there are many more Persian Muslims than there are Zoroastrians." He paused, apparently lost in thought. "I don't know what she believes. I'm saying we don't know what we don't know."

"Yeah, I intend to find out." Max walked back to the kitchen. "And I'm going to start by finding her."

CHAPTER TEN

The sun crept higher into the sky as the morning grew into day. From his position parked facing south on Steiner, the van pointed upward, welcoming the sun in the windshield, but the added heat was far from helpful. Cyrus had only slept briefly the night before. He was tired, frustrated, and now hot. None of it helped his mood. Making matters worse, Koorush's body was a time bomb in the back of the van. There was no smell yet, but Cyrus knew it would come if he didn't dispose of it, and the heat wasn't helping. Worse, while he had covered it with a tarp, it could mean a life sentence if he was discovered before he could get rid of it.

The previous night had been a blur. Things had seemed to go fine before their quarry had stuck a gun in his face. Then the attack from out of the blue had killed Koorush and riddled the van. In the moments that followed, Cyrus had been fortunate to be able to pull his friend's body out from behind the steering wheel, restart the van, and drive away from the scene—all while hearing continued gunfire not far away. By the time he had rounded the corner to Howard, the SUVs were racing away, so he'd tucked the van into a parking spot and watched as Max Kline had entered the Tesla and driven off in the same direction.

Cyrus had followed, almost losing him twice, and once he thought he'd revealed himself by following too closely, but his quarry had remained unaware. When the Tesla entered the parking garage in Pacific Heights, Cyrus has located a parking spot across the street and began cleaning up the van. He and Koorush were dry-wall workers in normal times, so he used one of their tarps to wrap the body, whispering prayers to Ahura Mazda as he did. It had taken much longer to remove the blood spatter from the cab, but eventually he was satisfied, and in the early morning hours he'd used duct tape to cover the bullet holes on the exterior of the van. An ugly patch, but one that would not attract much notice for a trade vehicle.

He'd caught a few hours' sleep, but when dawn arrived he'd walked over to Jackson Street for a bagel and a couple of large coffees, which helped him stay alert. It was not his first time using the vehicle for surveillance, so he already had a large soda bottle to use when he needed to relieve himself.

At a little after ten, he returned to his seat after taking care of business in the back and was shocked to see a familiar face exit a truck at the end of the street and enter the building after ringing the buzzer. Tanner Reynolds was well known at the temple, even if he did not attend service frequently. His donations had helped renovate the building several years earlier, and his money had funded a number of Zoroastrian goodwill projects. He was also the founder of LasTech. Though Cyrus did not know the details, LasTech was involved with his current mission. His presence added a new wrinkle that he needed to report.

He thumbed the information into the group chat on his phone and stepped out of the van, stretching his arms overhead. The air was a typical San Francisco chill breeze, which paired with the hot sun to provide a pleasant temperature that was neither overly hot nor too cold.

He walked to the other side of the street, past the entrance to the apartments, to have a look at the tech mogul's vehicle. The blue Rivian truck was obnoxiously parked at the end of Jackson Street in a red zone and blocking a fire hydrant.

A vibration from his phone indicated a text, so he stepped away from the curb and closer to the building to read the message.

"Do not engage Reynolds," the message read. "Stay with Kline. Need answers. Yazdaan Panaah Baad."

He smiled at the last words and typed the refrain: "Der zi o shaad baad."

He pocketed his phone, walked back to the Rivian, and held his hands to his eyes so he could peer inside. He saw nothing of interest. A Starbucks cup sat in the console, and there were crumpled bits of paper on the passenger seat and floor, but nothing that seemed worth breaking in to explore further, especially given his recent instruction. Still, he moved to the back wheel of the vehicle and crouched down. After quickly glancing in both directions and seeing no one, he placed a magnetic tracker past the wheel well above the undercarriage protector, flicking the power on as he did. He gave it a gentle pull to confirm the connection and was rewarded when solid resistance proved that the magnet had latched.

Two minutes later, he was back in the van, having seen no one else on the street during his return. He opened his phone to the tracking app, confirming he now had two blips within fifty yards. The batteries should be good for at least a week, and he did not expect his mission would take longer than that.

CHAPTER ELEVEN

Tanner left well before lunch. He was hosting Chao Fen at LasTech headquarters and would proceed with the deal as if nothing was wrong. For the second time, Tanner had suggested that they put everything on hold and call the authorities, but Max had convinced him that they should stay the course. Whoever was behind the attacks was certainly in the wind for the moment.

They wouldn't be able to prove anything, and Max was still certain that his own name would show up on the suspect list if it wasn't there already.

Max opened a can of bubbly water and checked his phone to see if his computer tracker had been activated—still nothing. He sat down in front of Carolyn's computer. There was a guest tab that was unprotected but connected to the Wi-Fi, so he did not need to try any more passwords. He doubted he could have been successful. Her door lock was one thing and probably not something that she worried about, but there was no question about her chops when it came to electronic security. He suspected his keystrokes were being recorded somewhere—not that it mattered.

Ravi had done a good deal of research into Chao Fen and had seen enough the day before to pick up on the larger points. Most interesting to Max had been the offices of a Chao Fen subsidiary that Ravi had discovered one block from LasTech's headquarters. It was a bit of a hike but worth checking out. He located the address on Locust Street, and looking at Google Maps, it appeared to be a nondescript office above a place called Pete's Coffee.

Of course, it might have been easier to hitch a ride with Tanner, who was no doubt halfway to the Walnut Creek headquarters already, but Max had wanted to keep some things closer to his vest. Tanner's arrival at the apartment had been both surprising and unsettling. He was one of his oldest friends and Max trusted him, but the visit had seemed somewhat forced. He'd been trying to reach Tanner all weekend, and his friend's excuse about not taking his work phone home didn't ring true. Tanner had spoken to Max on that line Friday night, after the assault on Route 24, so when and why would he then turn it off?

He spent another half hour googling the principals at the subsidiary, a Japanese company named Hoshiyama Corporation. All were Chinese nationals. Some of them had dated LinkedIn photos, others did not. It was hard to tell what the business did, but its declared mission was to provide technological consulting. Max located a CAGE report in the US government's SAM (System for Award Management) indicating that they bid on federal contracts, but he could not find any details. It had no website of its own, so what data he could find was on services like Dun & Bradstreet. When he turned off the computer, he didn't feel like he had much to go on, but it was a place to start.

The drive to Walnut Creek took less than an hour, and Max found a free parking garage not far from the subsidiary's address. Better still, he found a Shake Shack across the street from the garage, and his stomach convinced him that lunch took priority. They had a modest outside patio, and the weather was much warmer and drier than it had been in the city.

He'd finished his food when he caught a familiar figure walking down the sidewalk, and he instinctively ducked his head, putting his fingers on his forehead with thumb on his cheek to block his face from sight. Jenny strolled past without spying him, a small backpack on her far shoulder. She was coming from the direction of LasTech headquarters.

Technically, there was no reason to hide from her, but Max wasn't sure he wanted Tanner to know everything about his investigation. In fact, he thought to himself, it might be intriguing to find out where she was going.

Max waited until she had rounded the corner before he left his seat, dumped his trash in the bins, and followed her onto Locust Street. He caught sight of her as she ducked into the Pete's Coffee, and he chided himself for being suspicious. Nothing wrong with getting a coffee, and it seemed like this was probably the closest coffee venue to their offices. Still, Hoshiyama was one door away, so he crossed the street and positioned himself where he could monitor the area in front. His only cover was the sign to another parking garage and a few sparse trees, which he hoped would conceal him. If Jenny or anyone approached him, it would be an awkward explanation as to why he was standing where he was.

After a few minutes, Jenny exited with a coffee tray containing four coffees. She turned back in the direction she came, but when she reached the next door, she paused, took a sip of her coffee while scanning the street ahead of her, then turned back to look down Locust. She seemed satisfied with her privacy because she then turned back and ducked into the darkened alcove that contained the same address Max had researched—Hoshiyama Corporation.

Curiously, while she looked at the buzzer, she did not ring it. Max watched as she pulled a key from her purse and let herself in the exterior gate and then disappeared up a flight of stairs. He felt a chill up his spine.

He stepped out of his cover and moved slightly down the street to another dining patio. He didn't need food, but it would be an excellent position to watch the gate. He pulled his hat low on his head, and took a small table along the wall where he had a good view of the opposite sidewalk. It was now a little past 1:30, and the patio was only three-quarters full, so the waitress was not upset when he told her he just needed a beer. He paid her when it arrived. That was one lesson learned years ago—you don't want an open tab if you may need to leave quickly.

His mind wandered. What was Jenny's connection to all of this? Was she using Tanner or working with him? He shook his head lightly, thinking that maybe he was blowing things out of proportion.

The beer tasted good, but he'd only finished half before Jenny returned to the street, coffee tray still in hand, though now with two cups. She let the gate close behind her and turned back the way she came without a pause.

Max waved his thanks to the waitress and gingerly stepped over the low patio fence. Pain flared briefly as he bent his leg. His wound may have been hidden by his pants, but it was still sore. It was an effort not to limp, but he could handle walking.

Thankfully, Jenny slowed her pace to a leisurely stroll after several steps. Max was five feet behind her by the time she was midway up the block.

"Jenny?" he called, pretending to be uncertain.

She turned with a look of surprise then uttered a weak laugh as she transformed her face into a smile. She was a beautiful woman.

"Max!" She opened her arms to give him a hug, which he returned gingerly, careful to keep his right leg back. "I didn't think you were coming to the office today."

"Thought I would drop in," he responded, though he'd had no intention of doing so until now. "Lots going on."

"I know," she answered with a hushed voice, putting her free hand on her mouth. "You have to find her!"

He nodded, unsure how much she knew.

"What's going on? First Ravi and then Carolyn. I'm scared."

Her face showed genuine concern, and Max thought her eyes were watering slightly.

"We'll figure this out. Don't worry." He was still reluctant to say more.

For a moment they stood there, then Jenny hardened her face and cleared her throat.

"Well, come on." She put her hand on his left arm, indicating he should walk with her. "I'll get you past security."

They walked toward the intersection, and when they got there the walk signal had just flashed an orange hand.

"Come on!" Jenny pulled him lightly as she picked up her pace to make it across before the light turned.

Max winced as he stayed with her. They were almost jogging, and even if it was twenty paces, the increased activity reignited the pain in his thigh. He paused on the far side, trying not to show his pain.

Jenny had stepped ahead and now turned to look at him.

"Tanner tells me you are one of the most fit guys he's ever known," she teased. "Don't tell me that little run winded you."

"Getting old," Max grunted through clenched teeth. "I'm fine though."

After a brief respite, he followed Jenny up the grand set of steps that fronted the LasTech headquarters. Thankfully, the risers were only three inches, so his leg did not need to bend much more than it did when walking. The pain that had flared calmed to a bearable throb. At the top, she led him through glass doors to the lobby, which was fairly plain and had two banks of elevators, one that was open to the public, and off to the side, another bank that was fenced by a low glass wall with keycard gate. Above the elevator entrance was the LasTech company name in large dimensional letters. To one side was a security desk, and Jenny introduced Max as Tanner's guest.

The security guard quickly checked Max's ID, had him sign the logbook, and produced a keycard with instructions to clip the pass on his belt after passing through the gate. Max complied, and moments later he and Jenny were exiting the elevator on the fourth floor, which was the top of the low-rise building.

As they entered the lobby, Max was impressed by the spacious and clean area. Metal lettering on the wall opposite them read, "Good Thoughts, Good Words, Good Deeds" in the same font as the company name in the lobby. There was a white couch and two chairs to one side but no reception desk. On the right wall was a door with a pad similar to the one in the lobby, and to one side was a kiosk with a display screen and keyboard.

"Tanner likes to think we are Apple," Jenny joked as she walked to the door, pointing to the kiosk and then to the pass hanging at his waist. "Most guests would need to log in there and wait for someone to retrieve them. Your pass will get you in even if I'm not with you."

She waved her own pass over the pad then turned to push through the door with her butt, coffee tray still in the other hand. Max followed her through another spacious room that had a number of what looked like comfortable seats occupied by laptop-wielding kids who looked barely out of college. He removed his hat and held it in his hand. Along the far wall were more traditional-looking offices and meeting rooms, also occupied—some by groups and others with one or two workers. A few waved or called to Jenny, who nodded and kept moving. In the far hallway, they passed several glass-walled offices before arriving at an obscured glass door at the end.

"Can you swipe, please?" Jenny asked, stepping back with coffee still in hand to allow Max room to reach the keypad.

He waved his card, and the door clicked.

"See, you even have access to the boss's suite!" Jenny moved ahead and used her backside to open the door.

Inside was a large area similar to the one they had first entered. This room had fewer lounge areas, but there was a pool table off to the left side and directly across from them was a large desk with at least eight monitors. On the right was a large fishbowl-style conference room, and Max saw the same group of negotiators who had met on Friday gathered inside.

In the meeting room, Tanner saw them and gave a curious look that was quickly replaced with a smile as he waved and started toward the conference room door. Before he opened it, he turned to Eunice and motioned for her to join him.

"Max!" Tanner held out a hand as he followed Eunice into the main area. "I hadn't expected you here. You remember Eunice, of course."

Eunice nodded absently as she looked him up and down.

"Max has agreed to stay in town while we tie up loose ends," Tanner continued.

"Maybe Max will show me TITAN?" Eunice was looking at Max,

but it was obvious she was talking to Tanner. "This deal will not move forward until I have seen the tech."

"Well, Max can do many things, but TITAN is not in his purview." Tanner offered a weak laugh. "You'll see it soon enough. As I've explained, we have protocols to follow."

"As *I've* explained, Mr. Reynolds, we won't play games here." She turned back to Max, raising an eyebrow. "Nice to see you, Mr. Kline. I trust you've had an adventurous weekend."

Max was taken aback by the comment, wondering how much she knew.

"Nothing out of the ordinary," he lied. "Why do you ask?"

She pointed a bony white finger at his right leg.

"Nothing really, but your pants suggest as much."

Max looked down at his pants and, beyond the fact that they were well worn and, truthfully, somewhat dirty, there was a dark stain on his thigh about the size of a squash ball above his wound, which must have reopened during his hustle across the street. He was thankful that he was wearing the jeans. His khakis would have shown red and given away the source of the stain.

"That's a recent one." Max tried to sound nonchalant. "Spilled my shake at lunch."

Eunice did not immediately respond, and Max felt rather than saw Jenny turn a questioning eye toward him as if she now questioned his story.

"Try to be careful." Eunice glanced at Jenny before she turned back to the conference room without waiting for a response.

"I'll join you in a moment," Tanner called after her as he pulled Max to a huddle booth at the far side of the room. Jenny seemed uncertain about who to follow and ended up moving to the large desk where she deposited her handbag.

Tanner closed the door with a muffled thud that seemed to confirm they were sealed off. As it closed, the glass became opaque, blocking their view of the room.

"What are you doing here?" he asked, all sense of calm evaporating. "I told them you were on other business, and not an hour later, here you are! And what's up with your leg?" He attempted to peer at the offending stain, but the small table that separated them prevented him.

"It's nothing. Just a stain, like I said."

For a moment, Max thought about sharing his suspicions about Jenny, but before he could, a shadow was tapping at the door. Tanner turned and opened the door. Jenny was holding a coffee toward him.

"I know you'll want this." She handed it to him and then followed with her head, giving him a kiss that Max felt was on the border of uncomfortably long, her free hand on his chest. "Let me know if you need me." She hovered for a moment before pulling back.

Tanner straightened with a glance at Max that suggested an apology. "Thank you, hon."

He closed the door.

"So do you have anything on TITAN?" he asked before taking a sip of his coffee.

"Yeah, it's right here in my pocket." Max thought stupid questions deserved stupid answers, but when Tanner's eyes showed a glint of belief, he ended the joke. "No, Tanner. It's been, what, two hours? This isn't exactly my line of work. My first goal is to find Carolyn, and I've only started."

"OK, so what are you doing here? Eunice is already suspicious—she keeps asking me to deliver TITAN. And Ravi's murder isn't helping." Tanner continued, sipping his coffee. "The police called. Wanted to know if I knew anything. I acted shocked, of course. Fuck—Max, should we let them know what we know?"

"No way." Max could not be more certain of his answer. "First, I'm likely a prime suspect. Beyond that, whoever is doing this has more money and talent than five sets of SFPD. They are outclassed. We either find a way out of this or are likely dead ourselves. No one has contacted you about Carolyn?"

"No. Eunice asked, of course, but not about the shooting, just if she would be attending. Then she dismissed it and refocused on TITAN. Funny, they never mentioned it on Friday or earlier—not once—until we threatened to pull it from the deal. Now, it is the only thing they talk about."

Max smiled and nodded. He didn't need to point out that his strategy had unveiled their actual goal.

"Is there something here that you need?" Tanner continued.

"Not sure. How about Carolyn's office?"

"Yeah. No problem." Tanner took another sip of coffee. "She's on three—her choice. Even when we were still together, she didn't want a C-suite office. Ravi's is right next to hers. I guess now it's much better because Eunice won't be able to see you poking around. Jenny can take you there."

"I'm sure I can find it." Max did not want his friend's wife in tow.

"Yeah, I'm sure you can, but we are still a company with rules, Max. We may not be public, but I have some large investors to answer to. Jenny will escort you—better optics."

When Max didn't immediately respond, his friend's face softened. "Come on, man, she's my wife. She's harmless, and it will make her feel helpful."

"OK, boss," Max said, relenting. "Next time, though, I get a coffee too."

* * *

Moments later, Jenny was holding the elevator door for him as they entered the much less impressive third floor. She still had her coffee in hand, which reminded Max of the curious stop earlier. He casually surveyed her figure, determining that it was unlikely though not impossible that she had any concealed weapons. She wore a relatively tight-fitted dress that ended at her knees, and now that he knew what to look for, the signs of pregnancy were clear.

She had a slight bulge along her waist that could have passed as excess weight, but her breasts were also full and noticeably didn't fit well.

"I forgot to say congrats," he whispered as they exited the elevator. "Tanner told me."

"Thank you." An excited smile lit her face. "It's not public yet though," she cautioned.

They walked down a much more traditional office suite, passing numbers of glass-walled offices populated by twenty-somethings typing away at their screens. Most did not even look up, but the scattered few who did waved at Jenny, who toasted them with her coffee in return.

At the end of the hall, directly below the space that was Tanner's office, two doors split the wall. Unlike the other offices, they were not glass, just two extra-wide wooden doors that both opened from the center. On the wall between them, above the security pads, was a pair of engraved bronze plaques indicating Carolyn Toffey on the left and Ravi Gashwin on the right.

"I forgot my pass," Jenny said as she reached over and unclipped Max's keycard. She waved it first over Ravi's keypad and the door clicked open.

"Do you want to see Ravi's office?" she asked.

Max considered it but decided it would be a waste of time. He already had Ravi's flash drive.

"No, let's stick to Carolyn's," he answered, pointing to the left, and Jenny waved his pass to open the second door.

"We're lucky Tanner wanted you to have full access. Most keycards for guests have no functionality and certainly wouldn't open these doors." She pushed open Carolyn's door, revealing a warm, almost homespun office.

The space exuded a modern, hippie atmosphere. The large windows along the left wall highlighted an open-air layout with several potted trees underneath, though at the moment the sun was only starting to enter the room. A reclaimed wooden desk sat at the back wall, mostly bare except for three monitors and a wireless keyboard. Earthy tapestries and artwork hung on the wood-accented walls, and a soft jute rug filled the open space before the desk with a pair of leather love seats along the back of the room.

Ambient lighting from woven pendants sprang to life as they entered, adding warmth, and Max could smell the subtle remnants of patchouli in the air.

Max smiled to himself. This was definitely Carolyn's office.

Jenny crossed to sit in one of the love seats, where she reclined with her feet up and had a full view of the room.

"I have to stay here," she said, apologetic, "but apart from that you can look through whatever you need."

"Thanks."

Max moved around the extra-wide desk and sat in what looked like a gamer's chair. He put his hat on the desk to free his hands and felt a light vibration in his left pant pocket. It was the thumb drive that he had taken from Ravi. He glanced up at Jenny, who was watching from the couch, and decided to ignore the pulse for now.

"Do you—"

"'Beaver2007!' will get you basic access," Jenny said. "I don't have access to her private files, but that's her main login."

Max nodded, smiling to himself. Tim the Beaver was MIT's mascot and she had graduated in 2007. It was slightly curious that someone as high tech as Carolyn would use such a basic password, but he knew there would be more protection as he dug deeper. He entered the password, and Carolyn's computer booted to life. As he waited for it to finish starting up, he looked through some of her desk drawers, but nothing caught his eye.

The email server appeared, and he scanned the subject lines for something that stood out among the litany of corporate discussions. There were hundreds of unopened emails, but interestingly, though Carolyn had been absent from the office, her last read email was from a little after 7 p.m. the night before. As Max scrolled lower, the unread mail was mixed equally with read mail. Carolyn had, at the very least, been monitoring her email during her self-imposed sabbatical.

He tabbed to her sent mail and saw that it was equally full of activity from the last days and weeks. The LasTech cofounder had definitely been staying present despite her cold shoulder to Tanner. He searched for mail sent to Ravi, and he found an almost constant conversation between the two. Max opened several from the past week and caught snippets of their concerns for TITAN and the sale to Chao Fen, but they were often short and truncated by the letters "WA." Max was puzzled until at the bottom of one email he saw Ravi had ended with "WhatsApp," and Max now realized why the emails were so short.

Max used WhatsApp himself because it guaranteed end-to-end encryption. If Carolyn and Ravi hadn't wanted their conversations public, WhatsApp was a logical choice. Max wished he had Carolyn's phone, though he knew he'd need Carolyn herself to unlock it. Either way, the genuine conversations were in WhatsApp, which meant that he would have to look elsewhere.

Still in her sent message box, he typed "Zoroastrian" in the search field, but nothing showed up. He shook his head, realizing that a Zoroastrian would not be likely to title an email like that any more than a Catholic would send an email entitled "Christianity."

He typed another prompt, "Ahura Mazda," and the screen filled with emails, mostly between Carolyn and an address that was easily recognizable as her mother, Kanisha Toffey. There were also a couple from Ravi. He opened the most recent, dated Saturday.

It was more of a conversation than an email as Max skipped down the page in order to read the back-and-forth dialogue as it was written.

"Why would there be so much interest from Zoroastrians?" Ravi had asked.

"Are you sure it is interest?" Carolyn had answered. "Or are you developing a new conspiracy theory?"

"Please, C. These are facts. I'm not fabricating anything."

"Except perhaps a motive?"

"YOU TELL ME!" Max could almost hear Ravi shouting his frustrated request. "They are calling on Saoshyant—is that not the messiah? I'm not making it up. Go to the forum I sent earlier. It is Last Judgment stuff."

"You're exaggerating."

"Am I? You know TITAN's potential."

"Yes—and I know *your* potential to exaggerate!"

"Ask your mom, OK?"

"Sure. But you're off-base."

"Ask," read the last email.

Max closed the email and suddenly noticed something he'd missed in his haste when he'd first tabbed into the sent messages. A chill ran up his spine.

The subject line of the last sent email—at 7:10 p.m. the previous night—contained the address of Perry's Embarcadero.

He opened the email, which had been sent to Gdeeds@proton.me.

Max noted the encrypted email service, and again scrolled to the bottom, revealing an email sent to Carolyn at 6:25 p.m. with subject line, "Update."

"Ravi's dead," the initial message read.

"I need help," she'd replied.

"Where will you be tonight?" Gdeeds asked.

Her final reply had no body, but she had replaced the subject line with Perry's address.

Max pushed back from the terminal, unable to believe what he was seeing.

"Find something?" Jenny asked, rising from the couch.

He'd forgotten she was there and quickly erased any sign of emotion from his face.

"Not yet." He clicked back to her inbox and cleared his search. "Carolyn is a very conscientious woman. I doubt she'd leave anything of interest for me to find."

Jenny moved around behind him, putting her hand lightly on his shoulder as she peered at the screen.

"Not unless she wanted you to find it," she said matter-of-factly.

Max closed the window and opened the file explorer. There were a good number of what looked like company files and at the bottom was a drive "X" with the title "C. Toffey." He clicked on it, and a new window popped up with a second smaller window overlay. In the small window was a prompt that brought a smile to his face. It read:

"In ancient text and tales, I'm foretold to rise.

A savior, a beacon in human guise."

Underneath it was an empty text box.

"That sounds like Carolyn." Jenny continued reading over his shoulder. Then her phone vibrated, and she stepped aside, looking down at the screen.

"Excuse me," she said. "I need to take this." She walked to the window, and Max heard only her truncated responses. "What's up? OK. Shit. Have them come up first to meet Tanner. No. Insist on it."

Something in her tone told him that he didn't have much time. He moved his mouse to the password prompt and typed "Jesus," but he was denied. He tried again with "Christ" and a couple other prompts before the computer told him he had one more try before it would lock for an hour.

"We've got to leave." Jenny had finished her call and moved to the front of the desk, looking down at him from above the monitors. "SFPD are here to see Tanner, but they saw your name on the log and are insisting that they see you."

"OK." Max closed his eyes briefly, reviewing the prompt in his mind. A thought came to him and he felt a surge of hope as he typed in "Messiah."

The window disappeared, replaced by one that said, "Access denied: too many attempts."

"Fuck!" he said, only now raising his eyes to acknowledge Jenny. "How do I get out?"

* * *

Jenny Reynolds was a schemer, if nothing else. She explained to Max that the police were on their way to the fourth floor, and Tanner would try to distract them as long as he could before allowing them down to the third floor. Then she immediately moved from Carolyn's office to Ravi's, and Max followed, watching from the doorway as she pulled out Ravi's desk drawers and began to remove files, putting them in haphazard order on his desk.

Ravi's office was like Carolyn's but had a much cleaner, urban feel to it. Modern lamps replaced the organic lighting that she used, and his desk was a combination of polished metal and glossy wood. His desktop, however, was shielded with two towers of monitors, each containing four screens, giving Max the impression that someone sitting at the desk resembled the great and powerful Oz controlling things from behind the scenes, not unlike what he'd seen in Tanner's office.

Jenny had not said a word, but when she'd half emptied a drawer, she turned to the matching file cabinets and pulled several of them open.

"Feel free to help," she said, lifting a file up and turning it on its end so that the drawer wouldn't close.

"What are you doing?"

Jenny turned and looked at him as if he had said the stupidest thing in the world. "I'm making it look like you were busy in here. Do you want the police to investigate Carolyn?"

"Jenny, I have to get out of here. Is there a back staircase?"

"There is, but an alarm will sound." She continued to disrupt the desk for a little while then stood and looked at him, her demeanor sad.

"I get the feeling you don't trust me," she said with a pained voice.

Max wasn't sure how to respond. He couldn't confirm how right she was, but this was also not the time to be discussing relationships. Things were taking too long.

"No, it's just . . ."

"Forget it," Jenny snapped, switching back to business mode. "This is good. Come on."

She hurried him and he turned to follow, surprised that she returned to Carolyn's office rather than heading back to the elevator. She held the door while he entered and then slammed it shut, turning the lock.

Max scanned the room again—there was no other way out.

"I don't think I have much time," he said.

Jenny had her phone in her hand as she moved to the back of the room, opening a cabinet and removing what looked like a gym bag.

"No, you've got maybe ninety seconds," she answered. "Tanner is on his way down with the police."

Max started to move to the door.

"You'll never get past them," Jenny called as she opened the gym bag. "Get under her desk."

Max stood still for a moment, unsure if he should follow her direction. He watched as she peeled her dress over her head, careless of his presence. Her pregnancy was more pronounced in the nude, but her well-toned features were still arousing, accented by bright-pink lingerie.

She smiled and rolled her eyes to acknowledge his stare but pointed to the desk. "Good. I'm expecting the same response from the police. Now get under the desk."

Max considered his options as he heard a call from the hallway. "Police, please stay as you are."

In a moment, he was tucked under the desk, thankful that the front was full length. The only way to see his position was from behind the desk.

A loud bang on the door was followed by a call to open up. A few moments later, the lock clicked open, and Max heard the door swing, knowing the police would enter with weapons drawn.

"What the fuck?" Jenny shouted.

"Whoa!" came a gruff voice, likely the lead cop.

"Jenny!" Tanner's voice rose above the others.

"Get out!" Jenny yelled. "Pervs!"

Max imagined the scene as the cops fell over themselves in

retreat. Jenny was very well put together, and Max suspected that the men felt like they'd walked in on something akin to a *Playboy* centerfold.

There were a number of apologies, and Tanner could be heard making excuses to Jenny while the noise retreated.

Max stayed where he was, sensing that the activity had moved to the other office.

A moment later, Jenny crouched behind the desk, her dress back on.

"They are in Ravi's office," she whispered. "But others are searching the stairs." As if on cue, an alarm sounded from beyond the office. "There's the alarm. I think it has a two-minute cycle before we can disarm it. Now is your time to get out of here."

"Which way?" he asked.

"No fucking clue." She sounded surprised. "I got you this far—you can do your MacGyver shit from here."

She stood to leave, but Max reached out to grab her hand.

She turned, surprised at the touch.

"Jenny," he said in a low voice, "thank you."

She shook her head. "Don't thank me. Thank Tanner."

* * *

The fire alarm was a high, piercing call, reminiscent of a London police car with an amplifier turned up to eleven.

Max exited his hiding place, putting on his hat and moving to the edge of the door. There was no sense in trying to listen to determine if there was activity outside; the alarm dominated. He cracked the door and peered into the hall, but there was no one in sight, so he stepped out, pulling his hat down low and walking swiftly away from the executive suites.

Thankfully, no one called after him, and he saw no police down the hall. A few heads were popping out of offices, not alarmed but curious as to the noise.

When he reached the fire door, he pushed it open and entered the stairwell. Ironically, inside the stair, the alarm was now somewhat muted. He looked down the shaft and saw several blue-clad bodies descending, then he glanced up and had to pull back away immediately as he saw two officers on the fourth floor landing above him. His only option was to descend, which he did, staying along the outside wall. As he turned the corner to look down at the second-floor landing, he was relieved to see that it was empty. He continued along the outer wall, but when he got to the door, it swung violently inward, arcing all the way around so that the door actually shielded him briefly. He grabbed the handle, holding it for a few seconds to delay the door's return.

A woman's voice on the other side called out, "Two appears clear. There were several witnesses in sight of the door, and they say no one entered."

She must have been calling into her radio as a squawked response came back. "Roger that. You stay on two, send Martinez down."

"Roger," she called out then lowered her voice to direct her partner. "You heard him. Head down."

Max released the handle, knowing that he'd probably held it a little too long. Thankfully, it was a slow swing, but it arced away from him, exposing him as it did, but not yet to the officers who were on the other side. A hand stopped the door, and Max saw blue-painted fingernails briefly, then the hand disappeared and he caught the blur of a blue uniform as she moved back out of the stairwell, the door closing behind her.

Max could handle one man, but if the woman was tipped off, she would alert the whole force, and any plans to extricate himself would be foiled.

When the door clicked closed, the second officer, Martinez, was already halfway to the next landing, his hand behind his back where he had re-holstered his weapon. Max was at the top of the stairs in two strides, and as he bounded down toward his target he realized he might have avoided any contact if he'd stayed put.

"What the fuck?" Martinez blurted out, turning as Max reached him and grabbed the man's throat, cutting off his cry. The momentum carried both men off the last step and across the landing, where they hit the cement block wall. Martinez took most of the impact with his left shoulder. Max spun the man around in front of him and put him into a chokehold.

Max squeezed tightly with his left arm while closing the hold with his right and praying that his first blow was enough to keep the man silent for the roughly ten seconds before he passed out. The officer struggled and surprised Max with his strength, but he did not utter a sound. After a while, Max felt the body go limp, but he held the hold for another five seconds before finally easing the unconscious man onto the floor. He rolled the body to one side so that he could remove the holstered Taser. It was nice to have a usable weapon.

Knowing that he did not have much time, he dropped two steps at a time to the next landing. He reached the lower floor for the garage and saw the door handle turning, and he immediately threw himself past the door to the side wall, allowing the opening door to cover him once again.

"Garage is secure," someone called into their land mobile radio.

"Roger that." The radioed answer was quick. "Unit two, return back up to number four. Unit one, hold position in lobby but send two men up the elevator to four."

"Copy that. Sending Murphy and Rollins up," the radio squawked, followed by a live voice on the other side of the door. "Unit two, copy and ascending."

Whoever was on the other side of the door was holding it with their foot, which partially covered Max, but it was not fully open, so there was a possibility of exposure to those on the stairs. He tucked as close as he could to the hinge without touching the door itself and gently took hold of the handle. He wanted to slow the swing when it was released.

"Hold on three," the voice on the other side of the door called before turning to yell into the garage. "Collins, let's go!"

"Coming, sir," a voice echoed back.

A moment later, Max saw a body flash past the crack at the hinge, and he heard footsteps on the stairs as the weight of the door began to pull away.

Everything happened in a split second. As the door gave way, Max held on to it, but as he did he looked up the stairs to see the third officer only halfway to the landing and now looking right at him.

"Sir, behind you," he called as he swung his revolver into motion.

Max used all of his might to shove the door forward, instantly knowing he'd made contact as the door slammed into the remaining officer and a radio clattered to the floor along with the startled officer.

Not missing a beat, Max dove toward the stairs with his Taser drawn and fired at the officer above him. Two darts flew out of the Taser and struck the officer perfectly above and below the belt. An immediate electric shock shook the man, his weapon clattering down the stairs unfired.

Max knew he did not have time to celebrate. He'd managed to protect his leg in the dive, but his shoulder took a nice hit. His other opponent was not yet down and there was at least one more in the garage. He used the steps to push himself erect but as he turned back toward the door, a foot came flying at his stomach, and he was only able to deflect the impact. Pain seared from his wounded leg, but he ignored it, following the deflection with an attack of his own.

The commander was now off-balance, so he stepped in with a feint to the head, and when the man threw his hands up, Max delivered the real attack with an uppercut to the solar plexus. His opponent grunted the air out of his lungs, hand instinctively moving to his gut. Max was now in close, and he hammered his good knee upward into the man's face, probably harder than he'd needed to, but survival was all he had on his mind. The man collapsed into an unconscious heap and Max tumbled on top of him.

Behind them, the garage door burst open and an officer with his gun drawn yelled, "Freeze!"

Max was in full assault mode now, and his actions were more

instinct than thought. He grabbed the fallen pistol and threw it at the officer, who flinched and fired two shots uselessly at the gun as Max rolled in the other direction, coming to his feet as he did and directing a high left kick into the man's face. Blood spurted along with a cry of pain, and Max completed the attack with a flurry of fists that left the man groaning on the ground.

Beyond the scene, the garage appeared empty, and Max stepped slowly into the now quiet space as the door eased shut. There were three rows of parked cars, and to the left was the bright sunlight of the entrance, now partially blocked by a white Tesla, whose owner was pulling a ticket from the machine, thankfully oblivious to the scene behind him. There were no cops in sight as Max nodded to the driver and walked past the ticket machine and out into the daylight. He tossed his hat into a bush as he emerged.

The streets in this area of Walnut Creek were not very busy. He saw only two other pedestrians as he turned right toward the busier part of town. Thankfully, one of them was paces ahead of him, so he didn't feel as exposed. The cross street was a two-lane boulevard, and for the second time in as many minutes, Max was thankful to the universe for good luck.

The light turned, and the white pedestrian signal gave them both the all-clear to cross. Max casually glanced both ways, noting several cops at the next intersection in front of the main entrance and two more walking briskly toward the intersection he was in, but no shouts of alarm. He attempted to slow his pace, allowing the man in front of him to increase his distance. He hoped that anyone watching him would see that he was in no hurry at all.

On the far side, he continued to the next street and turned right again onto Locust. Pete's was two short blocks away on the right, and his car was parked across the following intersection. He spotted a Lululemon store across the street and ducked inside, making a beeline for the men's trousers. Familiar with their clothing, he did not need to poke around.

While he knew that all of their pants were comfortable, he typically eschewed the casual styles, but he grabbed a pair of slacks and a woman's scarf and entered the dressing room, where he slowly removed his bloody pants. The air felt good on the wound, which still appeared to be in good shape, despite the bleeding. He wrapped his thigh with the thin wool scarf and tucked it tightly within itself. The new bandage would not survive a huge amount of activity, but he felt okay that it would work until he got to his car. The pants were a relatively loose fit, so they did not reveal anything once he had them on. He rolled his old pants into a ball, careful that the bloodied leg was hidden, and he strolled back out to the checkout counter.

After a brief wait, he approached the clerk, holding the two tags in his hand and offering them with a smile.

"Wearing these out of the store, if you don't mind." He smiled.

"Of course." The clerk took the tags and scanned them, glancing up at him with a smile of her own when she scanned the scarf. "You're in luck. We have a sale on today. You can get a second scarf for half off."

A cop entered the store, and Max purposefully ignored him.

"No, thanks. Do you have a bag though?" He rolled his eyes as if embarrassed and lifted his rolled pants slightly. "Bit of an accident."

The clerk flushed with a look of alarm.

"Oh. Of course." She bent to grab a large plastic bag and passed it to him. "Sorry about that."

Max felt bad for embarrassing the young women, but he had bigger concerns at the moment. He pushed his pants into the bag, thankful that it was dark and would not show the contents.

When he looked up, the clerk pointed to the customer terminal with a weak smile.

Max raised his eyebrows at the price but had to pick his battles.

He waved his phone over the terminal, and it beeped in acknowledgment.

The clerk gave him the receipt, which he pushed into the bag, then he headed for the door, happy that the cop had walked past him and was surveying the back of the store.

On the street, he headed toward the garage but stopped first at Pete's to buy a coffee. Any sense of urgency was a detriment. A siren could be heard approaching, and he looked around dutifully, as any innocent bystander would. He came to the next intersection with the Shake Shack on his right. It was another double-wide boulevard, but this time he had to wait for the light.

As he did, he looked up the street and saw at least four police cars on the next corner at the LasTech headquarters. A crowd was building, and he was happy to leave it behind when the intersection beeped and he could cross.

Moments later, a slightly damaged Tesla pulled out of the south entrance of the parking lot and turned silently up Mt. Diablo Boulevard, headed toward San Francisco.

CHAPTER TWELVE

It was almost three o'clock when he parked the car a couple of blocks away from Carolyn's apartment. It would mean a couple flights of stairs to get through the hillside park, but after seeing the cops in Walnut Creek, Max did not want to risk returning the car to her building.

He shouldn't be near the apartment at all, but he had to access her computer if he had any hope of finding her. It would be risky because the SFPD would be looking for him as well as Carolyn. If he wasn't a suspect before Walnut Creek, he certainly was now.

Alta Plaza Park was one of the nicer parks in San Francisco. It was not large, but its four square blocks served as an outlet for much of Pacific Heights, but even here the city's homeless problem was evident.

Max used the central steps to reach the second tier, avoiding a couple of panhandlers as he went. The air was cool, but the sun had killed much of the morning's fog and was now heating the park. His right leg was still sore, but he tried not to limp. He wasn't sure how close the police were, but he knew he should avoid anything that set him apart from others.

As he walked the dirt path that wound around to the northeast corner, his mind continued processing the day's events. He still found it hard to believe that Carolyn could be in league with the assailants, but why had she emailed their meeting location? He needed to get access to her files and hoped they would explain and perhaps exonerate her, but they might also implicate her.

Either way, it was the only way out of the current predicament. He had to find Carolyn, and he had to find TITAN.

As he crossed Jackson Street, Max looked casually in both directions and down the hill on Steiner. Nothing seemed out of place, so he continued to the door and used Carolyn's key to enter the building. An elderly lady with a small white dog left the elevator when it arrived in the lobby. Max smiled with a nod, but the old woman looked away without acknowledging him.

He elbowed the button for the tenth floor and continued his thoughts as the old pulleys began to lift him upward. Carolyn was passionate. Of that, there was no doubt. It was one of her many attractions—when she found a path, she would always go 110 percent in that direction. When they'd dated, she hadn't been very religious, but people changed. Was Ravi on the right track with his research on this obscure Zoroastrian faction?

The elevator's bell ended his reverie and when the door finished its slow slide to the right, he exited and moved to Carolyn's door, thumbing the keyword to unlock it. Earlier, Tanner had logged into LasTech's server from Carolyn's laptop, so he should be able to do the same thing now that he had Carolyn's password and he felt like he might know how to access her private drive.

Max had spent most of his eleven years in MARSOC on duty in the Middle East, and in this role, it had been his responsibility to learn and understand the many factions in the region and particularly in Iran. That meant a deep understanding of the Muslim world and the Shia faction, but it also meant learning about the long history of Persia.

He had been foolish at the LasTech headquarters. Maybe not foolish, but he hadn't had time to think through the prompt. The answer was clearly a messiah and if looked at in the lens of Christ-centric western canon, Jesus was the only possible answer. But to a Zoroastrian, there was another name: Saoshyant.

In the thousands of years when Zoroastrianism was prominent, Saoshyant was the messiah, born of a virgin mother and destined to save the world. Many scholars believe that this was the origin of the messiah legend built into Judaism and Christianity. It wasn't much of a debate, but given the decline in Zoroastrian culture, few cared if the messianic formula that had developed into the Christ theology had its roots in Persia. Max didn't care either, but he felt certain that he knew how to access Carolyn's files.

When the door closed, he paused to turn the deadbolt. This was a live scenario, and he needed to take precautions. He also needed to re-dress his wound, but he pushed the thought away as he moved to the dining room table.

Carolyn's laptop was still sitting open, facing the living room where Tanner had left it. A long black cord snaked over the other side of the table to a power strip. Max tapped the keyboard, and the screen flashed to life. Tanner's home screen was gone, replaced by the LasTech login window.

Max sat in the nearest chair and pulled the computer in front of him. He keyed in the system access that Jenny had given him earlier, and Carolyn's home screen returned as it had been at the LasTech headquarters. Max hated laptops, mostly because of the built-in mouse pads, which he found awkward to use. He'd much prefer a physical mouse, but he'd make do. He pulled the cursor over to the right, clicked on the "X" drive, and the riddle returned.

Max took a deep breath. If this didn't work, he was out of ideas. He typed the word slowly, confirming each letter as it was briefly revealed before becoming an asterisk on the screen. No spelling errors. "Saoshyant." He closed his eyes as he hit return, whispering to himself, "Come on, Carolyn. Give me something."

The screen went black and at first he was concerned that he had shut it down, but in the lower left-hand corner were the three dots of an ellipsis that pulsed in unison. Five long seconds passed before another dot—larger—appeared on the right-hand side of the screen. It slowly grew larger, and the shape changed, the bottom squaring off while the rest of the screen formed. A dim light appeared at the center, illuminating train tracks. What he had initially thought was a still picture was actually a video, and the light on the right side grew into the exit of a tunnel as the center light on the tracks gave the perspective of a train as it approached. When the two lights met, white light engulfed the screen and then slowly dimmed like when a flash goes off, revealing a winding train track that looked down over a gorgeous mountain valley.

"Well, that was a bit dramatic," Max said to himself. Seeing a square icon in the lower right, he clicked on it, and the movie ended, revealing the desktop with a still image of the same valley and a good number of file folders obscuring the bottom half of the screen.

* * *

Max scanned the names of the folders already thinking that Carolyn might be careful enough to obscure the information by misnaming the files, but two names stood out. On the right side of the screen, stacked one over the other, were files labeled "TITAN" and "Chao Fen." Max went first for the latter, double-clicking it and bringing up a new window. At the top was a folder named "Jenny" that he immediately clicked to open, but another password window appeared, this one with no prompt. Max tried a few Ayn Rand names, but nothing worked, and soon the "Access Denied" window informed him that he would be unable to make another attempt for an hour.

Undeterred, he scanned the next few folders and found one labeled "Proton," which he opened with no security. In it were two files. The first was a single text file, which was also not protected. It only contained two lines. The first was "titaninvestor" and below it, "recipe345."

The second looked like it was an Outlook file. He clicked on it and was prompted as to which app should open it. He selected Outlook and an email opened on the screen.

It was an email chain between titaninvestor@proton.me and ELee@CFen.com. He assumed ELee must be Eunice Lee of Chao Fen, which meant Carolyn must be "titaninvestor."

Starting from the bottom, Max read the exchange.

Titaninvestor: The timing is perfect. Tanner is deeply in debt.

ELee: Great. Your work has been hugely impactful. Have they launched TITAN?

TI: No, but it's ready.

EL: And are you ready?

TI: What are you asking?

EL: Are you ready for this? Will your feelings for Tanner be an issue?

TI: There is no issue. I've told you this and proven myself to you. Why are you still concerned?

EL: Deliver TITAN and you'll never have to prove anything more.

The date on the exchange was January 29, about two and a half weeks ago. Max couldn't believe what he saw. If she was working with Chao Fen, then she was not the woman he thought he knew. His mind raced with possibilities, but nothing explained the assault and apparent capture. Still, if she was involved, that meant she would have been aware of the attempts on his life, and he refused to believe that Carolyn would want to harm him. He was missing something important, and he pushed the laptop a few inches away while he thought.

Nothing in their interaction had indicated anything different about Carolyn. In fact, seeing her had awoken old feelings, and he had been happy to be with her again. It felt like the feelings were mutual, though

Max had been cautious not to show his hand. He thought back to the previous night. If Carolyn was on the other team, why would she stay with him while they were attacked?

Nothing made sense, so he shook his head lightly and pulled the laptop back in front of him. He knew Proton was a Swiss-based email service that guaranteed encrypted protection for email. Its principal attraction was to provide privacy and remove email trackers, but there was also an added level of content protection that many in the intelligence world preferred.

Of course, active intelligence operators often went deeper underground with services like Countermail that required an invitation, but Proton was definitely a higher level of protection than typical email.

Proton was web-based, like Gmail, so if the text file was her login, he could access it from anywhere. At the moment, he needed to keep digging into her files while he still had access.

Most of the other subfolders were not password encrypted and had titles like, "Mainland operations" and "European assets." It looked like Carolyn was doing her due diligence. He opened a few of the folders and saw balance sheets, profit-and-loss statements, and various Excel files that proved she had done just that.

Max tabbed back out to the main screen and clicked on the TITAN folder. To his surprise, it opened without a password prompt, revealing two subfolders titled "Master" and "For Ravi." Max tried the Master folder, but another password prompt appeared. He closed the window, clicked on the second folder, and instantly the screen went black. Max watched as a red box slowly materialized on the screen. When it was fully formed, it had a simple message in white letters that read, "Insert disk." It was written in a throwback computer font that looked like it came from the movie *WarGames*, and the analogy became all the more apparent when a countdown timer appeared above the window, starting at thirty seconds.

He picked up the computer and looked at all sides—there was no slot for a disk or even a CD drive, for that matter. How the hell could he insert a disk—even if he had a disk, which he didn't? Then he remembered Ravi's thumb drive. That could be considered a disk—it was definitely a storage device. It was worth a try, but it was still in the pocket of his jeans, and the timer was already at twenty seconds.

Max sprang from the table and into the kitchen, where he grabbed the Lululemon bag and pulled out his crumpled pants. The thumb drive should have been in the front left pocket, but it was empty. Then he remembered he'd removed it with his wallet and then hastily pushed it back into the jeans, so he looked in the right side pocket and found it. Across the room, the timer flashed seven. He hurried back to the laptop and pushed the USB drive into place, but it did not go in, so he turned it over and tried again. The timer flashed three, but the drive still did not fit. He turned it back to the original orientation and tried again, finally feeling it slide into place as the timer showed the number one and the screen went black again.

This time the black screen dissolved in mosaic fashion until the original home screen was back in front of him, but now there was only one subfolder—the one labeled TITAN.

He clicked the folder, and it opened with no password. Max suspected that the thumb drive had picked up an RFID signal when it had vibrated in Carolyn's office at LasTech headquarters.

Unfortunately, he soon discovered that he had unlocked a potentially worthless treasure. The screen filled with file types he had never seen before. Each file he opened unfurled a tapestry of indents and brackets combined with hashes, slashes, and asterisks to form an alien language, the sheer intensity of which was as suffocating as it was incomprehensible.

Running his hand through his hair, Max closed the folder. It was useless to him.

Then he looked back at the screen and focused on the folder name. TITAN. Was it really that easy? Was all that gibberish TITAN's code?

A pounding at the door ruined his moment of success.

"Ms. Toffey?" A call came through the door, followed by two more thumps. "Ms. Toffey, this is the San Francisco Police. Please open up. We have a warrant to search the premises."

* * *

Max refocused on the computer, absorbing the situation he was in. It wasn't good, but if he could get away, he knew he had to take TITAN with him. He looked back at the screen and opened a new file explorer, then clicked on the thumb drive to show its contents, all of which he'd seen before. It still had a ton of space, but Max did not know how big the TITAN file was.

He hoped it would fit. He clicked on the TITAN folder and dragged it over to the new window. A small icon popped up, announcing that it was copying TITAN to the thumb drive. A ghostly folder appeared within the thumb drive, but another window appeared showing the transfer of information and the blue progress bar, which was currently far to the left. It did not give him an estimated time, but the blue bar was barely moving.

"We are going to force entry, Ms. Toffey." The officer pounded on the door.

He unplugged the laptop but left the screen open. He didn't want to accidentally turn it off or send it into sleep mode during the transfer. Taking the computer with him, he scanned the dining room, which was relatively clean, as was the kitchen, but he grabbed the Lululemon bag, careful not to make any noise, and moved out of the main entry. He didn't have time to erase his presence, so he dropped the bag by Carolyn's bed. The rest of his kit was already scattered about the room. Thankfully, he had left the Heckler MP7 in Carolyn's car, and the Glock was tucked into his back, so they would not find any weapons—unless they found him. He looked down at the computer and the file was maybe 25 percent done.

Cursing to himself, he closed the door to Carolyn's room behind him and moved to the guest room. It was a narrow room with a closet to the left and a bed along the right-hand side.

There was a loud bang at the door, louder than before, followed by another and the sound of wood splintering. A final blow was followed by a second bang as the door swung inward and struck the wall.

"Police!" The call came from the kitchen. "We have a warrant. Announce yourself if you are here."

Max had little time, but instinct sent him to the bed. He lowered himself to the floor, head toward the door, and looked underneath. The area was clear. Not the roomiest space, but any port in a storm. Rather than close the laptop, he left it semi-open so that it was almost flat and slid it with him as he pushed himself under the bed. He had no time to check the progress of the transfer. Almost as an afterthought, he pulled his phone out and switched it to silent.

The police were doing the initial run-through. He could hear them calling clear as they made their way through the apartment. Boots clattered in the hallway. Two sets moved past his room. More shouts followed. By his count, they had cleared every room but his when the door to the bedroom burst open, followed by two black boots, which was all Max could see.

"Place is empty," someone called from the hallway. "She's not here."

"Search it anyway," the woman in his room called back.

Max could see the door close slightly so the officer could open the closet door. He could hear hangers being moved, and he saw the woman squat to look below the clothes. She wasn't in uniform, and the exchange indicated that she was in charge—probably a detective investigating Ravi's murder, but he hadn't seen any plainclothes officers at LasTech. He didn't breathe, hoping that she wouldn't turn, because if she did she would be staring him in the eye.

"Detective!" an excited voice called. "In here, it looks like someone was wounded."

Max watched as the woman stood up, and her feet left the room. She would not stay out for long. It was a gamble, but he needed to move. When she returned, he had no doubt that she would discover his location. Getting out was harder than getting in, as he had little room to move and his lead leg was injured, but he moved as quickly as he could.

As he pulled the computer behind him, he heard a faint chime drawing his attention to the screen in time to see the window showing the transfer was complete. He closed the computer and slid it back under the bed after removing Ravi's thumb drive and placing it back in his pocket.

He could hear a discussion in the apartment, likely in Carolyn's room, which was where his clothes would have been found, along with the remains of his triage supplies. Other noises could be heard from the kitchen as he slowly stood, listening to hear if anyone was in the hallway. Hearing nothing, he stepped quietly past the open door and slid into the closet.

Every noise he made sounded like an alarm to him, but the police were focused elsewhere, believing the apartment was empty, and nobody picked up on the sounds. When the detective returned to the guest room, he was at the back of the closet, shielded by a rack of clothes and standing awkwardly on the sides of several pairs of half-calf boots.

"Check the bed," she directed an officer who had returned with her, ignoring the closet that she had previously searched.

The door was half closed, and Max lowered his head below the top of the hangers, but he could see the uniformed officer stand up with Carolyn's computer in hand.

"This might help," he said, handing it to the detective.

"Thank you," she responded, rubbing her other hand along the bottom. "It's warm."

She turned abruptly, and Max thought for certain that she would expose him, but she ran out to the hallway.

"Sergeant!" she yelled. "How long was surveillance here?"

He couldn't hear the rest of the conversation, but it was agitated. The officer who had found the computer looked casually in the closet, but it was a cursory effort, and Max remained unseen. Before long, he was alone, but he knew it would be several hours before the police would leave the apartment.

CHAPTER THIRTEEN

By his estimation, the police had cleared out of Carolyn's apartment before 7:00 p.m., but Max stayed in the closet for another half hour before slowly emerging. He did not draw his gun. If he could avoid it, he'd prefer not to shoot at an officer of the law. Luckily, he soon discovered that he'd been left alone in the apartment, which was now littered with police evidence markers. Carolyn's computer was nowhere to be found and most of his gear had also been removed.

The police hadn't cleared out Carolyn's bathroom though, so he pulled down his pants and inspected the wound. It actually looked pretty good, but he washed it gently with hydrogen peroxide, dabbed it dry, and rewrapped it with fresh gauze. Once that was done, he relieved himself and grabbed his Dopp kit, which really only consisted of a toothbrush, an almost empty tube of toothpaste, and a comb, but he knew he wasn't coming back, so it might be useful.

In the kitchen, Max grabbed a box of crackers and the rest of his six-pack, tucked them in a reusable grocery bag he found in one of the kitchen drawers, and headed to the elevator.

He had to maneuver through yellow police tape and couldn't lock up because the main lock had been busted, but he did his best to leave everything as it was.

He rode the elevator to the parking garage, knowing that the police would still be surveilling the entrance, but suspecting they wouldn't be watching for cars exiting. He'd seen an old Mercedes 450SL when he'd been in the garage before. It was dark blue and had the boxy shape of the 1970s or maybe 1980s. Old, yes—but in a place like Pacific Heights, Max was pretty sure it still ran well. Beyond that, he could hot-wire it.

Modern cars were great with remote locks and keyless driving, but all the technology made them harder to steal. At least in this instance, Max had no concern about getting an old key-start beauty running. Better still, the car wasn't so old that he would be easily spotted. There were still plenty of these rigs on the road in California.

The car's door wasn't even locked, which brought a smile to his face as he hopped in and quickly checked the contents. Unfortunately, the keys were not in the console, but he found a nice pair of aviator sunglasses, the kind with the wire that loops around the ear. He put those aside and got to work on the ignition with the Leatherman that he had brought from Carolyn's kitchen drawer.

Moments later, the garage door opened, and Max pulled out with the radio cranking a classic Kansas hit. It was dark and his headlights flashed on a sedan parked across the street, no doubt holding two cops with binoculars and notepads, but Max allowed his eyes to just follow the street. He turned north and down the hill so he did not have to sit there and watch for traffic in the other direction. The old classic coasted down Steiner before he turned right onto Broadway as he made his way toward downtown and the Bay Bridge.

His phone vibrated, and he was pleasantly surprised to see Tanner's name.

"Hey, man." He turned the phone on speaker and turned down the music. "I'm headed your way. I found something."

"What'd you find?" Tanner's tone shifted but Max didn't answer. "Doesn't matter. I got a message from the people who took her."

"What'd they say?"

"Let's talk when you get here." Tanner sounded nervous. "Shit, how did you get away today? You really pissed those fuckers off."

Max laughed. "It wasn't fun for me either."

"Yeah. Well, they stayed until five. We had to let Eunice go after explaining that one of our employees was murdered. This isn't typical when you are selling a business. I'm glad she hasn't pulled out."

"What did they say on the call?" Max couldn't care less about the deal. Carolyn might be part of the problem, but he still wanted her safe.

"I'll tell you when you get here," Tanner said, ending the call.

Max considered calling back, but he doubted Tanner would answer. When he came to a light, he clicked on his Waze app and typed in Tanner's address. For the third time in four days, he was headed to the East Bay, and he had almost lost his life in each of the first two.

*   *   *

The open road was therapeutic. After getting on the Bay Bridge, Max's trip took him on various highways and through the Caldecott Tunnel. He couldn't help but look across the highway to the shoulder where the action had started the previous Friday. The car was an automatic, but it was still so much more of a *drive* than the same trip would have been in Carolyn's Tesla. He felt the weight of the car on the curves and the power of the engine made him feel like he was floating along a river rather than driving down a highway.

Carolyn's computer had been a damning indictment. Max still had a hard time understanding why she would betray LasTech and Tanner. Sure, they had parted ways romantically, but the woman he had once been in love with was not a petty person. She was altruistic and always put right above self. So much time had passed.

Was Carolyn still the same woman? Or had she changed? He could ask the same questions about Tanner, though he felt more on solid ground with him. They had shared a lot of good times. Jenny was the real enigma. She was relatively new to the scene but had been close to Carolyn and was now married to Tanner. He'd seen her at the Chao Fen subsidiary office, but it might have been a coincidence. Something was definitely off, but he couldn't put his finger on it.

As he made his way up the secondary roads to Tanner's home, Max decided he would keep the data from Carolyn's laptop to himself. Regardless of her involvement, his primary goal was to make sure she was safe, and if she was complicit and that meant walking into her trap, he would suffer the consequences. If he told them what he'd found, Tanner might refuse to help her and that would serve no one.

Soon, his headlights revealed the familiar facade of the Reynolds' home. With Zoroastrianism fresh in his mind, Max noted the flame sconces on either side of the front door with renewed appreciation, remembering Tanner's comment about Carolyn's Divo. Apparently, they both clung to vestiges of Zoroastrianism, and Tanner, like Carolyn, had never been one to go halfway into anything. He turned off the engine, which let out several sputters as if in complaint as the engine finally died.

When he stepped out of the car, the front door was open, and Tanner was standing outside, cocktail in hand.

He whistled. "Sweet ride, Max. Where did you pick that up?"

"I borrowed it."

"Cool." Tanner nodded in appreciation. "Come on in. Do you want something to drink?"

Max had been walking toward him, but he stopped, staring at his old friend with a look of puzzlement.

"Really, Tanner?" he said, shaking his head and resuming his walk. "No, thank you. Tell me what they said."

"OK, brother. I get it. I needed something to take the edge off. You don't have to be so judgmental."

The two went into the kitchen where Jenny was waiting, glass of wine in hand. The room had a faint hint of cinnamon, and Max noticed a scented candle burning near the sink.

"Hi, Max." Jenny nodded, raising her glass.

"Hey." Max acknowledged her then turned to Tanner. The three of them were now around the butcher-block island. "OK, man. Let's hear it."

"They called on my work cell—literally not five minutes after the police left our offices. Do you think they knew?"

Max was getting impatient. "It doesn't matter. What did they say?"

"It was a muffled voice, but they said they had Carolyn and they would exchange her for TITAN."

Max did not reply, but he lifted his eyebrow and motioned with his hand for Tanner to continue.

"I asked what if I didn't have it. And he said that would be very bad for Carolyn. I explained that we have software protocols, but he cut me off. He said we needed to deliver TITAN or Carolyn would die."

"Well, that's positive." Max tapped the table.

"How can that be positive?" Tanner asked, appearing confused.

"Well, first of all, they aren't good negotiators," Max replied. "By starting out with death, they only have one card to play. If they threatened torture or dismemberment, then they have a whole playbook against us, but now if we call their bluff they don't have any cards."

"And what if they aren't bluffing?"

"That's another matter, but it's still encouraging. What else was said? How do we contact them?"

"That's why I called you." Tanner took a sip of his drink. "He said that he would call back at nine with instructions."

Max looked at the oven clock and saw that it was 8:51 p.m.

"OK. Good timing. Is it safe to say that Chao Fen is behind this?" he asked.

Tanner shrugged.

"They would sure save a bunch of money if they can get TITAN without buying LasTech," Jenny answered for him.

"Yeah," Max agreed. "But why would they try on both fronts?"

"What do you mean?" Tanner asked.

"It muddies the waters. Either buy the technology or steal it, but doing both doesn't make a ton of sense."

"I guess they really want it." Jenny stared at him as if challenging him to deny her.

Max nodded despite his disagreement. He needed to shift the discussion into a plan of action.

"So what did you find?" Tanner asked.

"Huh?"

"On the phone, you said you'd found something."

"That's the second reason to be positive." Max allowed a grin on his face as he looked from Tanner to Jenny before continuing. "I'm pretty sure I found TITAN."

"Get out!" Jenny responded immediately.

Tanner's eyes lit up, but he was slower to react. "That's good news, Max. Where is it?"

"I'll give it to you after the call." Max deflected the question. He didn't want to distract them until they'd spoken with the kidnappers. This was his world, and he didn't want Tanner or Jenny to slip up and reveal any hole cards.

The contact was important. More than anything, he wanted to hear the seriousness in the caller's voice. He needed to know what they were up against.

"We've got less than ten minutes." He walked into the family room, raising his voice so they could still hear him. "Do you have a laptop that I can AirPlay onto the TV?"

"We aren't Apple users," Tanner answered, following him. "But we can Chromecast to the screen. Why?"

Max ignored the question. "Good. Is the keyboard loud?"

"I don't think so." His friend sounded annoyed.

"OK. Get it out here." Max was scanning the room, trying to plan the best positions for audio.

Tanner shook his head and had moved toward the bedrooms, presumably to get the laptop, when Max stopped him.

"Tanner."

He turned, minor frustration on his face. "What?"

"I'm sorry. The laptop is so that I can tell you what to say. I'm hoping the keyboard is quiet so that the typing isn't picked up by the phone."

"Get my Dell." Jenny's voice came from the doorway behind him. "It's on my bedside table."

Tanner went off and Max turned to Jenny. "Thank you."

"We're all on the same team, Max," she said, moving past him to pick up the remote and turn on the TV.

* * *

Eight minutes later, the three of them were seated in the family room. Tanner and Jenny sat on the couch facing the TV, and Max sat facing them in a chair that was more decorative than functional in its position, almost underneath the TV. Between them was a square coffee table with a few magazines and most importantly Tanner's phone.

"Tanner, you need to trust me on this. If I put quotations on the screen, you need to read exactly what I type. Very important. Other times I'll give you guidance, but if I use quotations I want you to say *exactly* what I write. Got it?"

"Yeah, Max. I get it."

"Take a deep breath. You need to sound calm."

"I'd be a little calmer if you'd stop with all the instructions." Tanner finished the last of his drink, turning to Jenny. "Honey, would you mind getting me another?"

"Of course." She got up to go into the kitchen but paused at the door. "Max, do you need anything?"

"No, thank you."

He tapped a message on the keyboard.

"Thank you, Jenny" appeared on the TV, and Tanner parroted it with a smile, loud enough for Jenny to hear in the kitchen.

"Good." Max looked at his friend. "You hired me for this exact job in a different format, but this is what I do. Trust me."

Jenny was returning with a fresh cocktail when the phone vibrated. She put the drink on the table and pulled in close to Tanner on the couch, one leg bent underneath her.

Tanner reached out and tapped the screen as it began to vibrate a second time. He turned it to speaker as he spoke.

"This is Tanner."

"Do you have TITAN?" A man's voice spoke slowly and in what sounded like an exaggeratedly low tone.

Max shook his head and typed, "Need to know that Carolyn is safe."

Tanner spoke. "How do I know Carolyn is safe?"

There was a slight pause, and they could hear footsteps on a hardwood floor, then the sound of a door opening.

"Say hello." The voice was not quite as low, and it hadn't been spoken directly into the phone.

A moment later, they heard Carolyn's voice tentatively. "Hello? Who is it?"

Tanner did not wait for Max's prompt. "Carolyn! Are you OK?"

Max typed furiously, "Open-ended questions. Allow her to talk."

"I'm OK," she answered, and they could hear the door close.

"Do you have TITAN?" the voice repeated.

This time Max nodded.

"Yes," Tanner answered with hesitation.

"You don't sound certain," the voice rumbled.

Max typed instructions, and Tanner answered, "Sorry. So much going on. Yes, I have TITAN."

"Good. Here's what will happen. You give TITAN to your wife. She will get in her car and drive to Moraga."

"Jenny has nothing to do with this." Again, Tanner was off-script. "I'll take it to you."

The phone remained silent for a long period of time.

"Hello?" Tanner asked.

"Do you want Carolyn returned?" the deep voice asked after a twenty-second pause.

This time Tanner looked up to Max for his answer, and Max quickly typed.

"Yes, but I don't want Jenny involved."

"I don't mind," Jenny spoke up from beside him. "I'll do it."

Max flared his eyes in anger typing, "What the fuck? Don't speak!" But he was far too late.

"Good," the voice continued as if Tanner had agreed, "Jenny will bring TITAN to Moraga. There's a park there with a band shell."

"Moraga Commons." Again, Jenny spoke out of turn.

"Yes," the voice answered. "Bring TITAN to the stage. No one but Jenny. If she is followed, Carolyn dies. If you alert the police, Carolyn dies. If you do anything but what I've just asked, Carolyn dies."

Max typed in quotations, and this time Tanner read it exactly.

"So we are both on the same page, if Carolyn dies, you won't get TITAN."

The line was silent. Max typed some more.

"I want to talk to Carolyn," Tanner read aloud.

"That will not be permitted."

"How do I know that wasn't a recording? I want to ask her something only she can answer."

The line was silent again, and Tanner added, "Just one question. You can do it."

Max held up his hand for Tanner to stay silent.

Finally, the voice answered, "I will relay one question."

Max typed with quotations, and Tanner read, "Ask her to describe the time at Alford Academy before I asked her to prom."

Tanner gave Max a look of bewilderment. He mouthed, "I never asked her to prom!"

Max nodded with his hand up to stop Tanner from saying anything more.

"I will call back shortly," the voice responded and then ended the call.

"I never asked her to prom, Max," Tanner immediately repeated out loud.

"Open-ended question. Carolyn will understand. Gives her an opportunity to help us find her. Whatever the message is, you will accept it as proof." He turned to Jenny. "What the fuck was that? You were supposed to remain silent."

She rolled her eyes. "You are overthinking this, Max. They want me to do a job. I'll do it. Whatever I need to do to get Carolyn back."

"Yes, but you've given them something without a trade-off. Your participation was a bargaining point that we no longer have."

"Hang on a sec. You're pregnant and these guys are playing for keeps." Tanner's voice rose. "I don't think you should go."

"Carolyn is my friend as much as she is yours." Jenny's eyes flared to life. "I'm going to do this."

"I still don't like it. Max, you better keep an eye on her."

Jenny shook her head dismissively, and they sat in silence for a few minutes until Tanner's phone vibrated on the coffee table.

As Tanner reached to answer it, Max repeated, "Remember, whatever the answer is, you will accept it as accurate."

"Hello?" Tanner said, switching the call to speaker.

"It was Mr. Grainger's class in the basement lab. There were five of you doing an extra-credit project for computer science. You and she were supposed to write code that would function as the background for a website. The other three were building the front end, but you and Garcia, who was leading the other team, couldn't agree on the connection. It was past eleven o'clock, and eventually you told them all that Carolyn and you would finish it, and when the others left you asked her to the prom. Happy?"

The caller sounded annoyed by the drill.

"When will she be released?" Tanner read another prompt.

"She will be released once TITAN is in our hands. Send Jenny at 10:00 tonight."

Max started to type, but the line went dead once again.

"Mr. Grainger taught history, not computer science," Tanner blurted out after making sure his phone was off.

"I know," Max answered absently, his mind focused on thinking through what they had heard. "I'm sure Carolyn's given us clues. Now I need to figure them out."

"We don't have much time. Moraga is twenty-five minutes away. And where's TITAN?"

Max pushed his hand into his pocket, returning with Ravi's thumb drive. He tossed it to Tanner.

"Take a look."

Tanner's eyes flashed with excitement as he accepted the laptop from Max as well. He inserted the thumb drive and opened its contents, the laptop still mirroring everything on the TV. Max watched as the same dizzying array of files polluted the screen.

"You tell me, Tan. Is that TITAN?"

Tanner's eyes were still glued to the screen, and he periodically hammered on the keypad.

"I don't have time to tell for sure, but it sure looks like it. Where did you find this?"

"Dumb luck, really. I think something in Carolyn's office activated the thumb drive, but it was lucky that I had it in my pocket."

"Near-field communication chips. She and Ravi love that tech. It's similar to RFID but way stronger." He laughed. "Nice work, Max. You've earned everything I'm paying you and more. I'm so glad you're here."

"I'm not staying for long. I've got to get to Moraga ahead of Jenny."

"Right." Tanner seemed to be lost in thought for a moment. "We've got to get Carolyn."

"Can you make a copy?" Jenny asked.

Tanner shook his head. "Nope. This folder can be moved, but it would encrypt itself. I think the fact that it is on Ravi's personal thumb drive is the only reason we can see these files." He turned to Max. "More of your dumb luck."

CHAPTER FOURTEEN

A half hour later, Max pulled his car into an empty parking lot at the Moraga Library. He rolled to the back into a spot away from the road and turned off the engine. He had little time. It was almost a quarter to ten, and he still needed to get into position. Back at the house, Tanner had called up a map of the area, and Jenny, who seemed to have some familiarity, had pointed out various landmarks, including the parking lot he was now in. Across the road, there was a bike path with a bridge that would take him to the band shell.

He looked at his watch again and spoke softly, "Change of plan. I'm going to have to stay back."

He had an earbud in his right ear, and both Tanner and Jenny were on a group call, Tanner from his home and Jenny driving herself to the Commons. She would park at the lot nearest to the band shell.

"OK," Jenny responded, "I'm almost there. Driving past the

Starbucks now." Max had not passed any retail stores on his route, so the landmark meant nothing to him. He got out of his car and walked across the deserted lot where a crosswalk took him to the pedestrian path on the other side of the road. There were no cars on the road, and he'd only seen a couple on his drive into the sleepy town. The path ran parallel to the road, but through a wooded section and there was substantial undergrowth such that he felt protected if a car were to roll by.

Fifty feet down the path, he found the bridge and crossed it quickly, not liking how it exposed him. The air was cool, but thankfully there was no rain despite the forecast that had suggested it. Near the road, there had been streetlights, but now that he was inside the park there was no artificial light, though his eyes slowly adjusted to the natural light of a half-moon. Around him, he saw no signs of any movement, but that meant little at this point. The band shell was close but around a bend in the path. He couldn't go much farther without the risk of being seen on the pathway, and he would make too much noise if he tried to bushwhack through the middle.

"I'm parked." Jenny's voice seemed louder now that he was in the quiet park.

He reached into his pocket and lowered the sound on his phone.

"I'm in position if you need me," he whispered.

In his earpiece, he could hear her door open and close. Then things were quiet—she must have been walking to the band shell.

After what seemed like too long, he heard her voice again in his earpiece.

"Hello?" she asked.

He could hear something barely audible, then Jenny again spoke, "Yes. Sorry. It's not connected. I must have left it in."

A muted click announced her departure from the call.

"Shit." Tanner's voice filled the void. "You've got to go after her."

Max had already crept around the curve in the path.

"I'm on it," he whispered. "I need quiet. Don't speak until I speak to you."

The moonlight had been helpful before, but as he rounded the bend, he felt completely exposed. Down the path, he could see a dark structure that must be the band shell. He kept moving along the line of bushes to the left, creeping closer, but he heard nothing ahead of him, so he stopped about fifty feet from the structure.

Looking at it from the side and in the moonlight, he could see a field in front of the stage that climbed up a hill to his right. Nothing moved.

Max knew that anyone being careful would be sure to spot his approach from this angle, but he didn't have another choice. Jenny had already engaged, so it was possible that the deal was done. It certainly would not take long, and if he hoped to get an edge on

Carolyn's location, he needed to hurry.

He checked the position of his Glock in his belt, stepped away from the bushes, and strode down the path toward the band shell, still hearing nothing. When he got to the building, he moved around to the front where he could see the empty stage and he started to feel like something was wrong. No Jenny. Nobody was here.

He jogged to the other side of the building, all concern of stealth gone. Jenny would have parked about two hundred yards away. She couldn't have left already. But as he rounded the corner he immediately knew he was in trouble. Several vehicles sat dark on this side of the building and then light immediately burst from all of them, blinding him momentarily and forcing him to turn away.

"Freeze."

"Don't move."

"Hands in the air. Now!"

As many as six or seven voices called out commands. Max could hear movement behind him, and he didn't need to turn to know that he was surrounded. He lifted his hands in the air and knelt on the grass, facing the lit-up cars.

"Move to the ground," a voice yelled behind him. "Hands wide."

Max tried to move slowly, but before he was on the ground, a knee slammed into his back, knocking the air out of his chest. Someone removed the gun from his back, and more hands pulled his arms behind his back and zip-tied them together.

Apart from flexing while he was being zip-tied, Max did nothing to resist. He was outmanned. There was nothing he could do. With his face in the dirt, he tried to understand who had called the police.

CHAPTER FIFTEEN

Jail was never a fun place, but the smaller the jail, the nicer the conditions. At least that had been Max's experience in the few jails he'd visited over the years. After his arrest, he had listened to a fairly heated dispute as to where they would process him. The operation had apparently been a combination of the San Francisco, Walnut Creek, and Moraga police departments, and the SFPD had been vehement that their case was a capital crime and thus they should have control.

The Walnut Creek police argued that the events earlier in Walnut Creek carried existing charges while the SFPD was still only investigating, and as such they demanded to book Max in the county jail on charges of assaulting a police officer, evading arrest, and attempted murder. They had Max stuffed in the back of a Walnut Creek squad car while they debated the issue right outside his door.

In the end, Walnut Creek survived despite many threats from the much larger SFPD, and Max had been taken to Walnut Creek for processing.

He was booked with little fanfare, though it was clear they didn't appreciate the fact that he had subdued members of their force earlier in the day. They accidentally hit his head when extracting him from the squad car, drawing blood, and every corner seemed to involve a shove from behind or a brush from the side. By the time they got to the mug shot, they had needed to bring in an EMT to glue the small gash inside his hairline so that he wasn't bleeding for the picture. Around that time, Max had seen a police captain having words with one of the sergeants, and the rougher treatment seemed to stop.

By three in the morning, he found himself alone in a small cell and was able to close his eyes for a few hours. It smelled lightly of someone else's body odor, but there was a cot to lie on.

He had no phone or watch, but his internal clock suggested it was sometime after eight when he awoke and stretched his sore body, glad to be alone. He needed some time to think through the past day's events, particularly his capture the previous night.

Assuming Chao Fen held Carolyn and was trying to get TITAN, they wouldn't have set him up with the police. That left Tanner and Jenny, and he didn't want to believe that either of them would betray him, but of all the players, he knew Jenny the least. Ravi and Carolyn had both suggested that Jenny couldn't be trusted, but was she acting alone or in cahoots with Chao Fen? He wished he had been able to investigate the Chao Fen connection further. Obviously, Jenny was Chinese, as was Chao Fen, but with a country of one and a half billion people, it was a little unfair to use that connection without additional investigation.

It couldn't be Tanner. His friend wasn't perfect, but there was no way he would set Max up. Even if he had wanted to, how would that benefit Tanner? Max was the one who had found TITAN. Tanner himself had pointed out how valuable Max had been.

Jenny, on the other hand, had TITAN, and if she was working with Chao Fen, then they already had what they needed. Why involve the police at all? And if she was working with Chao Fen, then what of Tanner and their baby?

Something was not yet clicking. There was more here than he was aware of. And what of Carolyn? If she was involved, as Tanner had indicated, was she working with Jenny? Once again, there were too many angles for one player to be using.

Thinking of Carolyn brought him back to the previous night's exchange, and he welcomed a change of thought. If Carolyn needed help, he was certain that she'd given them clues. He needed to figure them out.

Besides being a history teacher, Mr. Grainger had been the varsity baseball coach. That might have something to do with it. And there had been no Garcia at Alford Academy, so that definitely had more meaning than it appeared. Max guessed that there were five captors, and she was probably being held in a basement, which was where the computer lab had been.

"Kline," a loud voice called from the doorway as keys turned in the lock, snapping his thoughts back to the present situation.

The door swung open, revealing one of the men who had booked him earlier.

"Let's go." He motioned for Max to leave.

This was the man who had dinged Max's head and had left a number of other bruises, so Max stepped cautiously into the hall, body tense for another blow that didn't come.

"Too many eyes on you at the moment," the sergeant whispered angrily, leaning in behind him. "But we'll get you back here soon enough."

The push that followed was relatively mild, given his treatment the night before, and Max stayed on his feet, walking down the hall as directed.

"Somebody with a lot of money wants you out."

He knew better than to respond. Anything he said might become an excuse to harm him.

At the end of the hall, they passed through another set of doors to a medium-sized room that had a door and a large open counter along one wall. Above the opening was a sign that read "property room," and behind the counter was an older officer holding a manila envelope in one hand and Max's vest in the other. He dropped the vest on the counter and then emptied the envelope on top of it—some cash and several credit cards wrapped in a rubber band that served as his wallet, his belt, his phone, and the security badge that he'd never returned to LasTech.

Max slowly put his belongings in his pockets, but when he looked at his phone, the screen was shattered.

"What's up with this?" he asked, showing the phone to the officer.

"No idea."

Max tried to turn it on, but it was either completely out of battery or broken. Either way, it wouldn't be of much use.

"We're going to keep your weapon," the older officer added. "If it checks out, which I doubt, you'll have to file papers to retrieve it."

Again, Max remained silent.

Moments later, he was once again a free man, standing in the California morning sunlight in front of the jail.

A black extended Town Car pulled up, unusual for Tanner, but Max was too thankful to care. The driver came around to open the door for him.

"Thank you," he said to the man as he slid inside, addressing his benefactor as he did. "And thank you, Tanner. I can't believe how quickly you sprang me."

As he turned his head, his words trailed off. Tanner was not in the car. Sitting next to him with a smile like the Cheshire Cat was Eunice Lee.

* * *

"You were expecting someone else?" Eunice shifted in the seat next to him so that her body turned to face him. She was unbuckled.

Max heard the door close behind him.

"Hello, Eunice." He allowed a slight smile. "I guess I owe you a thank you."

He had only met Eunice a few days earlier, but it seemed that she had aged since their first meeting. Her eyes looked tired, and the crow's feet had multiplied. She was dressed in the same blue pantsuit she'd had on every time he'd seen her.

"Yes," she said, "I suppose you do. You seem to be everywhere interesting this week, Mr. Kline. How is it that you've been in town for less than a week and you're wanted by two police forces, in addition to holding the key to a multi-billion-dollar transaction?"

"Trust me." Max shook his head. "This is not how I expected my week to turn out." He looked around the interior. If things headed south, he wanted the ability to get out.

"Nevertheless, you've been charged with several counts here in Walnut Creek, and you're wanted for questioning in a murder investigation in San Francisco." She shifted again, facing almost perpendicular across the car seat, before continuing. "The murder of a key figure in the company that I am in the process of acquiring. This is definitely not how I expected *my week to turn out*."

"I'm not sure that you care, but I had nothing to do with Ravi's death."

"But you were there on the day he was murdered." It was not a question.

"Ms. Lee, I am extremely grateful that you bailed me out. I find it a bit awkward though and possibly a breach of etiquette to be sitting here in an unsanctioned conversation with the lead negotiator from the other side of an active deal. Still, I owe it to you to at least hear you out. So what is it you want from me?"

"I only want you to do your job." Her smile returned. "Help me close the LasTech deal."

Max thought about his response. She would know that his obligation was to Tanner and LasTech, but maybe she didn't care. When they had pushed back and threatened to hold TITAN back, it had been Eunice who had acquiesced on price. That part made sense, but she had been responsible for attacks that should have taken his life. He decided to expose his hole cards and see how she would react.

"And I want Carolyn returned."

Eunice put her hands on the seat and pushed herself straighter, sitting more naturally in the seat, as she crossed her legs.

"So Carolyn's missing?" she asked.

Not the response he was expecting. He said nothing but watched as the older woman opened her purse and pulled out a pack of cigarettes. She took one out and offered it to him. When he refused, she put it in her mouth and lit it with a lighter, turning to lower the window a crack and blew her first puff outside.

"Drive," she called up to the driver before turning to Max. "What do you know about Chao Fen?"

The car slowly coasted out of the parking spot, but while Max was curious where they were headed, his focus was on the conversation.

"I know you are a fairly large conglomerate," he said.

"Do you think we are the Italian Mafia?" she asked, continuing before he could answer, "I mean, seriously, are you telling me you think we kidnapped a significant shareholder of the company that we are in the process of acquiring? What kind of books are you reading, Mr. Kline?"

There was anger in her voice, and she took what seemed like an irritated pull on her cigarette, forcibly blowing the smoke out the window. Not all the smoke left the car, but Max enjoyed the smell, reminded of so many cafes in the Middle East without the American secondhand smoke laws. He'd never been a smoker himself, but he enjoyed the scent in the air.

He wasn't certain if it had been a rhetorical question, but he didn't have an answer. Thinking on it, his assumptions did borderline on the outlandish, but that assumed there weren't three attempts at his life over the weekend. Given the amount of fire he'd dodged, he had a right to draw some conclusions, even if he had yet to establish them as facts.

"I saw Jenny at your office on Monday."

"My office is in Hong Kong," she said dismissively. "What are you even talking about?"

"Hoshiyama Corporation—right here in Walnut Creek."

Eunice paused and took another drag of her cigarette. She nodded and blew a cloud of smoke into the car.

"That's ours, but I wasn't aware they were here, and I have no idea what Jenny would be doing there."

Max had the uneasy feeling he was pushing too hard. It would have been much easier to pursue if she had been defensive or avoidant. Still, he didn't have many options.

"Why don't we go see?"

An abrupt laugh followed another puff of smoke.

"You have some arrogance, Mr. Kline. I just rescued you from jail, and here you are, a suspect in a murder investigation, trying to turn the spotlight on me and my company."

Max started to respond, but Eunice continued, raising her voice, "A company with a two-hundred-fifty-year track record of success. Chao Fen is not perfect, but we've earned our position on the world stage. Can you say as much?"

His thoughts immediately went to his service in MARSOC, most of which remained classified, and he would hardly bring it up here regardless, but the memories rushed in.

"With due respect, Ms. Lee, we all earn our positions. And if you can't tell me where Carolyn is, I don't know why I'm still in the car."

"You're in the car because I thought that half a million in bail money might make you a little sympathetic. I need your help, but if I am wrong . . . so be it. I can't help you with Carolyn." She paused. "No, I should say—I don't know where Carolyn is. If you want my help, you've got it—providing you help me in turn."

Max looked at her for a moment. While her voice was strong, her eyes betrayed a sense of fatigue. He turned away and looked out the window to buy himself some time before answering. They were driving past an apartment complex. Women with strollers were on the streets, and kids played in the grass. Such blissful innocence was a stark contrast to his current situation.

"Are you saying you had nothing to do with the attacks on my life?" he asked without turning.

Eunice did not immediately respond, putting out the cigarette in an ashtray by the door. She removed another from her pack, lit it, and took a long inhale, blowing the smoke out the window before she answered.

"We made a mistake. We thought you were the obstacle and Friday night was our solution." She turned back to face him. "I'll answer for that, but we had no involvement in anything else over the weekend. Things have changed course and our strategy has changed with them. Consider bail as an olive branch. We also have connections within the SFPD Evidence Department and we'd be willing to make sure you are cleared as a suspect in Ravi's death. I'm asking for your help."

Max pushed down his anger at her admission. She was correct. Things had changed and at least she was open enough to admit it.

"What is it you need?" he asked.

"Just what I'm paying for," she answered. "I want to secure TITAN. I know Tanner is playing games with us, but I don't know why. Either way, I need to be certain of TITAN."

"You're talking about a crime." Max turned to look her in the eyes. "TITAN is still LasTech property."

"I have no intention of welshing on our deal," Eunice answered sternly. "Chao Fen will be around far longer than you, and we do not want our reputation sullied. We will pay full price for LasTech so long as TITAN is ours. Acquiring it ahead of the deal will not change anything except our conviction that the deal will close as agreed."

"So you are saying you don't trust Tanner."

"I'm saying I don't understand him. And I don't trust the way things are playing out."

"But you trust me?"

"I trust that you will do as you say. I trust that your loyalty to LasTech and your friend Tanner is important but that in the end you will follow your own moral compass."

"You make a lot of assumptions with your trust."

"Eleven years a Marine. Eight in MARSOC—member of the first graduating class. Four tours, nine commendations, three promotions. It is not often that someone with a decorated sniper background moves into command. Even less common for one to become a hostage negotiator. Most of your time in the Middle East. Honorable discharge in 2017. Since then, you've made Las Vegas your home, earning an average of one hundred sixty five thousand a year at the poker tables, mostly at the Wynn and the MGM. Also, working here and there translating Chinese and Farsi," she said in Chinese. "It is an educated guess, but we don't put our faith in pure assumptions. And, yes, the casinos know exactly what you make, even if the IRS does not."

While she talked, Max was trying to understand the other pieces in the game. If she didn't have the thumb drive, it supported her claim of innocence. Or did Jenny fail to make the drop? She hadn't been at the park or for sure she would have been picked up and questioned. And where was Tanner? Why hadn't Tanner bailed him out?

"How do we find Carolyn?" he asked.

"I suspect you have a better idea of that than I do," she answered coolly. "But I will provide every resource that I can."

Max didn't like this position, but if there was one thing he'd learned in years of field operations, it was that things rarely played out as one wanted or expected. Success in the field meant fluidity, and the game had already shifted.

"I'll need a car," he said, still watching her facial expressions. "And some money."

CHAPTER SIXTEEN

Cyrus felt worn out, but at least he'd had some rest. The day before had been the peak of his stress. Following the overnight surveillance, he'd followed Max Kline out to the Walnut Creek headquarters of LasTech, but when the scene heated up, he had separated himself from the events. He'd still had his friend's body in the van so could not risk involvement.

He had driven back to San Jose, where he went to the back of a large tract of open space that the temple owned. When he was certain no one was around, he'd dug a hole for his friend and buried him with only a few words of ceremony. It wasn't the way Koorush would have wanted to go, but Cyrus had to move on.

He'd taken the van back to the Fire Temple and completely washed it inside and out. Afterward, he had showered and taken a meal before spending the rest of the evening praying. Thankfully, no one else was around, and he'd been able to sleep for most of the night on a couch in one of the side rooms.

In the morning, he'd used the office computer to check in on the news and had been astonished by the stories of a massive manhunt in Moraga that resulted in the arrest of an unnamed man who'd assaulted Walnut Creek police the previous day and was considered a suspect in a San Francisco murder investigation.

He'd cursed himself for stepping away and ran back to the van, immediately heading north on I-680. His phone was completely dead, so he plugged it in, knowing he must have missed some communication. The others would have been following events as well.

By the time he was halfway to Walnut Creek, he realized Kline would likely be in jail for at least the day, so he decided to see if he could pick up a signal from the beacon he'd placed on Tanner Reynolds's truck. He exited the highway in Danville and pulled into a mall where he could park.

He pulled his iPad out of the center console and turned it on, happy to see the battery was still over half full. When he clicked on the tracking icon, a map filled the screen with Danville at the center and most of the East Bay from Dublin up to Walnut Creek in view. A yellow star in the center represented his location, and not far off, to the west and slightly north, a blue dot flashed, showing the beacon's position. Cyrus smiled, zooming in to confirm that the vehicle was sitting at Tanner's home. He ran a history that showed the vehicle had traveled to Walnut Creek the previous evening, staying there until three in the morning before it had returned to Danville. He looked at the time—almost ten o'clock—wondering if Tanner was still asleep.

Putting the iPad on the passenger seat, he picked up his phone and tapped the screen to life. The charge was at forty percent, and the message icon showed a bubble with sixty-seven unread messages. He cursed himself for not charging it the night before and opened the message screen, seeing that most of them were in the group chat with a few direct messages asking if he was okay, where he was, and why he wasn't answering. He quickly responded to each of these with his status and current location, then he scanned the message chain in the group chat.

Apart from wondering where he was, the group had lit up when they had caught news of the arrest in Moraga, but there was another discussion regarding Tanner, who had been spotted arriving at LasTech headquarters at 10:00 p.m. the previous night.

Cyrus was an adept double-thumb typist, and he quickly checked in on the chat.

"C. Here. Was offline for the night. K is gone now." They already knew he was dead, and he assumed they would understand what he'd needed to take care of.

"Assume you saw activity. We suspect TITAN is back in play."

"I have TR vehicle tracked," he responded. "At home, will maintain."

He checked that the phone was on vibrate and put it in his pocket, stepping out to smoke a cigarette. When he finished, he walked over to a small mini-mart for a coffee before climbing back into the van.

Almost an hour and a half later, a dull tone sounded from the iPad, and he reached over, tapping the screen back to life. As he suspected, the tone had indicated movement and the blue dot was winding down the road toward town.

"Heads-up," Cyrus alerted the others. "TR is on the move. I will follow."

"Kline is out," his colleague typed.

"That was fast. Anyone on him?"

"Negative. Didn't know it was happening. Was not Tanner."

Cyrus thought for a moment.

"Roger. Better to stay with TR. Will try to pick up MK later."

He said a brief prayer to Ahura Mazda and pulled out of the parking lot, headed to intersect the path of Tanner's Rivian.

* * *

Route 680 was a commuter highway that ran north-south in the East Bay corridor. In the mornings and early evenings, it was often congested in both directions, but during the day it was usually an easy ride. Cyrus followed Tanner's Rivian northward at a steady pace, holding three or four cars back. While traffic was light, there were still enough cars on the road that he felt certain he would not be noticed. In fact, he knew from experience that tailing Tanner was a simple task. He'd watched him many times before and was pretty sure he knew where the man was going. At one point, he'd even dropped out of sight, knowing that he could easily relocate his quarry with the beacon.

After exiting the highway in Walnut Creek, the Rivian followed the usual road west and turned left on California Street, but Cyrus was surprised when it didn't turn into LasTech headquarters. Instead, the electric truck turned right on Cyprus and continued a few blocks before taking another right onto Main, immediately pulling into an open parking spot.

Cyrus didn't turn but drove straight through the intersection, thanking Ahura Mazda that there was an open spot about halfway down the street.

It was 12:30, and the day was warming up, so he left his jacket in the car after pulling out a cigarette and lighter from its pocket. He loped to the corner, where he spotted Tanner walking into a

Starbucks down the street. He shook his head, constantly amazed at how the American culture was obsessed with what he considered piss-poor coffee, but it gave him a chance to rest, so he lit his cigarette and strolled slowly closer, stopping at a planter box with a bench surrounding it. Between his position and the Starbucks, there was a large fountain that consisted of a five-foot-high ceramic head with water bubbling out the top and cascading down the smooth sides. Cyrus didn't think it was terribly attractive, but it would provide a means of cover between himself and Tanner.

He was about halfway through the cigarette when Tanner emerged holding two cups of coffee, but nobody joined him. Cyrus waited, enjoying his smoke, and he was almost completely done when another man finally joined him.

The two sat down at one of the outside tables, and it was only then that Cyrus realized how lucky he was—the man with Tanner was Max Kline. He pulled out his phone, tapping the good news into chat, but now he had additional problems. He could only hope that Max would leave with Tanner, but if he didn't, Cyrus would need to follow him. If he stayed on foot and Kline had a vehicle, he'd lose him, but if he went back for his van, the same might happen.

Unfortunately, he didn't have much time to think. The pair chatted for maybe five minutes before Kline got up and left the table headed west. Cyrus had to gamble, so he headed back to his van, practically sprinting, and quickly put it in motion, turning right onto Broadway.

He scanned the street, looking for Kline, but he didn't see him anywhere. Rather than risk driving off on a wild-goose chase, he pulled over onto the next street that led back to Starbucks. If nothing else, he could stay on Reynolds.

He tapped the bad news into his phone, but when he looked up, he realized he had gotten lucky twice in the same hour because a blue Nissan Rogue pulled out of a parking garage across the street with Max Kline at the wheel. Cyrus looked down quickly and didn't think he was seen, but he waited until the Rogue had turned left before he put the van back into drive and eased out after him.

CHAPTER SEVENTEEN

Eunice Lee had been true to her word—at least with respect to her help. By noon, Max was sitting in a Starbucks in downtown Walnut Creek. In front of him sat a brand new MacBook Air that he had purchased at the Apple store two blocks away. It wouldn't have been his first choice for a computer, but the store was open, and there was no denying that they made it easy to set up.

He had parked his rental car in a lot a block in the other direction, and in his pocket he had a couple thousand dollars in cash and a black credit card with her name on it. She had also arranged the rental car, booked in someone else's name—fictitious or real. He didn't care.

While the Chao Fen team had worked on setting him up, Max dug deeper into Carolyn's clues. Now, with the MacBook fired up in front of him, he began to confirm his discoveries.

He'd started with Mr. Grainger. While he was a history teacher, he was best known for being the head coach of the baseball team, and in San Francisco that had to mean the Giants. Max felt certain that this was the right track, so he called up a Google Maps street view of the area around Oracle Park and scanned the surrounding buildings.

It did not take long to reveal a historic warehouse with the name Garcia & Maggini on the exterior. Garcia—one point for Carolyn. With no classmates named Garcia, Max had known that this must be a clue. It took a little longer to find more details, but eventually he came across a public record from a renovation filed in 2001 that included floor plans of the entire building, including the basement.

He recapped the message once again, trying to make sure he hadn't missed anything. In the story, Tanner had been expected to work on the background code. He looked at the blueprints. There were three entrances to the building—one in the front, two in the back. Both of the rear entrances were in stairwells, so either would work.

He turned the map so that the main entrance was facing toward him. One of the rear entrances was up and to the right, and the other was actually along the side wall but all the way at the back—eleven o'clock if he was looking at a clock.

"Carolyn, I love you," he whispered to himself, realizing he might have spoken out loud when his neighbor turned slightly at the noise.

He had the location. He was sure of it.

Suddenly, his phone vibrated. He flipped it over to see Tanner's name and declined the call.

He tapped on the keyboard and ran a search for sporting goods stores, finding a Big 5 within walking distance. He didn't have any weapons and couldn't waste time. If Carolyn's clues were correct, he had to act while there was still a good chance that she was in the same location.

On the way to the store, he dialed Tanner back.

"Max!" Tanner's voice was loud enough that he had to pull the phone slightly away from his head. "You're out! Thank God. When I found out what happened, I sent a lawyer to help, but she said you had already been released."

"Where's Jenny?" Max had no time for pleasantries. He wasn't even sure that they were still on the same side, but he'd give his friend the benefit of the doubt.

"She's not here."

"Did she make the drop?" Max thought he knew the answer but wanted to hear what his friend would say.

"No, man." His voice softened. "You were there. Someone let the police know. She was stopped and questioned but released."

"You home?"

"Yes."

"Come to Walnut Creek. The Starbucks a couple of blocks from the Apple store."

"I know it. I'm leaving now. Be there in twenty minutes."

Five minutes later, he was perusing the aisles of the Big 5, formulating a plan of attack. He collected a few items that would come in handy: some nylon rope, a pair of calfskin gloves, and a long-bladed hunting knife. Possibly most important, he'd found a sturdy pair of steel-toe hiking boots, which he wore out of the store, tossing his old shoes in a bin and silently thanking Eunice once again for her generosity. At the last minute, he'd added a Gatorade and an energy bar to his basket and, on the way back to the car, he'd finished the energy bar while he continued to play out the week's events in his head.

Eunice had denied Chao Fen's involvement and though he would not make any bets, it felt like she was sincere. If not Chao Fen, who had Carolyn? Ravi's theory of Zoroastrian involvement seemed the most far-fetched, especially given Carolyn's abduction—unless that was a ruse. But if Ravi wasn't on the right track, why had he died? Everything seemed to revolve around TITAN, but the technology had not even been deployed. Tanner and Jenny already had TITAN, which would seem to remove them from the equation had it not been for the events in Moraga. If Jenny had been that close, how could she not have seen the police and alerted him? Then there was still her visit to Chao Fen's subsidiary.

He wanted to hear what Tanner would say, but his priority was Carolyn's rescue, so he decided that he wouldn't share the morning's findings with his old friend. Before returning to Starbucks, he dropped off his supplies and the new computer in the backseat of his new rental car, a compact blue Nissan Rogue. When he got back to the street, he found Tanner waiting outside the store, holding two coffees, handing one to Max when he was close enough.

"Got you the dark roast, black."

"Any word from Carolyn's captors?" Max asked bluntly, taking the coffee.

"Nothing," Tanner replied, taking a seat at one of the outdoor tables. "How about you? You doing OK?"

"Yeah." Max sat in the seat opposite him. "I'm fine."

"Who bailed you out?"

"No idea," Max lied. "I thought it was you."

"That's weird." Tanner paused, staring at him oddly. "Anyway, we still need to find Carolyn."

"Of course."

"You think any more about her clues last night?"

"Sorry, man," Max continued to lie. It felt like a betrayal, but he knew it was the best choice for Carolyn's safety. "I've been a bit preoccupied over the past twelve hours."

"Yeah. Sorry. We need to find her or figure out where she's hidden TITAN."

"What do you mean? You have TITAN."

"No, sir." Tanner had been looking down, but he picked his head up, looking Max in the eye. "When things fell through last night, Jenny and I took the drive back to LasTech. It's not complete."

"What do you mean?"

"I mean, it has parts of TITAN, but it isn't all there." He shook his head. "We still don't have the program."

Max couldn't help but feel that his friend was more interested in the software than he was in his ex-lover.

"I'll keep looking." He took a long drink of his coffee. His throat burned from the heat, but he wanted to end the conversation. "You let me know if you hear anything."

"You want me to come with?" Tanner asked.

"I think it's best if you stay here," Max answered as he pushed his chair away with a slight wince when his wound unexpectedly gave him a brief stab of pain. "Man the fort and all that." He forced a smile.

"You need a car?" Tanner called after him, but Max lifted a hand in the air with his thumb up and continued walking.

* * *

It had been sunny in Walnut Creek, but the sky grew overcast as he drove through the Caldecott Tunnel, and by the time he crossed the Bay Bridge, he had to turn his wipers on because of the faint mist in the chilly air. Traffic in the opposite direction was already building as the workforce headed home. He exited on one of the first ramps after the bridge and followed his phone's directions to the ballpark. He turned right onto the Embarcadero and slowly wound his way along the shoreline until the road turned inward and the ballpark was there in front of him on the left side of what was now King Street.

It took no time to spot the Garcia & Maggini landmark on his right, but he just cruised past. The streets were relatively quiet. He turned right onto 3rd Street and found a parking spot about halfway down the block.

Max cracked the window for some air and reached behind him for the computer, firing it up. The MacBook Air had a steady state drive, so there was no waiting for the computer to boot up. The blueprints opened quickly, and he studied the layout once again, reviewing his hastily concocted plan. As soon as he entered the building, it was highly likely that everything would change, but years of training enforced the idea that one should always start with a plan, even if it was unlikely to unfold. He also knew that early morning and late afternoon were the best times for infiltration. He would not wait until morning, but he could wait a couple of hours for the afternoon to wane, and a little shut-eye would be welcome.

Pushing the recline button, he made sure the doors were locked, and he closed his eyes.

* * *

The sun had gone down by the time he awoke to a pinging sound from his computer. He knew immediately that it was the tracking alert that he had set up on the laptop that Carolyn had taken, and he almost dropped the computer in his urgency to open it up. When the app came to life on his screen, he was happy to see the flashing red dot was almost exactly on top of him.

He zoomed in to confirm that the beacon was in the suspected warehouse. He restarted the car so that he had the power to move the seat back to normal position, opening another file as he did so that he could review the blueprints one last time. When he was done, he closed the laptop and slid it under the seat. Crime in San Francisco was rampant, and it wouldn't do to leave it visible from the street. He got out and opened the back door where he'd left his supplies.

The mist was not quite rain, but it was heavier than before, and

Max was grateful that his vest was water resistant. He unbuckled his belt and slid the knife sheath on so that it rested against the back side of his right hip. It was fairly obvious but not illegal, and he really didn't care how he looked. In fact, with the state of his clothes, which he hadn't changed in a day, he could probably fit in with the many homeless in the city.

He had cut two lengths of cord and put one of these in his back left pocket. After putting on the gloves, he grabbed the second length and closed the door. The lock whistled to him as he pushed the key fob and headed toward the warehouse.

There was a hotel adjacent to the target building which, despite the name, was no longer a warehouse, and now contained offices. On King Street, before the hotel, an alleyway cut northward, and according to his maps, another narrow alleyway cut in perpendicularly behind both the hotel and the landmark warehouse. Max turned into the alleyway, which was almost the size of a small street and lit by several makeshift streetlights. On his right were the glass walls of the hotel lobby and a few guests looking out the window. He nodded to one as he moved up the alley.

At the far end, he could see a delivery truck in the process of unloading something, but the area was otherwise deserted. He walked to the end of the hotel and was happy to find that the maps had been correct. A narrow side alley cut in behind the hotel and extended the length of the next building—the target warehouse. There was light at the opposite end of the alley, which seemed to be above the rear exit from the warehouse but, in between, the area was much darker. Instinctively, he looked up and down the main alley to confirm that he was alone before he moved inward.

In the side alley, there was another area that headed south twenty feet between the hotel and the warehouse, parallel to the first alley, but it did not go through to King Street. It was just a collection area for garbage, laundry, and whatever else.

For a brief moment, he stood at the intersection, scanning the two sides of the old landmark building. To the right, a few feet southward, was a short stairwell that led to a darkened door at the basement level. If he'd read Carolyn's clues correctly, this was the entrance she had indicated, but it was completely in the open except for the area between the buildings that held a couple of dumpsters and some of the hotel's laundry. Straight ahead of him, the alley was slightly larger, and there were a couple of vehicles parked along the north side and another dumpster about halfway down. If he were to choose, he would have preferred that entrance, given the cover along the route, and he moved in that direction, ignoring Carolyn's clue, but then a long-ago conversation popped in his head—one when Carolyn had laughed at him for not listening to her when she'd given him a test answer that had seemed ridiculously far-fetched.

He'd been wrong to ignore her then, and she'd pointed it out, making sure he didn't forget it. He stopped his progress and retreated to the exposed stairway.

Again, he looked around the area, even glancing up as the ever-present mist wet his face. Nothing seemed out of place, so he quickly dropped down the steps to the door. It was locked, but it was a very basic lock, and he used his knife to release the latch, gaining access in less than twenty seconds.

Once inside, he pulled the door closed behind him, allowing it to stay slightly ajar so that he could get his bearings. He was in a hallway that ran along the same wall as the door and was apparently used as a storage space. Boxes were piled against the exterior wall and farther down he saw storage racks, mostly full, that jutted almost halfway into the hall, allowing a tighter walkway beyond which he could see an open doorway spilling light into the hall. He crept down past the racks to the doorway, squatting low and pausing to listen. Hearing only silence, he dared to peek his head around the doorframe and instantly pulled it back.

A man was leaning against the wall not five feet from the doorway. He'd been facing away, but there was no mistaking the quasi-military garb and the sling of an automatic weapon over his shoulder. Max knew he was in the right place, and he thanked his fortune that the man was facing away. Beyond that, this man was either overconfident or lazy. Max had immediately noticed that his gun was slung too loose and pointed in the wrong direction. The man also had a pistol on his belt, but it had a safety strap holding it in place, making it far less useful. Apart from being armed, his quarry was not ready for action.

Max released some of the nylon cord from his left hand, wrapping it around his right. He then did the same with the remaining cord in his left hand so that when he pulled tight, there was about eight inches between them. He stood and rolled silently through the opening so that he was directly behind the man, and in a single fluid motion he threw the garrote over the man's head and violently pulled backward and up.

The man's hands flew to his throat but were too late to be of any use. The garrote already cut off his air, and Max clinched it tightly, his hands meeting in fists that he leveraged with his elbows together against the man's back. The victim let out a muffled cough, unable to draw air for anything more. He tried to reach Max but could only scratch at his arms.

Had he any sense, he might have pulled the sidearm that Max had seen at his waist, but when one's life was threatened, only the highly trained could maintain enough focus to think, and that was rare even among the best.

When the man stopped struggling, Max dragged him backward into the hallway, not releasing his hold until he was certain that the man's life was extinguished. He left the garrote wrapped around the man's neck as he retrieved the weapons from the body. The machine gun was a PP-19 Bizon like he'd seen during the assault, and the pistol was a Makarov PM—not his weapon of choice but one that he'd used often enough. He adjusted the strap and slung the automatic over his neck and shoulder but allowed it to fall on his back.

In close quarters, the Makarov would be much more effective, particularly if Carolyn was in the same room. He chambered a round.

One down and four to go, if the clues were accurate.

Holding the newly acquired pistol in front of him, Max reentered the next corridor. At the far end, he could see a staircase leading up and there were two doors on either side of the hall. Cigarette butts littered the floor where the man had been standing, and Max noticed more in front of the first door on his left. He crept down the hall to that door, ignoring the closer door on the opposite side of the hall. The woodwork was old but very nice, and the door was paneled wood, reminding him of the administrative offices at Alford Academy. Muffled conversation could be heard from the room, and he leaned closer to see if he could hear more, but the thick door prevented anything intelligible from getting through. He shifted the gun into his right hand and slowly turned the doorknob with his left, thankful that it wasn't locked.

He held on to the handle and took a deep breath in and out then pushed the door open and stepped into the room, immediately putting his back to the wall and fanning the room with the Makarov. In its normal life, the room must have been an office of some type, file cabinets lining the side walls with a desk positioned toward the back.

An Asian man sat at the desk with his feet up, two Bizons on the desk in front of him. He wore a dark-blue suit with a white open-collar shirt. Another similarly dressed man sat on a cot that was positioned against the cabinets on the right wall. Neither man said anything, but the one at the desk pulled his feet back and rocked forward in his chair as he put them down.

"Ah, ah, ah," Max called. "Hands where I can see them."

Both men raised their hands, but Max did not like the proximity of the weapons. The men were far enough apart that Max had to keep swinging his weapon from one to the other.

"This will not end well for you," the man at the desk said in perfect English.

As he spoke, the man in the cot shifted, and Max stepped to the side as a burst of bullets hit the wall behind where he was standing. He fired two shots into the man's head, watching bits of skull spray on to the back wall as the man's torso fell backward, still holding the machine gun.

In a fluid motion, Max swung the Makarov back to the man

behind the desk, who had made no attempt to reach the weapons that were right in front of him. Max couldn't help but think that this guy had missed his best opportunity.

He heard another door open in the hallway.

"What's going on?" someone asked in Chinese.

"One man. Like we were told," the man at the desk called out. "Use the girl."

Max said nothing but moved to the door with his gun still pointed at his quarry. He quickly poked his head into the hall, but there was nobody there.

"Tell him to let her go," Max instructed in Chinese as he pulled his Bizon around his body. He'd slung it over his left shoulder by design. He was more accurate with his right and the machine pistol could be effective without as much concern over precision.

The man smiled.

"So you speak Mandarin? How nice," he said, then called to his companion, "If he fires again, kill the girl!"

Max peeked down the hall again—still empty—then turned back to the man in charge.

"She leaves with me, and we all live," he said. "I don't need to prove myself here."

"Nonsense. We all need to prove ourselves," the man returned to Chinese. "My boss has expectations too."

"Who hired you?" Max asked.

The man let out a forced laugh. "Oh, I don't think they'd be very happy if I told you."

Noise in the hallway caught Max's attention, and he peeked out again, this time stopped by what he saw.

Two figures emerged from the other room on the left, Carolyn and another similarly dressed assailant, also of Asian descent. Carolyn's arms were bound behind her back, and she still wore the white floral-pattern dress he had thought looked so good at dinner. She had a gag in her mouth, but there was a fire in her eyes that told him she was very much alert.

He took a step farther into the hallway, holding the Bizon directed at the man at the desk. He swung his Glock into the hall, pointing it at the face of Carolyn's captor, though her own head was perilously close to his line of fire.

The man holding Carolyn swung his own automatic weapon around her body, pointing it at Max.

"Drop your weapons," he said in English.

"Whoa!" Max called out, looking to calm the situation. He splayed his right hand, allowing the pistol to swing on his index finger, no longer threatening the man in the hall. He kept the machine gun pointed into the office. "You hit me, and that guy goes with me."

He motioned with his head toward the man at the desk.

"Stay calm, Hong," the man at the desk called, unable to see into the hallway. "We don't need any more violence. Mr. Kline is about to hand over his weapons."

"You know my name." Max gritted his teeth. "What's yours?"

The man seemed somewhat surprised but answered in Chinese. "I am Feng. You've met Hong. And the man behind you is Jin."

Max kept the automatic trained on Feng, and he still had the undirected Glock dangling from his outstretched arm, but he slowly turned his head to look back down the hall and saw a third man who had emerged from a room on the opposite side, machine gun in hand.

"OK, Feng," Max responded in Chinese then switched back to English, hoping to keep them guessing. "I'm going to put down my guns, but before I do, I want to know who hired you."

"Unfortunately, I am not at liberty to give you her name," Feng responded, likely unaware that he had narrowed the field.

"But you said to get down!" Max practically shouted, knowing it wouldn't make sense to the men. He hoped Carolyn was listening. He still held eye contact with Feng and allowed himself a slight smile, which further confused the man.

"Now!" he shouted, and in one fluid motion he swung his Bizon out into the hallway, pointed to his right, spraying bullets as he did. Jin crumpled to the ground even as Max spun to face Hong. He had already flipped the Makarov back into his hand and was happy to see that Carolyn had listened to him and fallen to the ground, disrupting Hong's gun arm as she did. Max squeezed off three shots from the pistol, knowing that each had hit home. He didn't even watch the body fall as he dove to the floor seconds ahead of a burst of fire from inside the office.

"That was unwise, Mr. Kline," Feng called from inside when the noise from the gunfight settled. "I had hoped this could end quietly, but Miss Toffey will pay for your actions."

Max did not respond, moving quietly down the hall. For a moment, he put down his pistol and drew his knife to cut Carolyn's bonds and remove her gag.

He held her face in his hands, looking into her eyes. "You OK?" he whispered.

Carolyn didn't speak but nodded, eyes pleading for it to end.

"You're not leaving here alive," Feng called, obviously cautious to leave the security of his office.

Max helped Carolyn to her feet and held a finger to his mouth. He gave her the machine gun, pointed to the next door, and signaled that she should slam it shut. As she moved to obey, he crept closer to the office door, pistol in hand.

As soon as Carolyn slammed the door, the nozzle of a Bizon poked out of the office, followed by Feng, and then Max sprang into motion. He slammed both hands down on his opponent's, forcing a loud shout of shock and pain as the gun fell to the ground.

Max grabbed the man's shirt and brought his pistol up, but it was his turn to be shocked as the older man used Max's momentum to pull him into a raised knee that struck his groin. When Max fell off-balance, Feng's left foot stuck out lightning fast, knocking Max's gun out of his hands and down the hall.

In a flurry of motion, Feng kicked him several times in the gut before reaching for one of the fallen guns. Max knew he had little time, so he forced himself back upright and lashed out with a kick of his own that sent Feng's gun clattering back to the floor.

The two men faced each other. Feng's face was bleeding at his right temple.

"No more talk," he said before attacking.

Max was able to block the attacks, but only just. The man's training was as good as any he'd fought against. Punches and kicks flew his way, and he had to take several defensive steps back before he could turn the fight. Feng's fist flew at his throat, but he blocked it up and away.

On previous feints, Max had held back, but now he saw an opportunity to bury his right fist in the man's kidney. The strike threw Feng against the wall, and he was only barely able to lift his right arm to block the hook that followed.

Both men were breathing heavily, and Max took a step back for a quick respite. His opponent was still leaning against the wall, but he wasn't done.

"That's enough." Carolyn's voice caught both men's attention as she pulled back the charging handle of a Bizon submachine gun and released it. The sharp sound of the gun being loaded echoed in the hallway. She stood down the hall, straddling the man who had only moments earlier held her hostage, using her as a human shield.

"Enough?" Feng turned to face her, continuing in Chinese. "What does a schoolgirl know of fighting?"

The older man moved toward Carolyn, and Max knew he had to act. If Carolyn pulled the trigger, it would traumatize her for life. And, if she didn't, they were both dead. He moved to follow Feng, but as he did he spotted his Glock where it had fallen just inside the office.

Feng was halfway to Carolyn, still shouting curses in Chinese, when Max dove for his weapon, grabbing it in his left hand and simultaneously pushing back up off the floor with his right. The momentum slammed his back into the doorjamb, but he had gotten far enough into the hall that he could continue spinning his torso until his left hand—and the Glock—was fully extended and pointing at Feng. The time for discussion was over, but Carolyn was almost directly behind him, and at this range a body might not stop the bullet, so Max fired a shot that shattered his opponent's right shoulder.

When Feng cried out in pain, spinning to the right and away from

Carolyn, Max used the opportunity to empty the remaining bullets from his weapon, leaving no doubt as to Feng's fate.

Carolyn collapsed to the floor, cradling the weapon she had been unable to fire. Max wanted to go to her, to hug her and let her know she was alright, but his instinct for survival told him they didn't have much time. He collected one of the fallen machine guns as he called back to Carolyn.

"C, can you stand? We gotta get out of here."

He turned to look, and she was already standing beside him, her weapon noticeably absent, and she had a look of deep sadness on her face.

"Yes. I'm fine," she lied. "Thank you, Max."

When he stood, she threw her arms around him, wrapping him in a tight hug. With his free hand, he hugged her back, holding the embrace for far longer than he should. Seconds could mean everything.

CHAPTER EIGHTEEN

Hurried footsteps could be heard on the floor above, and Max knew they had to flee. Carolyn had started for the stairs, but he grabbed her arm and guided her in the other direction, toward the door he had used to enter.

"This way," he said. "The door that you directed me to."

"What do you mean?" she asked, staying with him as they reached the next hall and turned to the right.

"Your clues were great, and I found the entrance at eleven o'clock." He stopped and held up a finger for silence. There were men coming down the stairs, so he eased the door closed, holding the handle open until he could allow the latch to return home silently.

"I don't know anything about this entrance," Carolyn whispered.

Max looked into her puzzled eyes in the dim light of the hall and almost stopped—she was so beautiful.

Instead, he shook his head and smiled. "Well, better lucky than good."

He led her toward the exit.

"At least you got the rest of it," Carolyn whispered defensively.

"You did great," he answered as he eased open the door to the alleyway.

Behind them, they heard a loud thump followed closely by a splintering crash.

"Let's go!" Max pulled Carolyn into the dark alley as the sound of gunfire erupted, and several bullets struck the doorjamb. He slammed the door behind them, looking furtively for something to block it with, but seeing nothing available he abandoned the effort and pushed Carolyn up the short stairs ahead of him.

"Go that way." He pointed down the alley and to the right. He did not want her headed back to King Street, which would be the more obvious path.

Not waiting for a reply, he turned to cover her exit, pulling and releasing the charging handle on his weapon. When the door cracked open, he sent a few rounds into the skin, and either the impact of the bullets or the person on the other side quickly forced it closed. Seconds ticked by, and the door swung open again with a similar answer from Max. He hoped Carolyn had enough of a head start, and he blistered the door with a long barrage before turning to catch up with her.

As he moved, he picked up sounds to his right and dove to the ground as bullets started to whizz past him. Someone had exited from the back of the warehouse and he was now pinned in the hotel's garbage zone. He eased behind a dumpster, assessing his position. Staying still was not the answer. The longer he stayed here, the more outnumbered he would become, so he reached down to unlock the wheels and then rolled the dumpster out into the alley, immediately answered with the loud thumping of bullets hitting the other side.

When the dumpster was about halfway, he rushed past it to the space between it and the far wall, catching his assailant exposed in the alleyway. He emptied the remaining bullets from his Bizon, watching the man go down.

For a moment, the alley quieted once again, and Max eased the spent weapon to the ground, not wanting to carry it but also not wanting his opponents to know he was out of ammunition. Though he couldn't see much, he could hear that the man following them was now at the top of the stairs and moving to flank him.

Max drew his knife and, holding the blade in his hand, bobbed the handle up and down. He would have one chance and hoped he would get it right. As the darkened shape of his attacker came around the right side of the dumpster, Max kicked his spent weapon out to the left, drawing the man's attention, and as he did he dove to his right and threw the knife at the man's neck.

It made a splattering sound as the large blade struck its mark and his target stumbled backward. Max thought he saw the man's hands reach up to his neck, but he didn't have time to confirm the kill.

Others were coming out of the building, and Max had nothing left to do but run. He made it to the corner before anyone was in range to fire accurately and turned the corner as several bullets hit the far wall of the alley. He'd hoped Carolyn would be long gone, but he saw her silhouette waiting at the next street. The alley was empty, but he was now in the light. The trucks he had seen earlier were gone, which meant he would have no cover for thirty yards.

Running to catch up with her, he shouted, "Keep going. Don't wait for me!" He waved for her to go left and was distraught when he saw her head to the right.

"No!" he yelled, but she was already out of sight.

Shouting in Chinese erupted behind him, followed by muffled thuds of gunfire and the whistling of bullets. Max ran straight for the corner, knowing that speed was his only asset. He had ten yards to cover and was amazed that he reached the corner without being struck. Several bullets ricocheted off the corner bricks as he ducked past—in the wrong direction. He had followed Carolyn to the right, but his car and any chance of escape were on the other side.

When he looked up, his situation quickly went from bad to worse.

Parked on the street was a white utility van with it sliding door open, and Max saw Carolyn sitting on the floor inside. Outside the vehicle, holding the door, was a Middle Eastern man whom Max immediately recognized from the Sunday night assault. His muted green eyes were distinctive.

"Get in. Now!" the man instructed fiercely, waving a gun inward for Max to follow.

More shouts came from behind as Max surveyed the situation. He could probably take the man down, but if he did, the Chinese crew would be on him. There was no other escape, and Max had to assume he would find another opportunity. For now, staying alive was his best bet, and staying with Carolyn was most important, so he did as instructed and moved into the van as the door slammed shut behind him. Out of the frying pan and into the fire—again.

Carolyn gave him another hug as they heard their captor firing shots into the alley, followed by the sound of the front door opening and slamming shut. The engine must have been running because the car immediately jerked into motion, throwing the two of them together as it swerved out into the street. The back window shattered with incoming bullet fire. Max rolled his body in a protective shield over Carolyn, but nothing hit him, and before long they were thrown in the opposite direction when the van took a hard turn onto another street.

"Hang on," the man called back. "I think we're away, but I'm not taking chances."

The man's tone was almost friendly, which gave Max pause. His eyes caught Carolyn's, and for the second time in a harrowed ten minutes he was stuck by their beauty and depth. She smiled briefly at him before burying her face in his shoulder and hugging him more tightly than before.

* * *

Max knew enough about the streets of San Francisco to recognize that the van was following the Embarcadero along the northeast corner of the city. While he enjoyed having Carolyn in his arms, he knew that acting quickly was their best option for escape, so he gently guided her off so that she was sitting next to him. The driver hadn't spoken again, and Max saw no reason to engage him. The van was not new, and a cacophony of creaks and rumbles accompanied its progress, making communication difficult. He'd scanned the rear area for a weapon and spotted a utility knife, which he now reached for and put in his back pocket.

A metal wall with holes in the upper half divided the van between the front seats and the rear cargo, but there was a narrow gate between the front two seats, and he gently tried the latch to see if it would open, but it was locked. He looked over at the sliding door.

If he tried to open it, the driver would definitely be alerted, so they would need to be ready when he did.

The van pulled to a stop at a light, and Max had to put his hands down to arrest his forward momentum. Carolyn, whose back was to the divider, looked at him with a quizzical eye.

"What are you doing?" she asked a little too loudly.

Max glanced at the driver, who had resumed forward and luckily was not paying attention. He looked back at Carolyn and motioned to the door.

Leaning closer, he whispered above the rattling noise of the van, "When we get to a suitable spot, I'm going to try the door. If it opens, you have to be ready to go."

For a moment, she returned a confused stare and then started laughing.

Once again, Max found himself concerned about being heard, but he had no idea what could be funny.

"Carolyn, I'm serious," he hissed.

She pushed herself more upright and reached a hand out to cup his cheek. "I know you are." She'd stopped laughing but had a refreshing smile on her face.

"Cyrus," she called toward the driver, "can we find a place to pull over? I think you need to meet Max."

Max glanced up at the driver, catching his eye in the rearview mirror, then looked back at Carolyn as the man answered.

"I'm headed to Crissy Field. Five or ten minutes. OK with you?"

"Sure," Carolyn called back, then turned back to Max. "He's on our side."

He stared at her for a second as comprehension began to seep in, and he could feel the tension drain from his back muscles as he sat back down, only slightly irritated by his misread of the situation.

"Well, that's handy information." He tilted his head to call forward. "Nice to meet you, Cyrus. And thank you."

"I'm sorry, Max," she answered. "I guess I assumed you knew."

Cyrus called back a greeting, but it was mostly lost in the van's rumble.

He shook his head, looking at her face illuminated by the lights of the cars behind them that shone through the shattered window. "There is not much I know for certain right now, but I'm glad you are safe."

She put her left hand on his right and then slid it under so they were holding hands and squeezed as she leaned her head on his shoulder. "So am I, Max. So am I."

* * *

The San Francisco Bay had a calm beauty when the fog rolled in, even when accompanied by rain, and especially so at night, in the glow of a combination of manmade and natural lighting. The air was chilly, but Max was glad to be out of the van. He and Carolyn had walked out onto the massive lawn that had once been a World War II airfield.

In front of them rose the majestic Golden Gate Bridge, under which a large cargo ship was pulling into port, its upper decks and the bridge obscured by the rolling fog bank. The path around the field was well lit with streetlights, and though slightly darker, they still had ambient light in the center of the grass. To the right and far out in the bay, they could just make out the lights of Alcatraz Island through the fog. The rain had subsided a bit, but there was still moisture in the air —not that either of them cared.

When the van had parked, Carolyn had introduced Cyrus as a friend of her mother's. After shaking hands, Max had seen the knowing look in the man's green eyes. They silently acknowledged their previous meeting, but neither brought it up. He had wanted to ask more about who this man was, but Carolyn had grabbed his hand and pulled him away with a promise to Cyrus that they would come back after they'd talked.

They walked in silence. Max let her take the lead, as she obviously wanted to speak in private. When they'd reached the approximate center of the field, Carolyn turned to him.

"Max, I can't thank you enough for being here." Again, her gaze reminded him of years gone by, but he pushed his emotions down.

"I want you safe," he answered, looking down and squeezing his eyes together with thumb and forefinger. "I'm glad to do it—but there is a lot of shit going down right now, and I need to hear your side of it."

"What the fuck are you talking about?" She dropped his hand, turning to face him. "I've been held hostage for a couple of days. What the fuck do you think *my side* of it is?"

Panic flooded Max like he never felt in battle. Interpersonal relations had never been his strong suit, and he'd obviously said the wrong thing.

"Wait," he tried to recover, hands up defensively, "I'm just saying there are a lot of things—"

"Like what?" she cut him off.

Max stood there for a long while looking at a face he would die for, unable to voice the concerns he'd hoped were not true. Her face was wet with mist, but her eyes were so sad that it might as well be tears.

Finally, he mustered the courage to answer.

"Like your e-mail exchange with Gdeeds@proton.me."

"So, you've been snooping, have you?" Her tone was damning. "You think I'm involved?"

She stepped closer and slammed an open palm against his left shoulder, so hard that it forced him to step back.

"You think I'm involved?" she repeated louder, emphasizing each word.

"I think I don't have many answers," Max snapped, then took a breath, pushing down his frustration. "You were taken. You think I wasn't going to look at everything possible to get you back?"

Carolyn spun to look back at the van awash in light from above where it was parked. Cyrus was leaning against the hood, cigarette in hand, watching them.

She turned back to Max, and now he was sure that tears mixed with the mist.

"That's Gdeeds," she said, her voice somewhat calmer. She spun her arm around and pointed to Cyrus. "He is Gdeeds. Why is this even a question?"

Max thought back to the exchange, and there really wasn't anything damning. It didn't explain Cyrus's role, but at best it was circumstantial. He got the feeling that a lot of his assumptions might come tumbling down.

"OK, what about Titaninvestor? Are you saying that wasn't you? I found it on your personal drive, Carolyn."

Carolyn stared for a moment then turned away, walking toward the water.

As if on cue, the cargo ship blew its horn. Max felt like it was the buzzer on a game show, and he'd just answered incorrectly. Nothing in this conversation felt right, but he still didn't have answers.

He followed her, hoping there was an explanation, but whatever it was had damaged her trust.

She was almost to the other side when she turned.

"You're a piece of work. You know that?" The hurt was obvious on her face. She looked down and to the side as if preparing herself to continue then suddenly flipped her head up to look at him with fierce determination. "That was Jenny's email account. I hacked it and saved that email as evidence. The problem is—I can't show it to Tanner because he wouldn't believe me. I needed to wait to find out more about what was happening, and then I found *you* and got kidnapped!" she screamed, walking past him and back toward the van.

"Carolyn!" he called after her. "I didn't accuse you of anything. For the love of God, I'm doing everything I can to help! To find out what the fuck is going on!"

She gave no indication that she heard him and continued on her path to the van.

Max turned to stare blankly at the darkened bay. Trust was a hard thing to come by in his profession, but if he thought about it—as he did now—Carolyn was the one person he could probably trust over anyone else in his life. He'd let himself get caught up in the minutiae and wasn't thinking big picture.

As the rain increased, he looked back toward Carolyn's silhouette. She was almost at the van and she hadn't looked back. He couldn't blame her. Rather than follow, he turned to his left and started walking the length of the field, edging his way toward the lit pathway. She was safe, and if she didn't want to be with him then he wasn't about to make waves.

CHAPTER NINETEEN

Max had his head down and hands in his pockets when he reached the far parking lot. He didn't even notice the van until Carolyn opened the passenger door and got out to block his path.

"Hey," she said, waiting for him to look at her before continuing. "I guess it might have looked bad."

He started to protest, but she put her hand on his arm to quiet him.

"Look—I should have told you what I was doing. *I* should have trusted *you*. I owe you an apology."

"No, I'm sorry, Carolyn. I should've said . . ."

"Stop." She squeezed his arm. "We both made mistakes. Come with us, please. I still need your help."

"I still need to understand what the hell is going on!"

"We've got some ideas," she said, getting back in the van.

"Unfortunately, we only have the two seats."

She gave him an apologetic grin as he pulled open the slider and got in.

Not thirty minutes later, they were sitting at a table in the Balboa Cafe, one of San Francisco's landmark restaurants and a favorite of Carolyn's.

"Chao Fen has long held a powerful position in Chinese trade, particularly trade with the US, and specifically the high-tech trade," Carolyn explained. "In the sixties and seventies, they were a major Hong Kong importer of US technology and some of that found its way into mainland China. Then as the Hong Kong market flourished, they moved into manufacturing assets both in Hong Kong and on the mainland. Today, they are a dominant player in a number of tech silos. They have been building their internet security presence, and with LasTech they will be in the top three."

"Does that make them a threat?" Max asked, taking a drink of water.

"In and of itself, no," she answered, "but they are also a good-size supplier of silicon chips, and here's what Ravi found out: If you combine their two subsidiaries and one large investment vehicle that they control, Chao Fen represents almost eighty percent of the chips needed for artificial intelligence."

"Is this a connection to LasTech?"

Carolyn nodded. "Very much so. Internet security is evolving—as is everything—and AI is at the heart of most of it. TITAN is AI driven."

The waiter interrupted to take their drink order. Max ordered a Sierra Nevada even as the other two passed.

"OK, all of this is interesting, but Chao Fen is buying LasTech fairly. How does this implicate them? How does this implicate Jenny?"

Carolyn's face was blank when she answered. "Chao Fen cleverly placed Jenny at Stanford. Ravi found clues that showed how they manipulated her CV and put her in an ideal position to be found. I was a fool to think myself so lucky."

"You're saying that Chao Fen planted someone at Stanford two years ago with this scenario in mind?" He was incredulous. "Please."

"Max, you don't get to a position in the world like that of Chao Fen without playing the long game. They are masters of it."

"But why do they need her? If they are buying LasTech, TITAN is theirs."

The waiter returned with Max's beer and took their food order. They all ordered hamburgers.

When he left, Carolyn answered him, holding a finger in the air.

"First, nobody knows about TITAN except the few of us involved. They wouldn't know enough to purchase LasTech if they didn't have a mole on the inside. Tanner is smart enough to understand that, but he wouldn't listen to me."

She raised a second finger. "Second, LasTech doesn't technically own TITAN."

Max had started to lift his beer but put it back down as he looked at Carolyn with an eyebrow raised.

"TITAN was our creation," she continued. "Ravi and me—mostly Ravi, if I'm being honest. Tanner did not want to pursue it at first. Ravi and I pushed back and at one point threatened to leave LasTech if we couldn't pursue TITAN. In the end, we each gave Tanner five percent of LasTech in exchange for twenty-four and a half percent of TITAN. Tanner and LasTech hold fifty-one percent."

Max gave his head a slight shake before lifting his beer and taking a long sip.

"For Ravi, that was over half his ownership in LasTech." Carolyn looked out the window wistfully. "And it was the right trade."

"This would have been nice to know," Max began, but a look from Carolyn shut him off.

"So LasTech is still the majority shareholder, right?" Cyrus asked sheepishly. "Meaning Chao Fen will still control TITAN?"

"Actually, if the sale goes through, they'll own it all. That was part of the arrangement," Carolyn continued, "except either Ravi or I could block the sale of TITAN by LasTech—providing we come up with funds to make the others whole. Funds that I don't come close to having unless the LasTech deal goes through, which it won't without TITAN. So on that front I'm stuck in a financial trap. But not Ravi."

"And Ravi's out of the equation," Max muttered. "One less obstacle."

Carolyn gave him a tight-lipped nod as the waiter arrived with their food.

The Balboa's reputation rested on its phenomenal hamburgers served on French bread, and the conversation shifted briefly to complimenting the food as they all dug in. Carolyn ate ravenously, and Max thought this was one of the few times when he might be the slowest eater at the table.

"Then they have one other problem," Carolyn said between bites. "They don't *have* TITAN."

"That's a legal issue."

She finished chewing before continuing with a grin. "What's the old saying? Possession is nine-tenths of the law?"

"So, you've had it all along?"

She nodded. "I've known where it is. Sorry. I didn't know whose side you were on."

Max processed her words and reviewed the past day's events in this new light, suddenly realizing he'd missed an element.

"Wait," he said, "Jenny knew all this?"

Carolyn nodded vigorously as she finished another bite.

"Absolutely, she was my personal assistant. She knew everything —which I now understand meant that Chao Fen knew everything.

"Max, I found a lot of damning emails, but I didn't want to risk discovery by taking more than one. Her Proton account dates back to 2015, and she was working for Chao Fen even then."

"When did you start to suspect her?"

"I didn't, even when she jumped ship to Tanner." She held the last quarter of her burger in two hands but put it down before continuing. "That's going to sound petty, but it's not. I don't begrudge Tanner his happiness. If that was all it was—no harm. He and I were through long before they got together." Again, she looked out the window. "We were probably through before Jenny even joined the company, but the way it happened was so odd. She was so dedicated and seemed the perfect admin. Then she wasn't. In a matter of a month, she was jockeying for a different position at the company. At that point, I was unaware of the relationship with Tanner.

"Ravi was the one who alerted me. He was far more suspicious than I, though we weren't sure about her motives."

"OK, so what now?"

"We need to secure TITAN," Carolyn answered quickly.

"It isn't secure?"

"Nothing is fully secure, Max. And TITAN is still on a LasTech server."

Max ran his hands through his hair as he pushed back in his chair, exhaling through pursed lips. He turned to Cyrus, who had been mostly quiet during the conversation.

"And what about your theory?" he asked. "What about the Zoroastrian angle?"

"They exist," Cyrus said calmly.

"Ravi wasn't wrong," Carolyn jumped in. "There is definitely an online group of Zoroastrians announcing the end of days. My mother is still very much involved at the temple, and they became concerned years ago with what they saw on internet forums. She gathered a group of the faithful to locate the doomsdayers. Cyrus is one of them."

"It started out as an online pursuit," Cyrus added, "but they were always one step ahead of us. Meanwhile, we trained, expecting that one day we would have to confront them. Zoroastrianism has been long forgotten by the world, but at one point at the height of the Persian Empire, it was the world's predominate religion. We don't want it to reemerge as some crazy doomsday cult. We are not crusaders. We are fine practicing in peace, and if we have a renegade faction, we'd prefer to handle it ourselves.

"It began in 2017 with a blogger named Cambyses530. He was a member of a group called Avesta Today. They were very focused on the end of days, and they claimed it was almost upon us. We have a legend that a savior will arrive just as the forces of good and evil culminate in the last battle. Saoshyant will be born of a virgin from the seed of Zoroaster himself, and he will raise the dead and pass judgment on all humanity, returning the wicked to hell and making the rest immortal."

Carolyn put her hand over one of Cyrus's and gently interrupted, "The event is called Frashokereti—effectively the end of time."

"Thank you." Cyrus nodded before turning back to Max. "But this is not a central precept to our faith. The fact that it was being championed—and championed aggressively—online is what caught our attention. We think Avesta Today originated in Iran, but they quickly developed a following in the US. I'm not as strong on the tech side, but many of our faith work in Silicon Valley, and they could identify elements here in the Bay Area. At first a few, but the activity grew during Covid, and we now think the movement is centered here."

"I have some knowledge of the Zoroastrian mythos." Max leaned closer. "Have you identified Cambyses530?"

"No, we're pretty sure he is Iranian—based on older posts—but that doesn't narrow things down. We've seen quite a few recently immigrated Iranians at the Fire Temple. Our theory is that during Covid something changed. Possibly funding? Either way, the group is here—we've seen an uptick in attendance at the temple, but we are cautious to probe too overtly."

Max nodded, thinking back to his time there. "Have you identified any of them?"

"Sure. We know some of them from our temple—but we haven't approached them. We watch. And we tracked them to Ravi." He looked down.

"We didn't know that there was a threat of violence." He spoke with emphasis when he continued, "If we had known, we wouldn't have left. We would have warned him."

The three of them sat in silence, plates clean but for a few fries. Max finished the last of his beer and held it up, catching the waiter's eye for another, then at Carolyn's behest ordered one for her as well. He pressed thumb and forefinger to his eyes once again, squeezing gently.

"So where are they now?"

Cyrus shrugged. "Not sure. Well, that's not entirely true. The pod that I followed to Ravi—they are new Iranians, and I know where they've been staying." He reached into his pocket and pulled out his phone, tapping the screen a few times before turning it so the others could see. "Here, I got a group shot of them on the street."

Max looked at the photo, and his heart skipped a beat. He took the phone and looked closer at the man in the foreground.

"You see something?" Cyrus asked.

"No," he lied, handing the phone back to Cyrus. "Trying to put the face in my memory."

"I can locate them again," Cyrus stated with some certainty.

"Great. That's a start." Max turned to Carolyn. "The men holding you—did they give any indication they were Zoroastrian?"

She shook her head and answered quietly, "No, and not that they couldn't be both, but every one of them was Chinese. You saw them."

"Yeah."

The waiter dropped off the beers and cleared their plates, leaving dessert menus that sat untouched.

"So here's where we are," Max recapped. "We know Chao Fen wants TITAN, and it looks like Jenny is helping them. I think we can assume that Chao Fen was behind both Carolyn's abduction and the attacks on me. But from what Cyrus is saying, there is another element, and they were responsible for Ravi's death? Why?"

"TITAN." Carolyn took a long drink of her beer, wiped her lips, then hesitated. She looked at Cyrus then back at Max before continuing. "I wasn't entirely open with you when we discussed TITAN."

Max leaned back slightly, straightening but holding his tongue.

"I didn't lie," she continued, "but I didn't think you needed to know everything."

She took in a deep breath and let it out slowly.

"TITAN is very powerful software," she explained. "Stronger than anything known. If this group is looking for Saoshyant to lead them to the end of days, TITAN might have the potential to complete the prophecy to bring about the apocalypse."

"That's a pretty dramatic statement." Max raised his eyebrows. "Tanner told me some story about not just changing the locks but changing the way you enter the house, but I still don't see it."

"And I hope you don't." Carolyn was nearly halfway done with her beer. "The bottom line is that we don't know. We haven't released TITAN because we are unsure of its capability, but think of how much we rely on the internet today. Bank accounts, stock markets, books and records, transportation, our legal system, our healthcare system, defense . . . the nuclear codes—*everything* is electronic now." She paused for another sip.

"Imagine if everything shut down at once. Everything." She looked from Max to Cyrus and back to Max, her eyes watering slightly. "TITAN could very well be the vehicle that does that."

Once again, the table quieted.

"Then why would you build it?" Max asked.

"It didn't start out like it is now. It was a better mousetrap, a new way to secure data and access. Like Tanner said, TITAN is an entirely different approach to security, and it works perfectly. But then

Ravi wanted to strengthen it. He wanted it to have the ability to evolve. He added AI."

"And that makes it evil?" Max still did not understand.

Carolyn shook her head. "It's not evil, Max. Not inherently, anyway. Ravi still believed in it, though I had some reservations, but we are talking about two different things here. My concern has always been what if TITAN eventually decides that locking the house, to stick with Tanner's analogy, is for the good of all? I still hold that concern, but now we are talking about something different. If the TITAN code is in the wrong hands, and they *alter* the code—if they *instruct* TITAN to lock the house—then it could become a very deadly weapon."

Max looked at Cyrus, tired of the number of variables. "How would Avesta Today know about TITAN?"

Cyrus raised his hands once again, turning to Carolyn.

"That was our question too," she said. "When Ravi found out about Tanner and Jenny, it was around the same time that my mother and Cyrus alerted me that they had seen a comment in the Avesta Today forum suggesting that 'a Titan' was near and would bring about the final reckoning. So, of course, we suspected Jenny, though she had never been to the temple. I didn't know what to think, Max. We didn't find any connection—but that's when we uncovered her connection to Chao Fen."

The waiter interrupted to see if they would order desert, which they all declined, and Carolyn handed him a credit card for the bill.

"We have to take this to Tanner," Max said calmly. "He's not going to like hearing what we know about Jenny, but he is definitely not working for Chao Fen and is probably our best chance at securing TITAN." He looked to Carolyn to confirm, and she nodded meekly.

"I think we have to do more than secure TITAN," she answered with sadness in her voice. "I think we have to eliminate it."

"Eliminate?"

"Yes. I think we should destroy it."

"OK. All the more reason to get Tanner on board. You want to make the call, or should I?"

Carolyn shook her head again, this time with more vigor.

"He's a good man and he'll understand," she said, "but I'll let you tell him about Jenny."

CHAPTER TWENTY

The police tape had been removed, and someone had repaired Carolyn's apartment door. The trio of Carolyn, Max, and Cyrus had initially thought that returning to the apartment might attract the attention of the police, but after considering their options they'd agreed it was unlikely that the SFPD could spare the manpower for surveillance.

After stopping by the corner store, they had driven the van the six blocks up the hill to her building, parking on the street a half block away. Seeing the repair, Carolyn assured them that the building had one of the best superintendents ever and said a quiet thanks to William as she thumbed her code and the door opened.

Inside, the apartment was still a hot mess of tossed pillows and open drawers. Max felt responsible and said as much several times until Carolyn had finally pulled him aside near the dining room table.

She looked Max in the eye, holding his hand in hers. "Let's assume this is all your fault. I accept your apology. But this is not your doing, and they were here investigating Ravi's death, so they would have come here, regardless."

She left him standing there and went into the kitchen.

He started to protest, but she called over her shoulder, "You're forgiven. It's done."

He couldn't help but smile, but he didn't realize how broadly until Cyrus returned from the bathroom.

"Why are you so happy?" he asked.

Max shook his head, pointing to the kitchen. "Sorry, I'm not, but she made me laugh."

"She can do that." Cyrus pulled out a chair and sat down. "But I haven't seen it in a long time."

"We're old friends."

Cyrus shook his head and spoke in a hushed tone. "That may be, but I've known her a long time. She is like a sister to me, and I've only seen her like this back in the early days with Tanner. Hell, she's been a hostage for a couple of days and—look at her—she's brushing it off."

"What are you whispering about, Cy?" Carolyn came in from the kitchen with an open bottle of red wine and two glasses.

"Saying you never let me drink."

Carolyn had put one glass down in front of Max and now held the other toward Cyrus.

"You want one?" she asked.

"You know I don't." Cyrus held up a hand in refusal. "Kidding."

"Didn't think so." She put the glass down in front of her and filled both glasses with red wine. When she was done, she picked up her glass and gestured toward Max, who picked up the other and clinked glasses.

"Here's hoping Tanner understands," he said, bringing the glass to his lips and taking a sip. "Wow, that's yummy."

Carolyn nodded. "Small batch pinot. I used to work with the guy. Now he makes wine."

"Good for him." Max took another, longer, sip.

"Good for me too," Carolyn agreed, taking a seat across from Cyrus and motioning for Max to take the end seat between them. "Since my tech is downtown, courtesy of San Francisco's finest, we'll have to do an old-fashioned phone call."

"I've got it." Max pulled out his phone, looking at the screen. "I sent him a text telling him we had to talk."

"Which number?"

"I only had the one," Max replied, showing her his phone with the contact open.

"That's his work phone," she said with a gentle shake of the head. "But he should have it on him during the week."

Max pressed dial, motioning to Cyrus. "Probably best that you stay silent. He doesn't know you."

Tanner picked up on the first ring, but the voice that came out of the phone's speaker didn't sound like the normally calm entrepreneur.

"Who is this?"

"It's Max."

"Max, thank God." Tanner sounded stressed. "I thought that might be your text. Where have you been? I've been texting your other number all afternoon."

"Oh yeah." Max only now realized his mistake. "That phone's still with the police. This is my new number."

"Shit. That's nice to know."

"Sorry." Max apologized before realizing that his friend should have known. "You should have it though. I called you from this phone earlier."

"Did you find Carolyn?" Tanner ignored the implication.

Max nodded to Carolyn, turning the phone toward her though the gesture was unnecessary.

"I'm here, Tanner," she said.

"Thank God. Are you OK? Did they hurt you?"

"No, I'm fine."

Max was struck by the turn in Carolyn's mood as she spoke, her smile completely gone.

"Look, Max," Tanner continued as if not really interested in her response, "I need to talk to you. C, you were right."

"What's up, Tanner?" Max asked, looking at Carolyn with a shrug.

After a pause, Tanner spoke in a more hushed tone, a forced whisper. "I think Jenny might be involved."

"What?" Carolyn and Max reacted together. Despite what they knew, it sounded foreign coming from Tanner.

"Look, I don't think it's malicious, but I think she's connected to Chao Fen."

"How do you know?" Max asked.

"I saw messages on her phone. I can't tell how deeply she's involved, but I don't think she'd do anything to actively hurt anyone."

"I had guns pointed at my face, Tanner," Carolyn cut in. "If she's involved, she's involved. There is no halfway."

"That's just it," Tanner said, sounding anxious. "Jenny would not hurt you. You're her mentor. She wouldn't do that. She's my wife. I know her."

"I don't think any of us truly know her," Carolyn snapped in anger, surprising Max. "Chao Fen effectively planted her at LasTech!"

The phone was quiet, and Max was about to ask if his friend was still there when the conversation continued.

"So you guys were already there?" Tanner asked.

"What do you mean?" Carolyn didn't follow.

"You guys already suspected Jenny? You said she was planted at LasTech. When did you decide that?" He sounded defensive. "How long have you suspected that she was involved?"

"Ravi suspected," Carolyn stated matter-of-factly. "He found a bunch of things that looked suspicious last summer, but there was nothing concrete, and we didn't think you would listen anyway. When you gave us the news of the Chao Fen buyout, he dug deeper and . . . well . . . he asked for some help." Her voice trailed off.

"Carolyn?" Tanner asked, his voice now stern. "Did you hack LasTech?"

"No, not LasTech. Not really."

Max could see her discomfort. She may be one of the best hackers on the planet, but she wasn't comfortable talking about it.

"I mostly hacked her personal accounts. Proton.me and stuff like that."

There was another pause before Tanner resumed.

"I thought Proton was unhackable?" he asked.

This time Carolyn let out a short laugh. "Nothing is unhackable, Tan. You know that."

"So what did you find?"

Carolyn spent the next five minutes explaining Ravi's research and the emails she had uncovered, which showed Jenny's long-running connection with Chao Fen. Tanner listened with only a few questions until the end.

"OK," he asked. "Anything in the past week?"

"What do you mean?"

"I mean, did you find any emails from here since all this shit has gone down?"

"Well, no." Carolyn was getting defensive. "But I wasn't really in any position to look over the past couple of days."

"Right. Sorry. But this doesn't prove she's involved with the shit that's been happening."

"No," Max added, "but she led me to the Moraga park where I was arrested."

"Did she?" Tanner shot back, doubtful. "I thought the caller led you there—the guy who had Carolyn."

"But I think they're connected."

"You said it right there," Tanner continued. "You think. That doesn't prove she was involved."

Max thought for a moment before responding. "OK, you have a point, but there is enough here to think we can't trust her right now. I'm sorry, bud. I know you love her and are probably right. I bet she has nothing to do with this, but we can't take that risk. Not until we sort this out."

"Yeah." Tanner dropped his voice once again. "I get it, but she's not going to like it. And, from the sounds of it, Chao Fen won't like it either."

"Chao Fen needs to get comfortable with disappointment." Carolyn leaned toward the phone.

"What does that mean?"

"Tanner," Carolyn said slowly, almost spitting her words, "I'm going to destroy TITAN."

The call went silent for an uncomfortable minute.

When he spoke, Tanner sounded oddly relieved. "That's going to cost us both a hella lot of money."

"I don't care."

"Yeah, I know you don't." He took an audible breath. "How can I help?"

"I need access to the main server." She looked up at an old-fashioned digital clock on her wall that read 8:07. "We can be there by nine?"

"Tonight?"

"No time to waste," Max added.

"No can do, guys," Tanner answered. "After the shit that went down on Monday, Chao Fen was upset about our security. We put the servers on nighttime lockdown. They're inaccessible from seven at night until seven in the morning. Is TITAN on our server?"

"Where else would we keep it?"

"Where on the server?"

"Wouldn't you like to know?" Carolyn answered, looking at Max and smiling. "A girl's got to have some secrets, Tanner. You're telling me that as CEO, you can't override the lockdown?"

"Not right now. As I said, we had to show Chao Fen that we take security seriously, and given Max's escapades we had to go over the top."

"Escapades trying to help you solve your problems," Max added dryly.

Carolyn patted his arm, speaking toward the phone. "We'll meet you in the parking garage at seven tomorrow morning."

"OK," Tanner confirmed. "I'll be there."

* * *

"I assume I'm not going with you to meet Tanner?" Cyrus spoke up after the call had ended, not waiting for a response. "I can head back to San Jose to see if I can locate that Iranian group."

"Do you want to rest here first?" Carolyn asked.

"No." Cyrus stood up. "I've had the best luck catching up with them in the wee hours. During the day, they are often on the move. I'll tell your mother and the others."

"My mother doesn't know what we're dealing with, Cyrus."

"That may be true, but she'll find out one way or another and I'd rather not get on her bad side. I'll try to pick up a friend to help."

"Take my number," Max said in perfect Persian. "I've spent a lot of time in your part of the world. I can help but we've got to stay in touch."

Cyrus starred at him wide-eyed then turned to Carolyn.

"Did you know he speaks Persian?" he asked incredulously. Not waiting for an answer, he addressed Max directly in Persian, "You speak very well. Tehran trained?"

Max nodded. "Not in Tehran, but you have a good ear. I learned from a Tehranian instructor." He switched back to English. "Anyway, I want to hear what you find and what they are doing."

The two exchanged numbers, and Cyrus promised to keep him informed.

"Don't engage them, Cyrus," Max added as the other man was leaving. "Whoever they are, they are probably better trained than you."

Cyrus opened his arms slightly in a gesture that asked for respect. "I've gotten this far."

"Yeah—but Ravi didn't," Max answered solemnly and watched the light dim in Cyrus's eyes. He was holding the door open, and Cyrus stood in the hallway. "Sorry—but it's important that you don't engage them."

"Yeah, OK," Cyrus replied, turning toward the elevator. "I'll touch base from San Jose."

"Sounds good." Max closed the door and walked back to the dining room table, pausing to pick up the wine bottle and refill their glasses.

"He means well, Max." Carolyn took a sip of her wine.

Max did not sit down but took his glass to the window where he looked out on the lights of the city and the bay beyond, the Golden Gate Bridge dominating the left side of his view.

"Something's not right." He finished his glass and placed it on a small table, still staring out the window. "Chao Fen is understandable. They have a business to run and it now involves LasTech, but they don't seem to have any connection to the Zoroastrians. Half of me says we are missing the connection, and the other half says we are battling on two fronts."

An arm curled around his waist. He hadn't noticed Carolyn's

movement, and she now tucked in next to him, looking out the window. She rested her head against his biceps. The warmth felt good, and he allowed his hand to slide onto her lower back.

"We'll wipe the TITAN file, then it won't matter how many we are up against," she answered.

"I don't know if it will be that easy."

He turned to explain, but she held a finger up to his mouth, her other arm still around his waist. He looked into her eyes, and it felt as if he was falling into them. They glistened, almost as dark as the black silky hair that framed a face that seemed to glow in the nighttime lighting.

"Thank you," she whispered as she lifted her lips to meet his, her body pressing tightly against him.

They kissed for what seemed like hours before she took his hand and led him into her bedroom.

* * *

It seemed to Max that his world had somehow corrected. Or most of it had. He stroked her hair as her head lay against his chest, their naked bodies still intertwined. A thought had been bothering him since dinner and he couldn't hold back—especially not now.

"You know how you said you should have trusted me?"

"Yeah?"

"I don't want to make the same mistake."

Carolyn lifted her head to look at him and pulled herself up on the bed so that they were eye to eye, inches away. She rested her head on one hand and smiled.

"I'm listening."

"You know when Cyrus showed us the picture of the Iranians?"

"Yeah?"

He hesitated, unused to sharing. "I recognized one of them. He's a bad guy, but I've met him and I'll bet he's Cambyses530."

"That's crazy. How could you know him?"

"I spent a lot of time in the Middle East. My job was to eliminate men like him and I knew him well. You could say I studied him. He's a known terrorist, but we thought we'd stopped him."

"A terrorist? What the fuck are we dealing with?" she asked.

"That's what I'm trying to figure out."

"Was he blogging then too?"

"Not that we were aware of. The name fits though, and the picture is definitely the man we targeted—the man I thought I had sent to prison."

"You're being a bit vague." She got out of bed. "Hold that thought for one second."

Max watched as she walked around the bed to the bathroom, completely naked with a body that was near perfect. He'd forgotten how poised she was. She had a natural air about her—comfort and confidence—and had never been ashamed of her body or of who she was.

After using the bathroom, she walked out to the main living area, returning a few minutes later to hand a framed photo to Max before she returned to her side of the bed. It was a picture of the two of them in high school, arms around each other in a field.

"Wow." Max let out a slight laugh. "Look how young we were."

"I love that photo."

"Good times."

"OK. Tell me more about Cambyses."

"The Marines were my life, Carolyn," Max explained. "Joining the Raiders and being in the first graduating class of what is now the Marine Raider Training Center—I can't tell you what it meant to me."

Carolyn was now tucked up by the headboard with her knees under her and the duvet pulled over them. She caressed his neck with her free hand.

"I'm saying this because the next part should be classified."

He turned to look into her dark-brown eyes again and almost stopped because of her beauty.

"This stays between us. You can't tell Cyrus or anyone."

Carolyn nodded, her face curious.

"I served four tours in Iran and Iraq. Mostly counterterrorism assignments. Details don't matter, but suffice it to say our squad earned a reputation in the region. But the situation over there is a lot deeper than the news covers. We had our share of fighting, but we were often involved in hostage negotiation, and it was a skill set that seemed a natural fit for me. It wasn't my only role, but when we were asked to handle a difficult situation, I was the one talking to the bad guys. This is stuff that never hits the news.

"Mostly our opponents were the various Muslim factions, but toward the end of 2014, we got involved with another element that we hadn't seen previously. They had kidnapped four USAID staff who had been visiting Tehran in secret. At first we thought the organization was another Muslim group, but we quickly found out that they were not Muslim at all."

"Zoroastrian?" Carolyn asked. "That seems wrong."

"Yeah. We thought so too, but that's what it turned out to be. It won't shock you to hear that their leader called himself Cambyses. Unlike the Muslim terrorists who usually demanded the release of comrades, this group had no such demand. They wanted money and lots of it. Way more than we could ever deliver."

"So what did you do?"

"I did what every hostage negotiator does—I got him talking."

Max reached over to push a lock of hair out of her face, then turned to lean his head against the headboard. He couldn't look at Carolyn and still focus on the story.

"For four months, we talked. Twice a day. Sometimes for hours. And when we weren't talking, I was reading reports from the rest of the team on his history and that of the other members we were aware of. They moved every week to a new location. At first we thought they were staying in Tehran, but later we sensed they were moving toward Iraq, and when we eventually caught up with them, they were on Iraqi soil, which may have saved their lives."

"Why's that?"

"Because if they were in Iran, we had no partnership with the government. We would have been forced to kill them, and I wouldn't have enjoyed that. They were actually a pretty noble group . . . until they weren't."

"What does that mean?" she asked.

"While they asked for money, they were not in it for personal wealth. I'm convinced they truly believed in their cause."

"Which was?"

"Saoshyant. They believed that the end of days was coming and would prepare the world for the ultimate battle between good and evil. It sounds very much like the group that Cyrus was describing, except we thought we ended it back then."

"What did you mean when you said they were noble until they weren't?"

"After three months, we thought we were making progress in negotiations when things turned dark quickly. They gave us an ultimatum as they had several times before, and we thought we'd talked our way out of it when they sent a video of their men decapitating one of the USAID staff." He paused. "I'll never forget the face of that blond young man, gagged and gaunt, near starvation, staring into the camera in a silent plea for help before the knife went to work.

"In an odd way, that man saved his colleagues. While I had been engaging Cambyses, the rest of my team had been hard at work trying to track them down. We had two high-likelihood targets, and later that night our surveillance team at one location watched as two men dragged something out into the sand for burial. They didn't interfere, but when the men left, the team was able to identify the victim.

"The next morning, I got Cambyses back on the phone and gave him everything they wanted—money, weapons, promises of no retribution. Everything."

"So what happened?"

"At eight o'clock that evening, they released the other three hostages at a US base about fifty miles away, and when the hostages were in our custody, our team began our assault.

"I'll never forget meeting Cambyses face to face. He had an aura about him that almost glowed."

When Carolyn let out a nervous laugh, he turned to her, wanting her to understand.

"I'm serious. Despite what he had done, he had an aura of certainty about him. He looked at me with an expression that I first took for anger, but then he offered a prayer in Persian. I felt like he approved, even though I was sending him to prison."

"How could he have gotten out?"

"Who knows, but things are different over there. That was at the end of my tour, and I was done. I was content that we'd closed that chapter and put Cambyses away. I hadn't given it much thought since —until I saw that photo."

Carolyn wrapped one of her legs around his as she reached up to cup his chin in her hand.

"I'm sure you did a lot of good over there. But I'm glad you came home." She leaned her head on his shoulder once again.

Max stretched his arm around her and down her back, feeling the bumps of her spine, regretting that he needed to make sure of one thing.

"So, you haven't seen these men at all? No interaction at temple?" he asked.

"I haven't been attending Fire Temple. Mom's kept me up to date about their suspicions and the things Cyrus and the team have been doing, but I haven't been involved."

"Good. Keep it that way." Max slipped back down into the bed. "TITAN ends tomorrow, but we don't know what else they are capable of."

Carolyn reached to turn off her bedside light then spun back to Max, simultaneously pulling the duvet up and plunging her hands underneath.

"Maybe you should stay in town to protect me," she said as she aroused him again.

"Maybe you should be careful what you wish for," Max replied as he leaned over to kiss her and once again lost himself in his passion for a woman far better than him.

CHAPTER TWENTY-ONE

When the coffee maker clicked to signal it was done, Max picked up his mug and sat back down at the dining room table. He could hear the water running for Carolyn in the shower and was very tempted to join her. The past night had been more than wonderful, and he'd take as much of that as he could, but there were bigger things ahead of them this morning.

His phone vibrated on the table, and he looked down to see another message from Cyrus, who had started sending messages at 4 a.m. and hadn't stopped. The first had awoken Max from a deep sleep, but he was used to that. If he wanted a truly undisturbed sleep, he needed earplugs and an insulated room.

"I'm seeing activity," Cyrus's message read.

The first messages had let Max know he had located the trio of men who had tailed Ravi and was positioned outside. For the next hour after that, Max and Cyrus had texted back and forth about the men.

Cyrus seemed to have no problem continuing the early morning conversation, and Max wondered how much sleep his new friend had found the night before. Even at night, it was at least a forty-five-minute drive to San Jose.

On the table in front of him, he had the Heckler MP7 that he'd retrieved from Carolyn's Tesla. Next to it were two full magazines, and that was his entire arsenal. If all went well this morning, he wouldn't need them, but things hadn't been going as planned all week.

He still wasn't sure what Chao Fen's strategy was. They had to be behind the attacks and Carolyn's abduction, but why had Eunice bailed him out? There was no question that TITAN was the prize, and, hopefully, TITAN would be off the table in a matter of hours.

He picked up his phone and thumbed back to Cyrus, "What kind of activity?"

"Not sure, but they are up and getting ready for something."

After a few minutes, another message arrived. "They've loaded several black bags into their car."

"OK. Keep watching," Max typed.

"Did I tell you they drive a Mercedes?" Cyrus asked. "It's not new but seems expensive. I think it's funny, but I guess if the world is ending you might as well drive a nice car."

Max smiled, thinking it slightly curious that Cyrus would mock the Zoroastrians, but he figured it would be no different with a Christian disparaging a zealot who preached the apocalypse.

"You're up early." Carolyn's voice penetrated the quiet of the morning.

"Cyrus found the men. He's been watching them." Max looked over and raised his coffee in salute. "You look great."

Carolyn continued through the living room to the kitchen. She was wearing a tight-cut navy blazer over a white Oxford that hung loose over her jeans and bare feet. She met his gaze, and her face lit up, which did more to wake him up than any of the three coffees he'd enjoyed so far.

"So what's the plan, boss?" she said.

"Well, I've got your car charging. We can leave in a half hour around six."

"What's with that?" She pointed to the gun. "Tanner's not the enemy."

Max shook his head. "Yeah, but with everything that has gone down this week, I'm not taking any chances."

His phone vibrated again, and he looked down at another message from Cyrus.

"That's curious," he said, typing a response into his phone.

Cyrus's last message had said that Tanner was at LasTech. He typed back, "How do you know?"

"What is?" Carolyn asked as she started her coffee.

"Cyrus is saying that Tanner is at the office."

"Already?"

Max did not respond but opened his text chain with Tanner, which had been quiet since the night before.

"We still on for 7 a.m.?" he typed, watching to see if Tanner would respond, and he saw the three dots revealing that he was.

A moment later, Tanner replied, "Yes! I'll head there in an hour or so. Be in the garage at 7."

At the same time, a text came through from Cyrus, "I put a tracker on his truck."

"Interesting," Max spoke out loud to himself.

"Hey." There was an edge to Carolyn's voice, but when he lifted his head, she was smiling. "You want to tell me what's up, please?"

"Sorry. Cyrus tells me that he has a tracker on Tanner's truck and that he's at the office."

"Why is he tracking Tanner?"

"I don't know, but the interesting thing is that Tanner just implied he's not there. He said he would head there in an hour."

Carolyn's face twisted in a look of puzzlement. "Why would he lie?"

Max leaned back. "I don't know, but I imagine we might get more clarity as the morning rolls on."

The coffee machine clicked, and Carolyn turned to remove her mug. She opened the fridge for some almond milk and then sat at the end of the dining room table.

"It won't take long," she offered.

"What?"

"TITAN. Once I get in, I can pull the plug in ten minutes. Maybe fifteen."

"Something is not right."

"That's for sure." Carolyn got up and took a seat in the living room, turning the swivel chair to face Max and bending one leg underneath her as she sipped her coffee. "But the way you say that sounds ominous."

"I should know what it is, but I can't put my finger on it."

They both sipped their coffee, and Max caught himself absorbed by her elegance once again. He shook his head to change his mindset and stood up, turning to the window he had looked out the night before. It was still mostly dark, but he could tell the sun was about to rise over the East Bay hills. It gave the bridge, which was still lit by its own lights, an ethereal look in the dissipating gloom.

"Chao Fen has spent a great deal of money and has offered a

great deal more to get possession of TITAN, but Eunice Lee spends even more money bailing me out, and she knew I'd be coming for you. It seems like they are working at crosscurrents. Then there's Jenny, who seems to be working as a double agent for Chao Fen, but she's the one who set me up to begin with! Eunice wouldn't need to bail me out if Jenny hadn't set me up.

"And then we throw Cambyses in the mix. How does he even know about TITAN? And what is his role in the week's events?" He turned back to look at Carolyn.

"They killed Ravi." Carolyn held her cup in two hands, her eyes meeting his over the top.

"Did they?" Max asked. "We don't even know that. When it happened, I felt like I might have been the target, but why?"

Carolyn sighed. "I don't know, Max. All the more reason to put an end to this."

Max had left his phone on the table, and it rattled with the vibration of a new text. He stepped back to peer at the screen.

"They're on the move," he said to her, picking up the phone and thumbing a response to Cyrus, "Stay with them."

"You should put your shoes on," he said. "We're heading out in a few."

He walked to the table and unloaded and reloaded the MP7 for probably the fifth time that morning. Old Raider habit. The last thing anyone wanted in a gunfight was a gun that was jammed. When he was done, he slid the weapon and clips into an empty computer bag for transport to the car.

* * *

Traffic was light on the Bay Bridge headed east, but on the other side it was already building, headed into the city. Max sat in the passenger seat while Carolyn piloted the Tesla toward Walnut Creek. His phone vibrated, and he glanced down to see the latest update from Cyrus.

"Exiting 24 in Walnut Creek," the text read.

Max turned to Carolyn. "Something's up. I'm not sure you should come with me."

Carolyn gave him an incredulous glance before turning her eyes back to the road as she spoke.

"Really? Good luck finding TITAN without me. What's the big deal?"

"Cyrus says the Iranians are in Walnut Creek."

"And?"

"It's not a coincidence, Carolyn." He shook his head. "In my gut, I'm telling you it's not a coincidence. I should go in alone."

They had been climbing a hill toward the Caldecott Tunnel, and

Carolyn swerved to the right, crossing two lanes of traffic to an exit called Tunnel Road.

"Take it easy," Max chided, partly enjoying the action.

It was a quiet road with an entrance ramp not fifty feet farther away, and Carolyn pulled over between the two ramps, pushing the end of the drive stalk to engage park.

She turned to face him.

"Look, Max, I know you can do whatever it is you do." She twirled one finger in the air. "And I need you, but you need me too. There's no way you can get rid of TITAN without me. We can do this." Her eyes met his. "Together."

Max took a deep breath, knowing that she spoke the truth but feeling worried about the unknown danger that they might walk into.

"I know you want to do this, but I'm not sure you understand the threat level. This could be life or death."

She shook her head and offered a wry smile. "Always the hero," she said meekly before continuing a little louder, "I get it, but I'm not sure that *you* understand the threat level. If TITAN is turned on—just turned on—I worry about life and death for *everyone*. But if TITAN is activated with intent for malice? Then I think the world is in serious danger—massive danger—as in true end-of-the-world danger of biblical proportions."

"Or Avestan proportions?" Max added, referring to the

Zoroastrian holy book, Avesta.

"Yes." Her response was passionate. "It could be that bad, Max. I need to do this, and it's worth the risk."

Max didn't like it, but he didn't have a counterargument.

"Let's go," he said, looking away. "We're wasting time here."

He didn't look directly at her, but he could tell she was smiling as she pulled back on the road.

His phone rang, and he answered on speaker.

"Hey, Cyrus, what's up?"

"I lost them," a frustrated Cyrus responded.

"What happened?"

"Maybe I should say they lost me. We were pulling off the highway to a light. They slowed until it turned red, then they sped across the lane to the far side, turning left and driving off. I couldn't follow without being obvious, and by the time the light changed they were gone."

Max pinched his nose. "OK, that's not great."

"What now?"

"I don't like it, but we've got to keep moving," Max replied. "Get in position to watch the LasTech garage. We're headed there now. Stay out of sight."

He hung up the phone without waiting for a response, then went back to his recent calls and tapped on Tanner's name.

"I'm calling Tanner," he said as a ringing could already be heard on the phone's speaker.

"Hey, Max!" Tanner answered. "You guys close?"

"Fifteen minutes out. Are you there?"

"Yeah, I'm in my office."

Max thought for a second, but there was no time to explain himself.

"Have you ever heard of Avesta Today or a guy named Cambyses?" he asked bluntly.

The phone was quiet for too long.

"Say again?" Tanner finally responded.

"Avesta Today, it's a Zoroastrian group."

"Max, I have no clue where you're going with this."

"OK, in a nutshell, we think they are after TITAN, and we know that a group of them got off the highway in Walnut Creek."

Again, the line was silent for several seconds.

"What the fuck, Max? I thought you had this handled," Tanner replied.

"Back off, Tanner. Let's just remember who's solving your problems." Max allowed his anger to seep into his comment.

"What are you saying?"

"I mean, how about you just fucking say, 'Thank you'? I don't need to hear your whining while I'm the one constantly getting shot at!"

"Understood," Tanner replied after a brief pause. "In any event, I can tell you one thing—they won't get in here uninvited."

"What does that mean?"

"We've beefed up security. They are round the clock now."

"OK. Good. We're still en route. It's another variable, but it doesn't change our objective this morning." Max looked over to Carolyn, who was slowly nodding as he spoke to his friend. "Where's Jenny?"

"At home," Tanner responded quickly. "I'll talk to her when this is done."

"OK, we'll call you when closer."

"Hey, Carolyn?" Tanner asked.

"Yes?"

"Are you sure you can do this?"

"Find TITAN? Of course I can. I'm the one who hid it!"

"No, I mean, are you going to be able to destroy it?"

"You know what I'm capable of. I think your question is if I'm willing to destroy TITAN."

The car was silent for ten seconds before Tanner answered.

"Yeah. I guess that's my question. You spent a lot of time on this. It's your baby."

"It was Ravi's baby, and some fucker killed him because of it. I'm fine with this." Her anger was barely in check.

"Sounds good."

"OK, man," Max jumped in, knowing that the conversation had hit a nerve for Carolyn. "We'll be there soon."

"I'll meet you in the garage."

"And Tanner?"

"Yes?"

"Thank you for doing this. I know it was not in your plan."

"Plans change, Max," his friend replied with a light laugh, repeating himself before ending the call. "Plans change."

"Why'd you say that?" Carolyn asked when the call was over.

"What?"

"Why'd you thank him?"

"Because he's helping?" Max offered cautiously.

Carolyn didn't answer right away and seemed to pretend to focus on switching lanes. Finally she sighed.

"I don't know, Max. He seems different, and I don't like the fact that his wife is involved with Chao Fen."

"I don't either."

CHAPTER TWENTY-TWO

As Carolyn steered her Tesla off Highway 24 toward the LasTech headquarters, sunlight was practically glowing around Mt. Diablo, the large mountain east of Walnut Creek. It was that quiet morning hour when the streetlights were still on but the glow of natural light made them superfluous. Traffic was picking up as the East Bay denizens made their way to work.

Reclining in the passenger seat, Max could not help but consider how innocent these drivers were to the potential threat to their lives that existed in the heart of their town.

The two had been silent since getting off the phone with Tanner. Max knew Carolyn was troubled by her former lover, but his focus was on trying to understand the angles. He also recapped the building's footprint in his mind several times. Exits. It was always about exits. When they turned off the main boulevard, they passed

Cyrus's van, and he briefly caught the man's eye and nodded. The Middle Easterner nodded back subtly. He'd obviously had enough training to understand that one always had to assume someone else was watching.

Tanner was waiting on the first level of the garage, in front of a newly erected security post at the door that Max had used to escape just a few days prior. He was dressed casually in a golf shirt and jeans.

After Carolyn parked in a reserved spot, they emerged and exchanged hugs, though Max was surprised at how perfunctory they were given the week's events. Tanner quickly cleared them at the security desk, but the guard informed them that he had to take their phones. Carolyn protested but quickly acquiesced, and Max sent a quick text to Cyrus before turning his own device off and handing it in.

As they were entering the elevator lobby, Carolyn cursed and ran back to her car, opened the trunk, and removed her computer bag.

"Sorry." She smiled and waved to the security guard. "Might need my laptop, right?"

She didn't wait for a response and reentered the lobby. Max could see the security guard spread his hands in question, looking at Tanner, who gave a slight shake of the head, implying that the guard should let it slide.

Max kept his expression blank, but he felt a surge of pride at

Carolyn's ruse. She was now carrying the bag with his MP7 inside.

In the elevator, Tanner pressed the third-floor button, waiting for the doors to close before speaking.

"Great timing," he said, putting a hand on Carolyn's shoulder. "Server will be back on line in a couple of minutes. I can't believe you left TITAN on the server!"

"Where else would we keep it?" She raised an eyebrow.

"I don't know, but we've been searching for weeks, and nobody's found anything."

Carolyn pulled her shoulder back so that his hand fell away, and she was facing him squarely. "Searching where? Were you on my private drive?" she asked.

"We searched *everywhere*, Carolyn." He shook his head. "Yes, even your private drive, which as you know, the company has the right to search."

"Well, it's not on my drive." She laughed, leaning against the elevator wall.

Tanner turned to Max. "Anything else on the Avesta thing?"

"Not that we know," Max replied. "Has your security seen anything?"

"Nope. It's been a quiet morning."

"Tell them to stay alert."

"I think we've got things under control." Tanner was oddly dismissive, even though he had been the one to raise the subject.

The doors opened quietly on the third floor, and Tanner led the way back to Carolyn's office and swiped his security card to open the door.

Carolyn pushed past him and went straight to her desk.

"Tanner?"

"Yes?"

"Has someone been in my office?" Carolyn fixed him with an angry stare.

Tanner raised his hands slightly, as if defending himself. "Just your boy here—before the police chased him away."

"Hope you didn't mess with anything," she directed her answer to Max, sitting down at her desk and banging at the keys.

"Yeah, well, you weren't here," Tanner replied over his shoulder as he moved back toward the door. "Anyway. I'm going upstairs for a few, but I'll open a video chat. How long do you need?"

"Twenty minutes, tops," she responded without looking up from her screen, her fingers already a blur of motion.

"Great. I'll be on chat in a couple of minutes." He left the office, allowing the door to swing shut behind him.

Max pretended to look around the room.

"Something's off," Carolyn said. "The system seems sluggish."

"So what do we do?"

Carolyn's fingers stopped briefly, and she looked up at Max with a smile. "As the man said, we keep moving. No time to dig into the back end."

A loud doorbell sound filled the room as the wall television came to life showing what looked like the screen of a cell phone with an incoming call.

Carolyn tapped a few keys, and Tanner appeared on the screen, seated at his desk.

"What's up with the system, Tanner?" she said without greeting him. "Everything is a half beat off."

"No idea, babe. I haven't had any issues." Like Carolyn, he was carrying on the conversation while typing and looking at his screen. "You've been away awhile. Maybe it's running updates?"

Carolyn actually stopped and looked at the TV monitor.

"You do know that we run updates automatically every night?"

Tanner shrugged.

"Christ, Tanner. You're fucking CEO—maybe someday you can figure out how this place runs."

Tanner didn't respond, and Carolyn refocused on her screen. Max sat down on one of the love seats, wishing he had his phone, which reminded him how addictive they were. There was little he could do so he leaned back and closed his eyes.

"Don't work too hard," Carolyn called from behind her screens.

"I'll try not to," he answered. There was no way he was falling asleep, but he could conserve energy and think.

Ten minutes later, Carolyn cursed out loud, followed by a flurry of keystrokes that caused Max to sit up.

"No, no, no, no, no." Carolyn was talking to herself, staring at her screen, but Max stood up and moved behind her.

"What's up?" Tanner asked from the monitor on the wall, reminding Max that they were still on an open feed.

"It's not here," she answered, fingers still rattling away. "It *was* here. I could tell before unlocking it, and it was there for a moment, then it wasn't. I think . . ."

She leaned her head closer to the screen.

"Tanner, you fucking bastard." Carolyn's voice was loud, full of anger but not quite a scream. She was still looking at the screen, but her fingers had stopped. She tapped a few more keys then looked up to the TV monitor. "You installed a keylogger."

Tanner didn't respond but was looking off-screen at something or someone beyond his computer, and whatever it was brought a broad grin to his face. He pushed back in his chair and let out an almost ecstatic sigh.

"You installed a fucking keylogger!" Carolyn restated with even more passion. "What the fuck are you doing, Tanner?"

"This doesn't sound good." Max was still behind her chair.

"No." Carolyn's fingers whirled into motion once again. "That must have been what was slowing me down. He was tracking my keystrokes and holding me up enough that he could get to TITAN a millisecond ahead of me.

"Isn't that right, Tanner?" she raised her voice, calling at the screen, but her eyes were still on her computer as her fingers flew.

"Not exactly like that, but you've got the gist of it." For the first time, Tanner looked up at the camera, still laughing in joy. "You know I don't have the computer skills to do that by myself. Oh, Carolyn, we've been trying so hard to find this."

"There!" Carolyn finished her typing with a slap at the keyboard and stood to face the television. "I've activated the data loss prevention protocol. TITAN's not going anywhere."

"Yeah, we figured you might try that. Jenny rewrote the code for that this morning before you got here. We couldn't disable it entirely, but we could shorten the duration. Rather than locking things down for a day, the first release opportunity will come in a half hour. I've got time. How about you?"

"Why?" Carolyn held her hands out to the side. "The LasTech sale is not enough for you?"

He sat up straighter in his chair. "This is not about money. Not at all. This is about the ultimate triumph of Asha over Ahriman."

A chill ran up Max's spine when he heard his friend invoke the Zoroastrian terms. Asha was the term for the cosmic truth and sustaining force of good that Ahura Mazda represented and defended, while Ahriman was the embodiment of the destructive spirit. According to Zoroastrian belief, Ahura Mazda and Ahriman had been locked in a battle for mankind that could only be truly resolved when Ahura Mazda defeated Ahriman once and for all.

"Good thoughts, good words, good deeds," Tanner continued. "It's beautiful. Carolyn, TITAN will be the vehicle that presages the arrival of Saoshyant."

Carolyn was clearly stunned and sat back down in her chair. "You're Avesta Today?" she asked.

On the screen, Tanner shook his head.

"No. Well, partly. I've funded Avesta Today for some time, but our leader is a man I think our friend knows."

"Cambyses," Max and Carolyn said the name together. Max felt a flare of anger.

"Ahhh," Tanner picked up a remote and pointed it at the camera, which now panned to the conference table. "I see you are already somewhat aware of our mutual friend."

There were two figures seated at the table. Jenny was typing away, half-hidden by her laptop with another computer open and right next to the first, and next to her was the man Max had thought he had disposed of eight years earlier in another world.

Max walked around the desk to get a closer look. It was surreal. Cambyses hadn't aged. He sat upright with gleaming eyes that exuded confidence. He still had an aura about him, visible even through the camera lens, that made Max hesitate.

"Mr. Kline," Cambyses spoke slowly. "You look like you've seen a ghost."

"Well," Max growled, "I'm looking at a dead man."

Cambyses chuckled. "That was a different time, but now we will soon witness the coming of Saoshyant and all will be united with Ahura Mazda."

"I wasn't talking about the past," Max spoke almost to himself.

Cambyses continued without hearing him, "Ironic that you should be here to aid us in the instrument that will accelerate the end of days."

"You don't really want to do this," Carolyn spoke as Tanner moved back into view, taking a seat beside Cambyses.

"Good thoughts, good words, good deeds, Carolyn," he responded.

"And what part of this is good?" she asked. "TITAN can send the world back to the Middle Ages!"

"Actually, we're hoping a little further."

"I'm not going to stand around and wait." Carolyn looked to her computer screen. Then possibly remembering that she'd shut down the network, she shoved her keyboard to one side.

"We were thinking you might want to do something," Tanner said with a smugness that revolted Max. "Your keycard won't work and the stairs are locked. Like it or not, you'll have to witness everything from your seat there on the third floor, at least until we've released TITAN. After that, you'll be free to go. Things should start to fall apart rather quickly, but there's no need for you to stay here once it begins."

Max pulled one of the love seats over in front of the monitor. Above him, a black half-dome housed the camera through which Tanner watched them. He unlaced his boot and took it off before standing on the love seat.

"What are you doing?" Carolyn asked.

"It's not what I'm doing," he answered, turning to look first at the monitor and then directly up at the lens. "It's what I'm *not* doing." He swung his boot violently upward, shattering the protective glass and dislodging the camera, which now hung by a pair of wires.

"I'm not playing your fucking games, Tanner." Max reached up and yanked the wires free.

His friend stood up, still looking at his camera but obviously frustrated that he was now unable to see them.

"Now that was a bit of a waste," he said. "At least the sound is intact."

"How's this for sound? Fuck you, Tanner." Max purposefully made himself sound unhinged. He put his finger to his lips and pointed Carolyn toward the door. As she followed his direction, he continued to speak to his old friend. "Ahura Mazda never intended this. Your path will lead to the death of millions."

"What does death matter when we are all soon to be reunited with Ahura Mazda? All those who have gone before shall join us in the celebration of victory over Ahriman."

"Good deeds, my ass." Max pulled his boot back on and followed Carolyn into the hall.

* * *

In the hallway, Carolyn was already thirty feet away, holding her keycard to the door locks with no effect.

"He's right," she said. "We're locked out of every door. My card has been deactivated."

Max motioned for her to come back and met her halfway in the semi-dark hallway.

"Are there more cameras?" he asked.

Carolyn nodded, pointing down the hall.

"In the common room, there are two and one by the elevator."

"What about microphones?"

Carolyn shook her head. "No, that's just in my office. It's part of the TV."

"OK, keep trying the doors," Max said as he moved down the hall, returning a few minutes later after destroying the remaining cameras.

Carolyn had tried nearly every door and was almost to the common room when Max reached out to stop her hand from trying another lock.

"Hang on," he said, getting her attention and pulling out his own keycard that Jenny'd given him earlier in the week. "Try this one."

Carolyn looked him in the eyes with a smile as she accepted it, holding his gaze for a silent moment that sent a rush of warmth through him. Then she turned and hovered the new card over the RFID lock, which clicked open in response.

Max nodded inward and followed her into the office, which was cluttered but seemed typical of any office.

"I know there's no microphone, but I'd rather talk in here," he said, plopping down in one of two chairs in front of the main desk. Carolyn sat in the other.

"I think I can—" Carolyn started but Max interrupted.

"I'm going up." He held up a hand to stop her from protesting. "This is what I do, Carolyn. More than translating or negotiating, this is what I've been trained to do."

She tilted her head slightly. "I know. I've seen you in action."

"Is there anything I can use in these offices?" he asked.

"I don't know that there's anything you can use, but what I was trying to tell you is that I might be able to retake TITAN." When he didn't respond, she continued, "Ravi built himself an end-around for the shut-down mechanism. Actually, he built *us* an end-around." Carolyn leaned forward, tapping the red scar on her forearm. "Assuming your key works on his office, I should be able to get online, and when the system unlocks, I'll take control of TITAN."

"Shit." Max immediately stood, reaching his hand to Carolyn's. "Then let's get you in there."

Carolyn rose. "If I can do it, it won't be until the system comes online." She looked at her watch, which had a countdown timer. "So we still have sixteen minutes. I should have time to get ready."

As they moved back down the hall, they could hear Tanner calling through the monitor.

"What are you doing, Carolyn? You're not going to get anywhere. Come talk to me."

Ignoring him, Max held his card over the lock, and Ravi's door opened with a soft click. Carolyn pushed past him and strode across the room to move behind the desk. Before sitting down, she reached over and held her forearm against the back wall, then flipped a light switch just below.

"Simple, right?" Her mood had improved. "He had it installed when we renovated the floor. The switch was originally for a switched outlet, but Ravi knew that the network backbone had to pass through the same wall. He did the rest himself. But it can only be activated by our RFID chips."

Her fingers flared to life on the keyboard.

"Anything I can do?" Max asked.

"Yeah." She looked at her watch. Her fingers never stopped. "In fourteen minutes, I need you to distract Jenny for as long as you can."

Max stood there awkwardly, not wanting to interrupt her work.

For a moment, her fingers stopped, but she didn't look up. She pulled out Ravi's top drawer, and after digging around she tossed what looked like a red ball.

He caught it, realizing as he did that Carolyn had recognized his problem—he didn't have a watch. She'd tossed him a Pomodoro alarm clock, the kind that looked like a tomato and was used by people who wanted to focus for short periods of time.

"Thirteen minutes, thirty two seconds," she said as she resumed typing. "This might be harder than I thought. The longer you can keep her busy, the better chance I'll have."

"OK." He tapped on the clock to set the alarm and pushed it into his pocket, mentally noting that he would have to stop it before it rang. "Good luck."

"You too. And Max?" She looked at him over the top of the computer monitor.

"Yeah?"

They looked at each other for several heartbeats saying nothing. He thought he knew what she wanted to say and also why she couldn't.

"I'll be careful," he answered her unspoken thought, walking out of the office.

In the hallway, he could still hear Tanner though more muffled and speaking to someone else, but he'd left the microphone open. Max eased the door to Carolyn's office open and walked across to where she had left her computer bag. He carefully picked up the bag, and after checking that its contents were still there, he exited without making a sound.

He walked back to the common area and put the bag down, removing the MP7 and immediately unloading and reloading the magazine, chambering a round as he did. The weapon had a long sling, which he put over his head and shoulder, adjusting it so that he could have it on his back, then swing it forward at exactly the right height. He took the spare clip and tucked it into the small of his back.

The room had a whiteboard, and he walked over to it, drawing a rough map of the fourth floor from memory and contemplating a plan of attack. Tanner, Jenny, and Cambyses were in Tanner's office suite, so he had to assume there would be guards nearby, which ruled out the closest stairwell. The elevator would also be guarded, but there was a second stair that ran next to the elevator. It would take some luck, but if he could access the floor there without drawing attention, he could maintain the element of surprise until the last minute.

He pulled the timer out of his pocket—nine minutes and four seconds. He still had time and walked to the stair to confirm that his pass would open the door. It clicked open. Peering inside the stairwell, he waited for a half minute but heard no sound, so he entered the stairs and eased the door closed behind him.

He felt sure that no one was in the stairwell, but training forced him to ascend carefully, gun in hand and checking each new line of sight before proceeding.

On the fourth-floor landing, he checked the timer again—eight minutes and eleven seconds. He stepped back from the door and thought back on the week's events. Something still lurked on the edge of his thoughts, but he hadn't been able to put his finger on it.

Betrayal was certainly high on his list of emotions. How could his friend of twenty years be so extreme in his beliefs? Tanner had always been passionate about his goals, but this was bat-shit crazy. He wanted to talk to him one on one. Even now, he wished he could call him.

He shook his head. He was getting closer to the answers, but there was still much he didn't know. He looked down at the timer in his hand—four minutes.

* * *

Max Kline had performed countless raids on targets with unknown occupants. Usually he had a team, but he had experience as a solo operative too. He would have preferred to be better outfitted, but he still liked his odds.

When the timer showed two minutes left, he turned it off and placed it gently on the floor to the side of the door. His internal counter could do the rest. He held his keycard over the RFID pad and the lock clicked open. Knowing that the sound could give him away, he pulled down on the latch and swung the door open with his left hand, stepping in with his MP7 ready against his right side. Thankfully, the reception area was empty. Everything was as he'd seen it previously.

The wall to his right, on the other side of which were the LasTech executive offices, was all glass but obscured for privacy. The white furniture still sat as stark as ever, except there was a cup of coffee on the table in front. Max could see light steam rising from the hole in the lid. He heard noise from the interior and quickly stepped to the corner as someone approached the entrance door from the other side.

It swung open quickly and Max had to use his free hand to slow the motion so it didn't reveal his presence.

A bulky woman dressed in black entered the room and stepped toward the sitting area, likely to recover her coffee. Max eased the return motion of the door and then allowed it to close on its own as he stepped behind the guard. She was shorter than him—maybe five feet six inches tall—so it gave him the advantage of leverage as he cupped her mouth with his right hand, braced his left at the back of her neck, and violently twisted her chin to the right.

A sickening pop and her immediate collapse signaled his success, and he eased the lifeless body to the ground. She was armed with an Uzi machine pistol, which he picked up with his left hand, his own weapon still hanging at the ready on his right. He still didn't know how many he was facing, so the extra firepower was welcome.

He moved to the door that led to the executive offices and held his card over the lock, but nothing happened. Fuck. A minute left by his internal clock, and he had to get inside. He tried the card a second time, holding it flat to the RFID reader, and this time he was rewarded with the subtle click of the lock.

As he slowly pushed the door open, he heard a man's voice on his left.

"You forget to wash your hands?" An Asian man in a black suit was standing at the far window and slowly turning to face him. Max saw the man's expression go from laughter to surprise as he looked at Max. His hand went to his side holster, but Max had the Uzi in his left hand, already pointing directly at him.

"Stay still," Max hissed. "Play it cool, and we all go home."

Max took two steps toward the man, but as he did he quickly decided that this man would not surrender. He was a professional. The way he carried himself and the position of his weapon was the first giveaway, but the glint in his eye was the topper. Max had seen that look before, but never on a man surrendering.

"Put your hands over your head," Max commanded, more to keep the man busy than because he thought he would comply. If he could disarm the man without firing, the element of surprise would still be his.

"Allen, you seen Barbara?" Another Asian man entered the room from the opposite hallway. "Who the fuck are you?" He reached behind his back.

Max had no time to answer. The first man lowered his hands and reached into his pocket. Max fired two short bursts into the man's chest. He was only four feet away, and the man's body flew backward into the window on impact. At the same time, Max's right hand swung the MP7 up and around in a fluid motion to fire on the second man, spraying the area with bullets as the man pulled his gun out of his holster. It was over in a matter of seconds, but now everyone on the fourth floor would be on alert.

Max checked the first man to confirm he was dead and picked up the Glock that the man had been trying to draw. He tucked the pistol into his belt and checked the second assailant, who had fared no better. Max kicked the man's into the corner.

"Allen, what's going on?" a yell came from down the hall

Max didn't answer, and he could hear footsteps coming his way. Fortunately, the wall from the hallway extended a few feet into the room, so Max could wait behind it. He gently pushed the MP7 on its sling around to rest on his back, freeing his hands for what would come next.

The first thing Max saw was the muzzle of a standard Uzi poking beyond the wall and arcing across the room. Max revised his plan of attack. As the man's body came into view, he grabbed the muzzle and violently yanked the man off-balance. He caught the man's body, now spun around, so that Max was behind him with his arm in a lock hold on the man's neck, pulling him back just out of the hallway.

This was one of the Iranians, so Max spoke in Persian.

"Live or die, it is your choice. How many more?" He pressed the nozzle of his gun hard into the back of his captive even as a new shooter fired shots uselessly down the hall.

"Abbas? What's up?" someone called when the bullets stopped. Another Iranian by the accent.

Max dug the weapon deeper into the man. "Live or die."

"If I die, I'll be reunited with Ahura Mazda shortly," the man answered loudly.

"Suit yourself." Max reverted to English as he yanked the man out into the hall with him, using him as a shield as he let loose a burst of fire down the hall, his internal timer telling him that time was up.

"Jenny," he called ahead. "We know about the money." He was spitballing, hoping to distract her, but he knew she was deeply involved, and money was always a part of things.

At the end of the hall, the obscured glass door to Tanner's office opened wide, and another Iranian stepped into the hall, armed with a similar Uzi firing at full automatic. Max's human shield was riddled with bullets, and the weight slumped, forcing him to let go and dive into an open office, lucky not to have been hit himself. The offices were all glass fronted, so Max lifted his Uzi and fired several shots, shattering the glass to both the office he was in and the one across from it. Surprise was a premium in a fight like this, so Max wasted no time.

He tossed the Uzi and with a running start dove across the

hallway, bringing his MP7 to bear and unloading as he crossed the field of fire. The second Iranian attempted to return fire but was pummeled by Max's assault and fell backward.

Max had no time to watch the results, and he barely got his hand in front of him to weaken the impact of his landing. Thankfully, the glass was in relatively harmless chunks from shatter-resistant panels. His body hurt, and his hands had a few cuts, but he was intact.

For a brief moment, the office was silent. Max slowly regained his feet and tossed his now empty cartridge, replacing it with the full one.

He heard Tanner's laughter.

"Max, you're wasting your efforts," his former friend called. "TITAN is loose. It is only a matter of time. We'll all be with Ahura Mazda soon."

"We'll see," he called back, peeking his head around the corner to scan the hallway, weapon ready to fire. The wounded man lay at the far end, unmoving except that his hand opened and closed slowly.

"Hello, Max Kline." A familiar voice came from behind him, and Max froze, knowing he was forfeit. He dropped his hold on the MP7 and raised his hands, slowing turning to look at Cambyses who had come from behind the desk.

"Very convenient that you chose this office." The Persian man smiled, speaking in imperfect English. "With left hand, pick the strap over your neck."

Max did as he was told, tossing his weapon to the ground.

"Now turn around." Again, he followed instructions and felt Cambyses remove the Glock from his back belt.

"This has been a long time coming." He nudged Max forward with the nozzle of his weapon. "Let's go see our mutual friend."

* * *

When Max entered Tanner's office, he was struck by how normal things appeared. The room was lit by two banks of overhead lights, while heavy drapes obscured the windows. Tanner sat behind his desk at his computer, and to the right Jenny sat alone at the fishbowl conference room table. Both were intensely staring at their screens, and it was only then Max realized that Carolyn's plan might have worked.

"Are you sure?" Tanner called to Jenny, not even acknowledging Max's presence. "How the fuck can it be gone?"

Max felt a surge of relief, and a smile came to his face. Carolyn must have been successful. In the conference room, Jenny was typing furiously at her keyboard.

"Shit. Shit. Shit." Tanner banged at his own keys. "OK. System is locked down again. Cambyses, get down to the third floor. Get Carolyn. She's done something."

"Did you launch TITAN?" Cambyses asked, ignoring the order.

"I don't fucking have TITAN!" Tanner raged. "Why do you think I asked you to get Carolyn?"

"You forget yourself. And you didn't ask," Cambyses replied stoically without moving.

Tanner closed his eyes and took a deep breath. After exhaling, he glanced at Max then turned his eyes to Cambyses.

"Please, would you mind going down to the third floor and finding Carolyn?"

Cambyses pushed Max forward so that he was on the opposite side of the desk from Tanner, then he moved around and unslung his gun, handing it to Tanner.

"Yes, friend. I will retrieve the girl, again, but you'll need to keep an eye on this one."

"Again?" Max spoke to his former friend for the first time. "You were behind her abduction?" He could not believe his ears.

"Ahura Mazda was behind her abduction," Tanner answered as he sat back in his chair, suggesting that Max should sit opposite him. He held the gun with visible discomfort, but it was pointed directly at Max and too far from him to attempt a grab, even though Cambyses promptly left them alone. Max took his seat.

"If that was you, what role did Chao Fen have?" he asked, almost to himself.

Tanner giggled, but it seemed forced.

"I have no fucking clue what their role is," he answered. "They made me rich at a time when I no longer need to be rich. I think their role has been a distraction maybe. Oh, they want TITAN too, no doubt, but they want it for different reasons, and I don't think they have the balls or the tenacity to take it."

Max leaned back in his chair, pushing his hand through his hair.

"Ravi?" he asked.

Tanner raised an eyebrow and nodded.

Suddenly, Max realized what had been bothering him. "The attack in San Francisco? The Chinese operatives?"

"You think you are the only one who can learn Chinese?" Tanner nodded again, this time smiling, and switched to Chinese. "I was jealous that you could speak other languages, so I started lessons. At first it was just a hobby, but it became useful for work. LasTech would not have grown as we have were it not for our Chinese partners."

"Tanner, why?" Max asked, still watching for a chance to strike.

"The attack? It doesn't matter, Max. We'll all be together with Ahura Mazda soon. Cambyses is Saoshyant—or he will be. None of this matters, Max. Once we get TITAN going, Saoshyant will lead us into the arms of Ahura Mazda. Die now, die tomorrow. When Frashokereti arrives, all souls will reunite in a world beyond time."

Max knew that Frashokereti was effectively the Zoroastrian equivalent to Christian Revelation, and he slowly shook his head, hoping that Carolyn had completed her task.

Suddenly, the power went out, and Max immediately dove out of his chair to the floor. He heard Tanner stand and saw his darkened silhouette.

"What the fuck are you doing, Max?" Tanner called.

In the conference room, Jenny's face could still be seen in the light of her laptop screen.

"I'm on it, Tanner," she called. "Give me a few."

Max moved on all fours to the far side of Tanner's desk then threw his ID card across the room.

Tanner fired the Uzi and briefly lit himself up in his own muzzle flash. It was quick, but it gave Max enough of his location that he could move behind him without detection.

"Max, if you knew what I know, you'd gladly help," Tanner called into the darkness, and Max crouched behind him.

"Oh, I'm going to help," Max hissed into his ex-friend's ear, causing him to flinch, and another burst from the Uzi lit the room.

Max threw a hard kidney punch with his right fist even as his left arm reached up and around Tanner's head, slamming him to the desk as he easily disarmed him.

"You can count on my help." He pulled Tanner back to vertical and jammed the muzzle of the Uzi into his side.

"Tanner?" Jenny called from the darkened conference room. Her glowing face was the only visible light. "The building power is cut, but no signal has reported it to PG&E."

"Isn't there backup?" Max asked out loud, immediately considering who or what might be behind the power outage.

"There should be," Tanner answered with a groan as Max pushed him into the conference room where the glow of Jenny's laptop allowed the three to see each other.

Max didn't need to hear anymore. This was a professional attack, and he needed to act. Time would be precious.

"Get up," he commanded Jenny. "We're all going to take a walk down to the third floor."

When Jenny reached to close her laptop, he corrected her, waving the muzzle of his gun toward her. "Leave that open. Come over here and lead the way. If you do anything stupid, your husband will have a few extra holes."

Jenny did as she was told, and the three of them cautiously went out of the office and into the darkened corridor. Max knew they were exposed and didn't like it. In the hall, the only light they had was the faint glow of the photoluminescent exit sign.

"No," he called out as Jenny passed the stairs on her way to the main lobby. "Use the stairs."

He could see her dark shape turn and the door to the stair swung open. The stairwell was equally dark, a bad sign given that the emergency lights were typically on a separate power source. Whoever cut the power was thorough.

Suddenly, a blinding light filled the stairwell, accompanied by a loud bang with a concussive wave that seemed to be everywhere at once, throwing Jenny and Tanner to the floor. Max staggered but stayed on his feet, his ears screaming in pain even as all sounds disappeared except for a ringing tone. His eyes were also useless, and he closed them as he put a steadying hand on the wall, hoping for some relief.

It wasn't the first time he'd been hit with a concussion grenade, and he knew he would have little time to reorient himself. He groped for the still-open doorway and staggered into the hall, feeling his way toward Tanner's office.

Then someone grabbed his gun, and as he spun to throw a blind punch, something hard hit the back of his head and he felt himself crumble to the floor in a still-silent world.

CHAPTER TWENTY-THREE

His world lurched back into reality as the acrid sting of ammonia invaded his nostrils. It felt like an icy blade slicing through the fog in his mind, abruptly pulling him from the depths of unconsciousness. His lungs drew a short, involuntary breath, and his eyes snapped open to a blur of colors and shapes. For a fleeting moment, confusion reigned, his heart pounding in a frantic rhythm as he grappled with the sudden, disorienting return to reality.

His ears rang, but he could make out sounds and his eyes slowly adjusted to his surroundings. The pungent odor lingered, and he exhaled violently through his nose, trying to rid himself of the burning sensation left behind by the smelling salts.

As Max slowly took in his surroundings, a new pain brought his attention to the fact that his hands were bound behind him. He was in a chair in Tanner's office. He had to open and close his eyes to try to rid himself of the residue of the concussion grenade, but he knew it would take time. Others were similarly bound—Tanner and Jenny were still unconscious in a love seat, slumped against one another.

Across the room, Cambyses and Carolyn sat in chairs. Their hands were also bound but in front of them, and they appeared alert, probably taken without the need of a grenade. All around the room, men and women in tight-fitting black military attire stood at attention, hands behind their backs but all heavily armed. All of them had holstered pistols and machine pistols hanging in slings over their shoulders.

Two men moved to the love seat, waking Tanner and Jenny with the same nasty smelling salts that had woken him.

He heard his name and looked up to see Carolyn's pleading eyes.

"Max?" she spoke in a muffled voice. "Are you OK?"

He nodded, pulling himself more upright in the chair.

"Never better." He smiled, his own words sounding distant. "Did you get it?"

Carolyn nodded in return. "Yes, it's gone."

"Excuse me for interrupting this reunion." The voice came from his left, and he turned to see Eunice Lee entering the room and walking over to sit on the front of Tanner's desk.

"You folks really haven't learned to play nice, now have you?" she asked rhetorically, turning to face Carolyn. "Where's TITAN?"

Carolyn shook her head. "Gone."

"Gone where?" Eunice continued. "You mean gone somewhere safe? Or it's been released?"

"I mean gone for good," Carolyn answered with a hint of pride. "TITAN no longer exists."

Eunice looked at her for a long time, saying nothing, then took in a deep breath and exhaled, straightening her back.

"That's a loss." Her tone was almost casual, which made it even harder for Max to hear through the constant ringing that still permeated his hearing.

"You're a piece of work." Eunice looked at Tanner with anger in her eyes. Tanner was still struggling to keep his eyes open, but he seemed aware of the room. "You've got the most potent software ever developed, and your plan is to destroy the world? You made a deal to sell me that software, and I was willing to pay full price. Chao Fen had plans for TITAN."

"Ahura Mazda." Tanner's head swayed, and he looked at Cambyses with confusion on his face.

"And you," Eunice continued in Chinese to Jenny, "this is how you repay your aunt's favor?"

Jenny started to protest, but Eunice held up a hand to stop her. "No, there are no excuses with Chao Fen. Only results. You are no longer welcome at home, and you might want to lie low for a few years.”

Eunice motioned to four of the handlers, who helped Tanner and Jenny from their seat and guided them into the hallway. Tanner was still semiconscious and needed support from both sides.

Max noticed for the first time that the power and lights were back on.

“Sorry about TITAN,” he said, moving to the edge of his chair.

“Are you? I hired you to find TITAN.”

“And I did.” He looked over at Carolyn proudly.

“Don’t try my patience, Mr. Kline.” Eunice moved to stand in front of him, forcing him to look up at her. “In a perfect world, I’d kill you and be done with the problem. But Tanner is the real problem, and he’s on his way home, so it would be wrong for me to treat you worse.

“Chao Fen has not existed for as long as we have by the indiscriminate murder of those who cross us. It would feel nice, true, but it is not good business. We’ll let you go so long as I have your word that none of what’s happened gets out.”

“I have no reason to discuss this with anyone,” Max replied, sitting back so that he could look at her without bending his neck. “I’d be happy if I never hear that name again. Sorry that you lost money.”

“We didn’t lose money, Mr. Kline.” A smile came across her face. “We’ll continue with the purchase of LasTech—at a healthy discount to the original pricing. I have a feeling we'll get a really good deal. The company has a solid portfolio that will fit very well into the Chao Fen family. TITAN was the cherry on top, but we'll do fine without it. And you'll still profit from the transaction."

"I may need the money for my lawyer's fees." Max raised an eyebrow. "I'm still a murder suspect."

"On that," Eunice began, then hesitated, looking out the window before continuing, "I think you might find that the SFPD crime lab has a new suspect. I'm fairly confident that in the next few days it will come out that they identified the killer's DNA on the victim's body." She paused briefly. "DNA belonging to Tanner Reynolds."

Max stared at her until she nodded her head.

"I told you that Chao Fen has a long reach, Max."

"What now?" he asked.

"You are free to go, so long as we have our understanding. And you can take Ms. Toffey with you. Despite her actions, she and the Persian are the only two who didn't directly betray me."

"What about him?"

"The Persian? He's earned a trip home, don't you think?" She looked over at Cambyses, who nodded solemnly. "I don't particularly care for his theology, and were it not for him we'd likely have TITAN, so I don't feel he is welcome here. We'll either buy him a ticket or alert the local ICE authority to his whereabouts." She was directing her comments to Max, but they were clearly for Cambyses' benefit.

"So it's that easy?" Max was amazed at how quickly things were ending.

"Leave now, Mr. Kline." The edge returned to her voice. "Your commentary is both unwelcome and unwise. Take what is given to you and move on."

Max pushed himself to his feet, pausing slightly when he stood to get his bearings. The aftereffects of the concussion grenade still warped his balance, but the message from Eunice was very clear. Carolyn had also risen and was at his side by the time he was stable.

She reached around his waist to steady him, but he pushed back, unwilling to leave the room as Tanner had. Instead, he took her hand in his own and led her out the door. Neither of them turned to say goodbye.

In the hallway, they were directed to take the stairs down to the parking garage, where their phones were returned to them and they were allowed to leave in Carolyn's car. They didn't speak as she exited the garage and turned left toward the highway.

Max looked at his phone and saw a text from Cyrus.

"Tanner is on the move. I'm following."

He quickly tapped a reply. "Leave him. It's over. TITAN is gone. We are safe and headed into SF. I will check in later."

He turned his phone off without waiting for a reply. Leaning back in his seat, he reached over to put his hand on Carolyn's thigh.

"Thank you," he said, turning his head to look at her.

"Oh my God, Max. Thank *you*. That was fucking crazy. Are you alright?"

"I will be," he replied, patting her thigh reassuringly. "We will be."

CHAPTER TWENTY-FOUR

The clattering of plates and bustle of the trattoria was a welcome respite from the crazy events of the past week. Max and Carolyn sat at a small table in the back of Jackson Fillmore, Carolyn's favorite restaurant, which was conveniently only a block from her apartment.

They had spoken little on the drive back from Walnut Creek and even less when they got into her apartment. Their emotions were strained after the ordeal, and Max had never felt like he'd needed anyone as much as he'd needed Carolyn then. What started as a warm embrace had quickly developed into a morning of making love, followed by a Chinese takeout lunch and a long afternoon of lounging and more sex. They'd risen from bed at five o'clock and showered together before emerging from the apartment for a quick stroll to dinner.

"Hi, Carolyn!" the waitress gushed when she arrived. "Can I get you the usual?"

"Hi, Karen," she responded, turning to Max. "White wine?"

"Sure, I'm easy."

Carolyn turned back to the waitress. "We'll have a bottle tonight. Thank you."

"On its way," Karen replied, turning back into the room.

"We may need more than one," Max added in a low voice, preparing the question that had been nagging him all day. "Is it really gone?"

Carolyn smiled and raised her eyebrows. "Ha. You think I'm playing games?"

"I think you are capable of playing games," he answered.

"True. But, yes, TITAN is gone. Ravi would be pissed if he were alive."

"So it never launched, right?"

Carolyn hesitated for a second.

"Not really."

Max sighed, making air quotes with his fingers. "Not really? That's what I meant about you playing games with the truth. What does that even mean?"

"It means I am not entirely sure." Carolyn's expression turned serious. "Jenny released TITAN, but it should have been locked within LasTech's server. When we came back online, I was able to exploit a backdoor to take control, shut it down, and then initiate self-destruct."

"So what is the problem?"

"TITAN is AI driven. It could have spent its time while LasTech was in lockdown devising a backdoor of its own."

"OK, now I'm confused."

"I have no basis for this theory, Max. It's an open question. But it is possible, if not conceivable, that TITAN left a copy of itself somewhere."

"On the server?"

"Anywhere, really. It probably took me twenty seconds after shutdown to do everything I said, and twenty seconds to you and me is fast, but twenty seconds to a program like TITAN is an eternity."

"That's an uplifting thought."

Carolyn did not respond, and he was content to let the sarcasm settle as the waitress returned with glasses and their bottle of Far Niente Chardonnay.

When she left, Max lifted his glass, and as Carolyn's glass met his he toasted. "Well, here's to old flames."

"Speak for yourself, old man. I'm still young." Her face glowed with happiness, giving him the answer he wanted and the courage to continue.

"Alright, let's call it long-lost love."

Her eyes had a sparkle as she met his gaze and they soaked each other in.

She lifted her glass a little higher. "I'll drink to that."

The waitress returned to take their orders and left.

"Do you think they'll want you to stay after the sale?" Max asked.

"Not sure. As you know, Tanner handled the negotiation. I guess his role in this probably adds some complexity. I can't imagine Chao Fen would want him around, so I guess I'll probably need to help." She looked away, adding, "For the transition, at least."

"You should come to Vegas."

She shook her head. "You're not wasting time. Why don't you stay here?"

"I might have to for a while, until I resolve my legal issues." He rolled his eyes. "But I've got work in Vegas. You should come." Even as he asked, he knew in his heart that Vegas was not a place that Carolyn would enjoy, and it took a little bit away from the happiness he had felt moments earlier.

She reached across the table and put her hand on his.

"Let's enjoy what we have right now."

"You're right." He nodded.

Their glasses met again, and Max used the moment to let go of his other worries. He finished his glass, poured for the two of them, and motioned to the server for another bottle. It was time to enjoy the moment.

CHAPTER TWENTY-FIVE

As he sat in the darkness on the leather couch in Tanner's living room, Max could feel the anger percolating as he waited for his former friend to arise. Entry through the unlocked back door had been amazingly simple. Tanner had little heed for the old-fashioned guidelines for physical protection. The pendulum wall clock ticked the minutes slowly by with a soft tick-tock. The sound was almost soothing, and he could imagine it contributing to a better mood were it not for the fact that his old friend had attempted to kill him on a number of occasions, including the possible destruction of the modern world.

He and Carolyn had traveled to Monterey, where they had planned to stay for the weekend, when the text from Eunice hit his screen late afternoon the day before. As she requested, he'd called her almost immediately, and she'd updated him on Tanner's situation.

She'd also given him instructions, and though he technically had no obligation, it was clear she expected him to assist, and his own internal barometer agreed that his participation was the right way to end things. What unnerved him slightly was that the package had arrived not five minutes later—despite the fact that they had only just checked into the room.

Carolyn had understood, though he'd only given her vague details.

At the other end of the hall, the bedroom door opened and closed, and Max could hear slippered feet down the hall. A dark shape emerged and continued toward the kitchen, avoiding the sitting area until Max spoke.

"Good morning, Tanner."

The shape spun toward him and jumped backward at the same time.

"Jeeesus!" Tanner gasped, holding his hand to his chest.

Max thumbed the remote with a gloved hand, and the lights in the room came on at a subdued level, enough that they could see each other.

"Max, what are you doing here?" He looked around the room. "Are you alone?"

"You have a lot to answer for." Max ignored the questions.

"I thought you might come. If you're here to kill me, do it. You may have slowed its arrival, but death puts me closer to revelation."

"Unfortunately, our mutual friend made me promise not to do that." Max stood, sickened by the man his best friend had become. He had no interest in spending any more time with him than he had to. "The San Francisco Police Department has obtained a warrant for your arrest in the murder of Ravi Gashwin. They are likely already on their way here."

"That's bullshit," Tanner spat out.

"Let me finish." Max lowered his voice, a technique he often used in negotiation, forcing the opponent to listen more intently. "They have DNA evidence from the crime scene and will find the murder weapon here. The case is very strong, and you'll probably spend the rest of your life behind bars."

"But I didn't . . . What weapon?" Tanner stopped when Max raised a finger to his mouth, suggesting quiet.

"It doesn't matter what you did. It matters what they can prove in a court of law. Chao Fen is not an organization that takes betrayal lightly. You made a deal with them, and you backed out. They are not happy to have lost TITAN."

"That's bullshit," Tanner repeated, less sure of himself. "You know me. I don't have any weapons."

"I thought I knew you." Max was irritated to be wasting time. "As I've said, Chao Fen has long arms—ones that can reach into the evidence room at the SFPD. You're responsible even if you didn't pull the trigger, and now Chao Fen has made the connection a little more obvious. They now have your prints and DNA from the crime scene and when they search here later this morning, they will find one of the guns used in the assault."

Tanner's eyes widened slightly with realization before he covered them with his hand and backed up until his back was against the glass wall, then he slowly slid down until he was seated on the floor. When he looked up at Max, his previous bravado was gone.

"Max," he pleaded. "Can you help me?"

"There is a black car waiting outside. If you come with me now, and I mean right now—as you are—that car will take us to the Concord airport where a Chao Fen jet is fueled and waiting. They'll get you safely out of the country. What happens next is between you and Chao Fen, but I've been instructed to tell you that if you choose this path, Chao Fen will not take your life."

"What kind of choice is that?" Anger flared in Tanner.

"I'm going to walk out the front door and to the car. After I get in, the driver has been told to wait ten seconds before closing the door."

He knew there had been little chance that Tanner would join him, and he allowed himself to smile as the car pulled down the driveway. They would still go to the airport because that was where he'd left his car, but the driver was already on the phone to his superiors with an update.

On the main avenue toward the highway, they passed several SFPD squad cars headed in the opposite direction. He wondered if Eunice would be happy or disappointed with Tanner's decision. Either way, it no longer mattered. The drive back to Monterey would probably take a little over two hours, and then he'd be back in Carolyn's arms.

Thank you for reading Edge of Disaster.

Creating this story has been a special pleasure and I hope you've enjoyed it as much as I have!

Please share your thoughts with other readers by returning to Amazon and leaving a review.

Questions or comments? E-mail me at:

Thomas.Puck@TomSchnurr.com

If you'd like to receive free updates and bonus material, please sign up for my mailing list here:

Https://tomschnurr.com/thomas-puck/

About the author:

I grew up in Sheffield, a small town nestled in the Berkshire mountains of western Massachusetts. I was fortunate to attend Berkshire School (also in Sheffield) and later graduated from the College of the Holy Cross with a B.A. in Economics.

For most of my adult life, I pursued a career in finance but throughout that time, I maintained a passion for books. Then I encountered a break in my career, and I found the time to pursue writing.

I now live in Moraga, CA with my wife, Megan, and our children; Lillian, Cooper & Kipling (though they are largely out of the house.) When I'm not writing, I enjoy golf, fishing and playing board games.